NEXUS CONFESSIONS:
VOLUME THREE

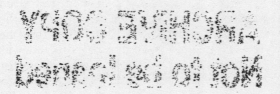

Other titles available in the Nexus Confessions series:

NEXUS CONFESSIONS: VOLUME ONE
NEXUS CONFESSIONS: VOLUME TWO

NEXUS CONFESSIONS: VOLUME THREE

Edited and compiled by
Lindsay Gordon

Always make sure you practise safe, sane and consensual sex.

First published in 2008 by
Nexus
Thames Wharf Studios
Rainville Rd
London W6 9HA

Copyright © Virgin Books Ltd 2008

A catalogue record for this book is available from the British Library.

www.nexus-books.com

Typeset by TW Typesetting, Plymouth, Devon

Printed and bound in Great Britain by CPI Bookmarque,
Croydon CR0 4TD

Distributed in the USA by Macmillan, 175 Fifth Avenue,
New York, NY 10010, USA

ISBN 978 0 352 34113 6

Mixed Sources
Product group from well-managed
forests and other controlled sources
www.fsc.org Cert no. TF-COC-002227
© 1996 Forest Stewardship Council

The Random House Group Limited supports The Forest Stewardship Council (FSC),
the leading international forest certification organisation. All our titles that are
printed on Greenpeace approved FSC certified paper carry the FSC logo.
Our paper procurement policy can be found at *www.rbooks.co.uk/environment.*

1 3 5 7 9 10 8 6 4 2

Contents

Introduction   vii

Perfect – *Seeking the further reaches of restraint*   1

Breastfed – *There are girls who like it too*   23

Under a Blanket in the Sky – *Never too old to misbehave on a plane*   30

He Touched Me – *You got to hand it to her*   36

'Have you got that in a size 16?' – *Forced to dress by a matron*   44

Effing Mablethorpe – *The cuckold, his wife, their holiday and her lovers*   67

Stranger on a Ten-Speed – *Opportunism rides*   79

Jan's Buyer – *Breaking every rule in the book*   87

Word of Foot – *Confession of a female foot sucker*   107

Cheating – *Reaching the heights of betrayal*   118

Gagging the Press – *You can never underestimate the benefits of fieldwork*   128

Family Girlfriend – *All for the love of MILF*   149

Moving On – *Good work if you can get it*   160

My Wife is a Lesbian – *For the purposes of home porno*   181

The Officer and His Bitch – *The strong arm of the law*   195

Pounce – *The more the merrier*   203

Annie's Bum Deal – *Sometimes, discomfort is underrated*   215

Introduction

Who can forget the first time they read a reader's letter in an adult magazine? It could make your legs shake. You could almost feel your imagination stretching to comprehend exactly what some woman had done with a neighbour, the baby-sitter, her best friend, her son's friend, a couple of complete strangers, whatever . . . Do real women actually do these things? Did this guy really get that lucky? We asked ourselves these questions, and the not knowing, and the wanting to believe, or wanting to disbelieve because we felt we were missing out, were all part of the reading experience, the fun, the involvement in the confessions of others, as if we were reading some shameful diary. And when Nancy Friday's collections of sexual fantasies became available, didn't we all shake our heads and say, no way, some depraved writer made all of this up. No woman could possibly want to do that. Or this guy must be crazy. But I bet there are readers' letters and confessed fantasies that we read years, even decades ago, that we can still remember clearly. Stories that haunt us: did it, might it, could it have really happened? And stories that still thrill us when the lights go out because they have informed our own dreams. But as we get older and become more experienced, maybe we have learnt that we would be foolish to underestimate anyone sexually, especially ourselves.

The scope of human fantasy and sexual experience seems infinite now. And our sexual urges and imaginations never cease to eroticise any new situation or trend or cultural flux about us. To browse online and to see how many erotic sub-cultures have arisen and made themselves known, is to be in awe. Same deal with magazines and adult films – the variety, the diversity, the complexity and level of obsessive detail involved. But I still believe there are few pictures or visuals that can offer the insights into motivation and desire, or reveal the inner world of a fetish, or detail the pure visceral thrill of sexual arousal, or the anticipation and suspense of a sexual experience in the same way that a story can. When it comes to the erotic you can't beat a narrative, and when it comes to an erotic narrative you can't beat a confession. An actual experience or longing confided to you, the reader, in a private dialogue that declares: *yes, if I am honest, I even shock myself at what I have done and what I want to do.* There is something comforting about it. And unlike a novel, with an anthology there is the additional perk of dipping in and out and of not having to follow continuity; the chance to find something fresh and intensely arousing every few pages written by a different hand. Start at the back if you want. Anthologies are perfect for erotica, and they thrive when the short story in other genres has tragically gone the way of poetry.

So sit back and enjoy the Nexus Confessions series. It offers the old school thrills of reading about the sexual shenanigans of others, but Nexus-style. And the fantasies and confessions that came flooding in – when the call went out on our website – are probably only suitable for Nexus. Because like the rest of our canon, they detail fetishes, curious tastes and perverse longings: the thrills of shame and humiliation, the swapping of genders, and the ecstasy of submission or domination. There are no visiting milkmen, or busty neighbours hanging out the washing and winking over the hedge here. Oh, no. Our readers and fantasists are far more likely to have been spanked, or caned, feminised into women, have given themselves to strangers, to have dominated other men or women, gone dogging, done the unthinkable, behaved inappropriately and broken the rules.

Lindsay Gordon, Spring 2007

Perfect

I'm paid to be right, maximising the chance of success; or, when events turn in the wrong direction, to minimise risk. The balance depends on attention to detail and the correct prediction of outcomes. But we can't stay on the professional plane, governed by rationality, forever. Personal lives involve erratic emotions.

In the mirror it's the power player I see with glossy black hair, expensively cut and combed to a casual style. Highly arched brows curve over intense hazel eyes. Flawless tanned skin glows with rouge on high cheekbones and into the hollows beneath. Broad sculptured lips glisten in complementary red. The charcoal-grey Chanel suit clings to my slender form. For timid women the outfit might be too revealing, its plunging neckline too wide and deep, but how should a Finance Director of an international company be expected to dress? And beneath the strictly formal covering no one could detect the wispy lace of bra and panties which leave no outward trace.

I slung the red crocodile bag onto my shoulder, picked up its matching briefcase, and left the washroom. Outside, the terminal bustled with confused human traffic. As I walked across to the bar, poised with diamond precision on high heels, the broad suspender straps – a souvenir of the Paris adventure – stretched down my thighs comfortably. Parisians understand chic underwear. Hoisting the skirt I arranged myself on a stool and, when the barman approached, ordered a Martini. While he poured and delivered I sat unconcerned by a rude examination that lingered over my face and drifted into the shadowed cleavage. In fact I inclined further to deepen his view as if hot for attention and finished the drink unhurriedly. But when I paid with a generous tip I gave him an icy appraisal to convey that sex, a commodity in the personal services sector, can be bought, just like Martini.

The Cartier wristwatch confirmed ten minutes to boarding. I returned to the waiting area and chose a seat well away from anyone else, where my thoughts drifted to the forthcoming meeting which could become nasty. In the distance the barman wiped the counter and caused me to reflect on my switch from alluring behaviour to puritan. I ought to discipline a girly game that I played too often. Discipline –

Interrupted by a chirruping phone I retrieved a slim silver model from my bag and opened the line.

'Morning, Sophie. Elaine here. What's the verdict? Out of ten.'

'I think . . . nine.'

'Exceptional, from you. I take it he made you come deliciously?'

'Several times.'

'Have you any immediate interest in another? As a regular client I like to keep you well supplied.'

'No, I'm in the departure lounge at Heathrow, en route to Geneva. But as a speculation what's the youngest age on your books?'

'Seventeen.'

'God! It must be like getting fucked by your son.'

'He's certainly virile,' Elaine chuckled.

'The oldest?'

'Sixty-seven.'

'That must be like going with your grandfather.'

'He has extraordinary skill and patience.'

'Do you always sample them personally?'

'How could I recommend them otherwise?'

'All that wrinkled skin – ugh!'

Elaine laughed. 'You're so fastidious I wonder how you survive in this wicked world.'

'By avoiding sordidness.'

'Whereas I'll try anything, or anyone, once. My clients deserve only the best, and if I learn something new that's a bonus.'

'You're an extremely bad influence. I'm beginning to think in a similar way. Recently I've been considering . . . an experiment.'

'Which particular one?'

I paused, then boldly revealed my hand. 'Restraint.'

'Now I'm really impressed! I had no idea a control freak could be so adventurous.'

'He would, of course, have to be completely reliable.'

'Your timing is fortunate. I have a candidate who –'

'Don't rush me. First, guarantee his reliability.'

'I understand. You wish to sample being controlled without losing your own control.'

'Precisely.'

'Even so, be careful of what you start.'

'I must go. My flight has been called.'

Ten days later, following a pleasant meal with friends, I returned after midnight to my towerblock apartment. Leaving all the lights off I crossed to the

3

uncurtained window to gaze contentedly at a sailing moon over the Thames, patterned by reflected lights, curving below. The potent effect of quality wine still thumped my heart and over the high view I drowsed sluggishly.

A loud buzz jerked me sharply awake. Puzzled, I lifted the security phone from its wall cradle. 'Yes?'

'Good evening, Sophie. My name is Bernard. We have never met but we'll start now.'

'Start what?'

'I am recommended by Elaine.'

'Elaine sent you?' I ransacked muddled thoughts until a hazy memory emerged of my speculative enquiry. 'Do you know what time it is?' I asked indignantly.

'I understood you were a serious client and not a time-waster.'

How dare he doubt my credentials! 'Who the hell do you think you are?'

'A mark of seriousness is to do as you're told, when you are told. I am here simply to meet you and shall make no further demands. Now, with that reassurance, let me in. At once.'

'Damn you!' I punched the Entry, slammed down the phone, and instantly regretted the overreaction. Slumped in a chair I struggled through fury to rationalise.

He could still be stopped at the apartment door –

Only a meeting –

And then goodbye, forever!

My heart pounded but not, perhaps, with the effects of the wine.

How long does the journey take in the express lift?

I stroked clammy palms on the fabric of my dress and jumped in shock when the doorbell shrieked. Then, motionless, I inhaled deeply to steady my nerves. Poised at the door I took another steadying breath before releasing the lock but the sight of a dark silhouette constricted my throat. Unable to speak I turned away.

Despite his bulk he moved with agile grace to the opposite chair. It seemed appropriate to leave the room in shadow although, by moonlight, I could see only glinting silver-grey hair and a part of his face with mature lines. I guessed his age at about fifty.

Bernard leaned back comfortably and glanced around before his black eye sockets turned on me. 'I approve,' he said in a rumbling tone.

Approve of what – sitting in dim light? The furnishings? Or approve of me? I rejected the last thought instantly. I needed no man to like me; rather, he needed me to accept him.

'I shall be demanding, of course –' he continued '– as you expect, with your inclination.'

What inclination? 'It's only an experiment,' I croaked.

He ignored the important caveat as if I'd not spoken at all. 'I know nothing of your tastes. Do you have anything to tell me, regarding those?'

Tastes? For what? I shook my head.

'Merely a reckless desire for restraint?'

Reckless suggested, impertinently, a simpleton.

'Do you have a preference for the means? Velvet rope, for example, or Velcro . . . Chains?'

I snorted angrily.

'Any particular scenarios in mind? A persistent fantasy? Have you thought about what should follow restraint? That, alone, is simply a prelude.'

He seemed so dark, and so large, and so much at ease in the interrogation. His deep calm tones transmitted authority. This stupid idea had suddenly come far too close and in too much detail for comfort. I cleared my throat with a strangled cough. 'What usually happens?'

'The whole point is for something unusual to happen.'

Of course it is. I felt ridiculous. 'You decide.'

He leaned forwards intently. 'Are you a masochist?'

'No!'

'Then why do you trust me?'

'I suppose . . . I'm trusting Elaine.'

Bernard stood up promptly. 'I salute the courage of a bold young woman.'

I really hated my surge of gratitude. Gazing up at the looming form I muttered, 'Where will it be? And when? My diary is full.'

'I shall choose the time and venue. My first instruction is to stand.'

'You said no demands!'

'Relax . . . and do it.'

I complied meekly. Large heavy hands clamped my arms to the sides and held my body rigidly. My brain revolved with an excited thought: I'm being restrained! Unable to shrink away from the kiss, I absorbed his warm and resilient pressure for the length of time he decided.

When Bernard pulled back, the dark pools of his eyes gazed into mine, and his voice sounded husky. 'I rather wish I hadn't made that promise.' Abruptly he released me and disappeared into the gloom. The door opened but then there was a pause. Through a blank silence my heartbeat stopped. As the door shut decisively, a sprung trap, 'Be careful of what you start' vibrated inside my head.

Early the next morning the Swedish acquisition fell apart and absorbed all my energies in complex negotiations. In fleeting moments of free time I remembered Bernard's allure and felt in my belly a sickening stab. But that experiment lay in a different world, remote from the daily reality of fighting clauses line by line, crunching the numbers urgently, and the analysis of results. Through sheer bloody-mindedness I rescued the key elements and the company gave me a raise together with a month's leave. A website offered a hotel in the old heart of Antibes. After leaving the number, and instructions for my team, I flew out the following day to the warmth of a golden autumn in the Mediterranean.

During the first days I poked into every corner and tiny shop in the narrow crowded streets, and sunbathed on the beach at a distant point from the busy port. The tensions of hard negotiation faded away. Relaxed, I ate in a different restaurant every evening and at night slept dreamlessly although, as the first week came to an end, I began to feel unusually lonely. At home the remedy would have been a meal with friends or a call to Elaine.

The telephone's shrill tones penetrated drugged sleep at some dark hour of absolute silence. I fumbled to switch on the bedside lamp and struggled to lift the receiver. Had the deal soured after all my work? 'Hullo.'

'It's Bernard here. Come now.'

'Who? . . . Oh, I remember. How did you know where to find me?' I glanced at my watch and said, disbelievingly, 'It's 2 a.m.'

'A blue Citroën is parked across the street. Come now, just as you are. Make no preparations.'

'I'm naked!'

'Then I won't need to strip you. Put on a coat, go to the car, and give the driver my name. I shall judge

7

your commitment by how long you take. Don't keep me waiting.' A painfully loud click closed the line.

Trembling on the edge of an abyss and stifled in suddenly hot air, I blocked my mind, fearing to lose the will. In the bathroom I threw tepid water over my face and dragged a comb through tangled hair. My heart pounded rapidly as I dressed in a light summer coat, thrust on my shoes, and locked the door. Shoving the key deep in my pocket I dared not consider stupidity. I was out on a limb and at risk having abandoned money, credit cards, identification; all security gambled on an experiment.

The corridors were deserted and so, too, the reception desk. Outside, shivering in cold air, I tightened the coat. Only one car stood at the curb, its engine idling quietly. I opened the rear door, sank into the seat and said, 'Bernard'. Without turning round or uttering a word in reply the driver steered into the empty street.

Beyond the town the car followed a winding route into the hills until I looked down on the harbour's lights; a diamond necklace in purple velvet. I could easily have fallen into a doze but for the electric pulses that raced through my belly, and noticed nothing more until elaborate iron gates, a gravelled drive, and a house with white shutters. The driver stopped at a stone staircase and pointed upwards to an open door.

I stepped out and the car swept away. In the crystal air, illuminated by glimmering stars, there was no sign of anyone else. Hesitantly I mounted the stairs and paused at the entrance. Beyond, the pitch black might conceal any kind of danger. 'Bernard?' My voice fractured. Screwing my nerve I moved forwards, stiff with tension, nervously poised for flight. After a few steps, completely blind, I halted and called out again.

'Do not turn round. Take off your coat.' Trans-fixed, I stood motionless. 'Do as you are told!' The commanding note unlocked my inertia and the garment quickly rustled to the floor. 'Kick off your shoes.' One by one they clattered somewhere ahead in the dark and my bare feet rested on icy tiles. I waited breathlessly.

Warm fingers touched the chilled skin of my shoulders and moved down, as if acquainting themselves with the length of my arms. The fingers coaxed my right wrist over the left and my heart thumped as soft leather strapped them together as one, a lengthy process involving elaborate connections, all handled fluently by touch alone. I tried to flex this way or that but changed nothing. A second strap above my elbows drew them unnaturally close and another series of links fastened my arms. Pressure forced my shoulders back and projected my breasts. Floating dangerously, elated at having given away my independence, I croaked, 'And if I asked you to release me?'

'It's far too late.'

'But I told Elaine . . .'

'That's irrelevant.'

From behind, a cupped palm lifted the bowl of my breast. A second hand came from the opposite side and both caressed the soft pulp, rotating and squeezing. Fingertips teased and stretched my nipples, enlarging and hardening them. I breathed heavily, my tension lifting. 'What now?' I muttered, my voice thick. 'Am I to be raped?'

Bernard's breath warmed my ear. 'An indulgent fantasy, unworthy of us both.'

'I can't prevent it.'

'Nor anything else I choose to inflict.'

The right hand deserted my globe and slid gradually down my belly. As it reached the pubic curls I instinctively pulled back, then between my legs fingers pressed into my crotch, stroked my slit, and widened the moistened labia. My back arched. Formed as a wedge, the fingers plunged into my passage and during a deep finger-fuck I writhed and groaned. 'Does this please you?' I gasped. Abruptly the treatment stopped and the second hand released my breast. Bewildered, senses reeling, I struggled to understand.

'You talk too much.'

A blank interval, then something – a cloth band – touched my lips. Twisting from side to side I attempted to avoid the inward pressure, but unremitting persistence separated my jaw. The band dragged hard on the corners of my mouth, and while it was being fastened at the back of my skull I desperately inhaled air through my nose. I had never imagined how much a gag could equal restraint in reducing me to a passive condition. Now, in removing my last shred of autonomy, Bernard had all of the power.

As a tough grip enclosed my arm and urged me forwards I gave a muffled, piteous moan. Hustled along a corridor, my feet thudded on freezing tiles until he pulled me into a room, as black as before. A soft edge pressed my legs and Bernard lowered me onto a bed. Above, his bulky body, sensed but unseen, arranged my limbs comfortably, thighs wide apart, arms protected by deep pillows from the weight of my body. Beside me the bed sagged with the additional load of his weight.

He was going to do it!

For tense moments nothing happened until, just beyond my chin, came the touch of a fat slug settling between my breasts and down my belly, ending on my pubes. A long shaft lay there, cold and inert, wobbling slightly with each breath.

Noiselessly, on the ceiling above, a movie began. A small flame-haired woman danced enticingly in a skimpy costume of gold chains that rustled and chinked. It displayed through gaps her areolae and red pubic bush. She danced for a bearded man, a giant; she scarcely reached his chest. When she paused to kiss him the woman reached on tiptoe while he leaned down.

As a captive audience I gazed distastefully at banal porn. The slug began to slide down my torso, dragged its head across my pubes and settled into my fork, nudging the entrance. When the crown bulged my labia I gasped in muffled explosions of breath, and more followed its gradual piercing. Eventually the slug's fat girth distended my passage.

Above, the scene changed. The tiny woman continued to kiss the giant awkwardly. Her bra, pushed up, allowed her breasts to squash into his bared abdomen. Below the waist he was equally bare with massive thighs, pillars of hairy wood, pressed into the woman's groin. She cupped the sac of his testicles and his penis, not yet erect, lay on her forearm. From her fingertips several pounds of inflamed meat, thicker than her wrist, stretched halfway along her arm!

Stifled, I fought to inhale more air and squirmed as the shaft slid rapidly in sloppy heat. During brief stationary moments, the dildo wedged in my sex, Bernard's thumb rotated my clit. I squirmed and moaned, hating being compelled so heartlessly.

The scene changed again. The giant sat beside the woman, and his full erection reared upwards. Her fingers, cupped over the bulging head, reached only a short distance down the stem. If, in her tiny body, she took his cock – Ah! – that cruel monster would split her in two.

At the unrelenting pressure of Bernard's thumb I gasped helplessly and drifted away, gritting my teeth, determined to resist him. The massive slug stretched me ruthlessly.

Another change. The woman, naked, nipples like stalks, lay with her head to the camera, her wide mouth shrieking either in pleasure or pain, as the giant loomed above, plunging vigorously between her thighs. And every part of her – Ah! I trembled violently – would be stuffed unbearably. At least the woman, a shadow, had some choice, while I had none and struggling only hurt my arms. Incessant pressure, circling over that vulnerable spot – Ah! A fiery wave surged up from my groin. The giant's thick bayonet – my slug – slurped in the flow of abundant juice and Bernard's ravaging thumb would never cease. Above, it was clear – Ah! Another surge shook me from top and toe and the room dwindled and faded away. With my last dregs of energy used up, I twisted into Bernard's body as if for shelter; the only way I could tell him to stop, please stop the unbearable torment.

Wincing, eyes tight, I screwed away from the window's glare, clinking the ankle chain joined to the bedpost. If I was lucky today Bernard would soon come to set me free. If unlucky, he would send Maria the cook, an old crone dressed in black from head to foot, with leathery wrinkled skin. Her eyes, glittering obsidian, were so intense that I feared her malevolence – and with good reason.

Draped over her lap, bound hand and foot, Maria's calloused hands had hurt like toughened boards during the spanking. The extra rope, tight in my crotch and separating my labia, emerged from its moist bed at the top of my slit and crossed the pubic bone up to the neckband. My first spanking, made more painful by being administered by another woman; an old unforgiving mother to an errant daughter! My bitter tears were compounded of pain, the rope's insidious stimulation, and humiliation increased by Bernard's obvious pleasure. When the mirror revealed the bruising marks etched into my pliant flesh I had found it hard to forgive him. But as the throbbing stings diminished, my feelings had also modified. I had, after all, granted him the power to rule and he had led me into a web, a maze, too intricate to understand. The remnants of my own power lay in tattered pride at never protesting. My reward came from heightened sensations.

A key rasped in the lock and the door swung open.

Bernard had studied every detail of my body but not, before now, revealed himself. I had never known a man to be so reserved; it drove me mad. Greedily I absorbed the sight of his barrel chest covered in fine silver hair, his broad muscular thighs, a flaccid penis dangling over his balls and the whole smothered in thick pubic hair. As he moved closer, my desire swayed to and fro and I wriggled onto my spine, breasts slumped in mounds at the sides of my ribs. Bernard leaned over to place my right wrist on the rail behind my head. As a bondage fetishist his favourite routine was to bind me intricately, positioning and winding thin white rope with meticulous care.

'You gain beauty with each strand,' he murmured.

For me the tedious process had a different outcome. How, when securely bound, could I feel free?

Bernard moved around the bed to secure the left side. During the entire silent period every motion of his slack tool tantalised my mouth until, at last, the hooded crown wiped my lips. In darkness he toyed with me, only allowing me to kiss and lick its supple smoothness, bathed in spicy masculine scent. I relished the daylight view and poked out my tongue to ripple against the sliding tube of flesh, widening my jaws invitingly. Briefly, raising my hopes, the voluptuous organ popped inside but out again, dragging saliva over my cheek. If only that wet streak could be his semen! Surging with lust I whispered, 'I'm so hot. Let me taste you this time.' He kept me waiting until, once again, I crumbled in shame and whimpered, 'Please!' It was so humiliating to be forced, once again, to plead. In my past experience men urgently wanted to fuck me.

Unexpectedly the miracle happened. When the weighty rod sank into my oral cavity I adored the feel of hot flesh throbbing and lurching. Starved, I sucked avidly while, in my mind, a pattern revolved. This man: my master. My master's cock with a sculptured velvet plum. This cock: my true master. Bernard, groaning quietly, gave in to my appetite and straddled my chest, his thighs squashing my breasts as he leaned forwards. Elated, I formed a smooth tunnel for the luscious sex which continued to swell. If my hands were loose they would pull the man's butt to encourage my master deeper inside. I squinted along the stiff length, moving rhythmically, and its broad blunt cap nudged the back of my throat. It made me choke but I didn't care; my master's pleasure was paramount. As he thrust steadily into me I imagined his pouring tributes and my frantic squirming strained the bonds. I wanted my master's surging spunk in my throat but also coats of his cream on my face; every drop, everywhere. The first impulse splashed on the roof of my mouth before he pulled out. A wad fell on my teeth, a strand blocked one eye, and more spattered erratically over my lips. From my chin a dangling thread crept down. Bernard looked at my soiled condition while I gazed amorously at the purpled knob and a creamy drool oozing from the tip. My master dipped once more, allowing my tongue to wash him clean.

Bernard released my right hand and murmured, 'Clean yourself.'

Patiently, following directions, I dragged the gifts from scattered locations and fed on it, piece by piece, quivering as I swallowed.

Maria's piercing eyes observed every move. Immersed in silvered water from the overhead shower, I ignored her and continued to wash. When I stepped out she approached, her black robe flapping behind, and gestured curtly, giving me no time to dry. A small lake collected on the tiles around my feet while I held out my wrists for the handcuffs. They snapped together and at the next command I turned apprehensively to face the shower. Raising my arms I gripped the rail above and waited tensely with water dripping from soaking hair onto my shoulders. I hoped she would not repeat –

Claws kneaded my buttock curves lasciviously and then insisted I open my legs. Investigating my cleft, a calloused finger crudely probed my anal hole. I gritted my teeth and held on desperately. Treatment like this, when it happened untied, destroyed my dignity but I knew better than to pull away – that earlier protest had led to a spanking I'd never forget. As one horny nail thrust into the dry, tight aperture I yelped, my hips bucked forwards and I only breathed again, shakily, when the invader withdrew. The crone moved under my crotch, rubbed my labia mercilessly, and I groaned aloud. These unspeakable intimacies were a terrible trial. Maria's voraciousness suggested not just simple play but actual desire. I flinched at a truly horrible thought: had Bernard cruelly given me to the witch? Tough fingers burst suddenly into my channel, plunging deeply to emphasise their ownership, stretching out my vagina's walls. I howled, squirming and clutching the rail, shamed by a flood that seemed to welcome the very thing I really hated. Into my mind flashed an image of the cook, lying back with her robe high, her naked wrinkled belly and spread thighs. Unkempt strands of black hair bearded her old, receptively parted, drooping lips. Bernard forced me closer, stifled by a stale smell in the ripe cleft, until I began to lap willingly –

'Ahhh!' Despairing orgasmic wails accompanied my helpless judders and pelvic convulsions. Throughout the spasms – and even after they'd subsided – the wedge of fingers, jammed inside, emphasised their domination. Finally, as they released possession, I vaguely heard Bernard's laugh. 'Let go and turn round,' he said.

I discovered Maria sniffing her fingers and licking my lubrication with signs of pleasure. She looked up with glittering eyes. Recalling my own fevered image my cheeks, already flushed, flamed in embarrassment. Bernard laughed again and lifted my chin to kiss my mouth while his free hand fondled my breast. Woozy from the climax, I leaned against his rugged chest and responded passively.

He pulled back, and gripped my right arm, and Maria my left. As they marched me along the corridor Bernard delivered an unexpected stinging slap to one haunch. I gasped and squirmed away, only to meet an equally sharp slap from the maid. Their sport continued through a beaded screen and onto the bright unshaded terrace. I screwed my nerve for another ordeal. The terrace overlooked a narrow street with apartments opposite, giving the top floors a grandstand view. Here, in late-evening gloom, I had received Maria's spanking and wondered how many spies had been attracted by regular cracks in the silent air. But now, men could be staring salaciously at my nakedness and I cringed, clearly exposed with nowhere to hide, never before so vulnerable.

My captors provided one important concession by leading me to a wrought-iron chair turned away from the terrace rail. Perhaps, with only my back visible, watchers would think I was sunbathing topless. I also welcomed the soft cushion for my pulsing butt while Bernard started to form elaborate links, fastening my left leg to the chair. When he widened my right to match the opposite leg I realised his intention. Nevertheless, lulled by the heat of the sun, I almost dozed, cuffed hands in my lap, and stirred only when Maria lifted them. Released, I had to place my forearms on the chair's arms for Bernard to resume his patient work.

At last, with a final flourish, he completed the binding and stepped back. I struggled to obtain the slightest movement but every limb had, of course, been locked. To him, bonds gave me beauty but, in a strange way I did not understand, I also felt beautiful. Ignoring Maria's dark scowl I smiled up at Bernard.

'Magnificent,' he breathed. 'Aesthetically pleasing. Your breasts hang splendidly, your pointed nipples are very fine, and your dark slit is pouting generously. It's inviting a shag, right now.'

I tensed. Here, in full view –

'Instead, I'll take photographs.'

'No!' I screeched. 'They could ruin my reputation . . . my career.'

'So – your first defence will lie in sunshades. Second, I'll use film so there's nothing digital to appear on the internet. Third, I'll give you the negs and prints.'

Given those assurances, the idea sounded appealing; I had few pictures of myself naked and none exposed so lewdly, open-crotched. Large round glasses disguised a substantial portion of my face and when the time came, moistening between my legs, I smiled alluringly into the lens.

After several shots Bernard said, 'You need decorations. Maria, fetch the box.'

Her gap-toothed grin looked ominous. Bernard knelt in my wide fork, lifted each breast in turn and sucked my nipples, tongue flicking, extending them in his lips. Unbearably aroused, my breathing deepened and, when Maria returned, tight stalks projected out from my breasts.

The box appeared innocuous and its opened lid masked the contents. Maria rummaged inside, prolonging the scrapes and rasps of metallic objects, trying to increase my nervousness. When she produced a long silver clip and opened its jaws I jerked in horror, screeching the chair's legs. The clamp extended across my breast and its jaws settled around my sensitive tip, squeezing hard. When they snapped shut I jolted violently, my eyes rounded in shock. Maria lifted another clip and tightened it ruthlessly onto the second. As the jaws snapped again my head craned back, mouth wide, and a leathery palm smothered my scream instantly.

'Mustn't alarm the neighbours,' Bernard said.

The reminder of watchers forced me to subdue my reactions and my deep gulps of air wobbled the weights eccentrically. My nipples, beyond their flattened bases, stuck out as luscious berries. In Bernard's subsequent shots my face, cleared of every artifice, could only register raw emotions.

'Next,' he called.

Maria applied a small nipping clamp to the delicate

surface of one breast. At the teeth's full force I gasped and wrenched. Identical clamps followed; another on the first, two more on its twin. Another pair snatched my belly and at each sharp bite I jerked involuntarily and cried out. Others, more painful, clenched the tender flesh of my inner thighs, a pair in each, but the most severe were two in my labia. My head fell back and Maria's hand again stifled a helpless scream.

Desperately I fought for control while Bernard continued to photograph. 'Really magnificent –' he called '– a total of fourteen.' At last he finished, released the awful nipple pressures, and I slumped forwards in massive relief. 'One day I'm sure you'll enjoy these pictures.'

Alone on the terrace my mind slowly cleared. The twelve remaining clamps were cold crystal jewellery but what strange process transformed their pain to pleasure, borne with pride? Later I realised that the people opposite must have known something sexual accounted for my writhing and stifled shrieks, especially with a photographer moving around. At least they couldn't observe the reason. In the silent heat I lost all track of time until Maria arrived to release the adornments and remove the glasses. When she held up a mirror I gazed in chilled awe at the puckered red marks deep in my skin. Each photograph would be that mirror, retaining the memory after they faded.

Gradually I realised my vagina's ache had not come from the clamps alone. I moaned, squirmed my pelvis, rocked and scraped the chair. I gulped and breathed harshly and called out, again tormented. Agonised minutes passed before they appeared and I cried, 'You must let me go.' My captors stared silently, as if unable to comprehend. 'Please!' They sat on chairs at both sides. 'You're heartless!' I shrieked. They leaned forwards, watching intently. Choking, I cursed them both, the words broken by wracking sobs. They smiled sympathetically. Tears poured down my cheeks as a stream of scalding fluid burst out, splashed and sprayed over the tiles in all directions. The disgusting disgrace went on and on, thighs and cushion shamefully soaked. Immersed in hot acrid scent, I quivered with tension and fear until, drained of every shred of beauty or pride, I moaned miserably, 'Why must I be so demeaned?'

'Why does a powerful executive ask for restraint with no stipulations?' Bernard's reply hit me with the force of a sudden slap. 'Is that due to naïve trust? Unlikely. Or does it allow you to claim, "I am not responsible?" '

Numb and soiled, hurting more than when gripped by clamps, I lowered my head. Amber spurts accompanied the tears that flowed again.

'Our time is almost up.' Bernard glanced at me, supine on the bed, and completed knotting the left bond.

'And you've never fucked me –' I grumbled '– not once.'

'Nor introduced you to the lash.'

I gasped in physical strain as he raised my right leg to match the left, forcing my body to a shallow V. My arms were stretched out from the shoulders and my wrists bound to the ankles. My feet, splayed out on either side of my head, had additional ties to the headboard. I had never experienced anything resembling the tough pull on my thigh muscles but worse, far worse, was to have my crotch opened to its absolute maximum. My genitals were completely unprotected from Maria's avid gaze and her loathsome talons had free reign to clutch the pleats of my labia, spreading them out to display my sex as a blossoming flower.

Bernard joined the crone and both examined the position silently. 'A beautiful sight needing no further decoration,' he said. I gulped and tossed my head, humiliated utterly and feeling grotesque. 'Maria can help with that.'

She came to my side, blotted out all sight by a thick mask over my eyes, and strapped it efficiently behind my head.

'Think about what you're presenting,' Bernard continued. 'Excellent tits. A gloriously stretched arse. A prominent cunt. A tempting anal ring.'

He had reduced me to some kind of basic object and moans of despair trembled my breasts like soft jellies. Later, I could hear no sounds and for a long blank time nothing occurred. My rigid pose allowed no opportunity to forget Bernard's brutal description, or the fearful implications. He suggested –

I tensed and strained to catch the words of male voices, murmuring too low to hear. Did Bernard intend to give me to strangers? Were there two? More? With my stark invitations how could they avoid arousal? What were they planning? Then I clearly heard: 'I guarantee she's ready for it.'

I fought the implacable bonds while a leathery palm stifled my breath. I had no choice but to take the cocks, however many, wherever they came. The bed sagged. At the first touch, a palm clamped down on my scream.

The mobile's muted chirrups interrupted discreetly. I checked the number, quietly excused myself from the meeting, and opened the line in the corridor.

'Well?' Elaine enquired mischievously. 'Have you a good report? Aren't I clever to find him?'

'I have. You are. However, I'm reluctant to praise him too highly in case he becomes fully booked.'

'It's me you should worry about. I'm denying all access until you agree to my terms.'

'Name them.'

'I'm dying to see those photographs. Tomorrow evening, seven o'clock. Our table's booked at the Savoy Grill.'

'You were that sure I'd agree?'

'We can discuss the merits of bondage, affecting our minds far more than a straightforward fuck can ever achieve.'

'Seductive . . . insidious.'

'Great antidote to the pressures of work.'

'The exhilaration! To give up and simply obey!'

'Remember my caution – be careful of what you start?'

'Well, I have, and mean to continue. For me it's just . . . perfect.'

– S.J., London, UK

Breastfed

Before anything else, I want to thank everyone at Nexus Books for making me realise I'm not alone in the world. I have the strangest fetish, and while I know there are men like me, for years I thought I had to be the only woman who'd ever had anything like it even enter her head. I'm twenty-nine, reasonably attractive I suppose, from a completely boring suburban background, and I like to be suckled at another woman's breast.

I don't know where it came from, or why, but it has been an important part of my sexuality for as long as I can remember. Not the most important part, maybe, and I'm not claiming I couldn't live without it or anything, but it is something I crave. I prefer other women anyway, and I'm not really into vanilla sex, which is just boring. For me it's all in my head, and when I come I like to feel completely relaxed and open, but above all, comforted. There is no greater comfort than lying in a strong woman's arms while I suckle from her nipple and she brings me gently off with her fingers.

As you may well imagine, it's not exactly easy to get what I want. It involves a lot of compromise for one thing, because while it's easy for, say, a girl who likes to be tied up to find a woman who likes to do the tying, or a girl who likes to be spanked to find a woman who likes to do the spanking, with my needs I've never even come close. That doesn't mean I don't get it, but it does mean I have to compromise.

They always seem to want to spank me. Maybe it's because of who I go for, or maybe it's something about me, but it seems that every time I find a partner I really fancy the first thing she seems to want to do is smack my bottom. I suspect it's something to do with fashion too, because of course if you want to find kinky people you need to go to kinky places, and it just seems to be assumed that bottom smacking is what you do.

So I get spanked a lot, and I tend to spend quite a bit of time in bondage or crawling around the floor in nothing but a spiky leather collar, or whatever it might be, simply as a compromise so that my own needs can be met in return for meeting the needs of my partner. Not that I mind the spankings so much if they're in private, because it's quite nice having a glowing bum while I'm breastfed, but it was never part of my original desire. Being naked was, and is. To be naked is to be protected, to me, and if that doesn't make sense to you, try thinking about it this way. For me, the whole thing is to give myself over completely into a partner's control, to have nothing hidden from them at all, which means not just having my body available to them, but having no clothes on whatsoever. My partner is my protection, and to hold her nipple in my mouth as she comforts me and brings me to ecstasy is incomparably better than anything I've ever experienced any other way.

Like I say, it's not easy finding a partner and I have to put up with a lot, but I do have an ideal. She's older than me, and a lot bigger, which is quite easy because I'm small, but when I say bigger I do mean bigger, and not just tall. She should be fifteen or maybe even twenty stone, and with a full, matronly figure, wide hips, a great big bottom and, of course, large breasts with big nipples, preferably big enough to get my whole mouth around when I suck. A big woman brings out the feeling of being cared for and protected, call it mothered if you like, in a way that nobody of even approximately my own size ever can.

There are two positions I like to be breastfed in, the original and best, and more recently, the post-punishment. For the original I am taken in my partner's arms just exactly as if she were suckling a baby, with my body curled into her lap and my head cradled to her breast and supported by one hand while she uses the other to feed me. After a while I let my legs come apart, exposing myself completely, which she should know is the signal to slip a hand between my thighs and bring me to ecstasy. The post-punishment position is how the woman who got me into spanking liked to feed me. First I'd go over her lap in the conventional punishment position to have my bottom smacked, before having my upper body lifted into her arms and my mouth put to her breast, still bum up, and she would cup my sex to masturbate me.

To come like that leaves me in a state of complete bliss, relaxed in a way no other technique can achieve, and believe me, I've tried plenty. It also leaves me feeling very pliant and grateful to the woman who's fed me, and completely uninhibited. I like to be cuddled for a while, and then I'll return the favour in absolutely any way she wishes. Most women are content with a nice slow lick, which I'm more than happy to give anyway, but after being suckled I've been put on a lead and treated like a puppy dog, given a milk enema, and worse, all of which I've accepted and even enjoyed, which I could never do normally.

My ideal is still to be taken to orgasm as I suckle, but some of my more inventive partners have added some wonderful details. One, who I shall call Ms X because too many people know her, and me (but not about our more intimate secrets), used to like to wrap a big fluffy towel around my middle and up between my thighs and pin it into place as if it was a giant nappy. That felt nice, soothing in a slightly different way to being cuddled while I'm naked, and especially when I'd let my legs come apart and her hand would steal down the front to give me my orgasm. She has lovely nipples too, very wide, and one of my happiest memories will always be of lying in her lap with my mouth completely full of her nipple and her hand pushed in down my nappy. Her great thing is to have me go about the house in just my nappy and a little top, and she loved to humiliate me by having me pee in my nappy and then clean up in the nude, all of which I'm happy to put up with for the pleasure of how she handles me. The only drawback is that we can only play when her husband's away on business, because while he's scene, neither of us feel we want any male involvement in our more private games.

I'm funny like that, because I do like men, but I can never achieve the same level of intimacy and relaxation as I can with a woman. Obviously they haven't got the right equipment to suckle me with anyway, but it's more than that, perhaps something to do with the way a woman's flesh feels or how her skin smells, which is completely different and really important to me.

Only once have I achieved what must be the perfect expression of my fantasy and, while it gave me a level of pleasure I've never been able to equal, I still feel oddly guilty about it. I'd played with 'Ms Z' before, allowing her to spank me at a club and kneeling between her thighs to be suckled briefly, but that was all. About a year later she fell pregnant and stopped going out except to the occasional market or munch, but we were quite close friends anyway and I still saw her occasionally.

All went well with her pregnancy and birth, but with her new baby she wasn't really in a position to go out at all and felt very tied down. I went round to cheer her up, and I swear it was only that, despite the fact that towards the end of her term I'd found her swollen breasts and the rich smell of her intensely exciting.

I did try to resist, but with nobody else around except the baby, who was upstairs asleep in his cot, it was absolute torture for me. She was producing so much milk that she was leaking, and had to change the pads in her bra every half hour or so. To see her nipples so dark and swollen, with the milk spots coming even as she removed the wet pads, was absolute torture, and in the end I offered to relieve her of some of the pressure. She was genuinely grateful, as having full breasts can be quite painful, so I came next to her and she fed me a nipple.

From the moment I tasted her milk I was completely lost to pleasure. To feel her milk flowing into my mouth as I suckled her was completely overwhelming, and I couldn't hold back. I asked if she minded if I stripped off so that she could hold me to her breast and bring me off as she suckled me, and after a bit of hesitation she agreed. I couldn't get my clothes off fast enough, and to curl myself naked into her lap and take her hard, milky nipple back into my mouth was ecstasy close to orgasm in itself.

She made me relieve both her breasts before she'd touch me, so I got a proper drink, not just a drop. Human milk is slightly sharp to the taste, and a bit odd after being used to cow's milk, but the knowledge that I was drinking it made the taste and the feel of it in my mouth so special I couldn't possibly put it into words. She held me perfectly too, cradling my head and putting her breasts to my mouth one by one, while she'd put on a lot of weight during pregnancy so she was lovely to cuddle.

My legs had been wide apart almost from the first moment I felt her milk squirt into my mouth, and I have never felt so completely surrendered and relaxed, or so badly in need of a touch. Her blouse was open and her bra cups unzipped, so that both her breasts were pressed to my bare skin, warm and naked and milky, so that my own breasts were a little wet with it as I suckled. She rubbed that in first, all around my breasts and over my nipples, then a bit more on the mound of my sex before she finally slid a finger between my lips and began to rub.

That moment was perfect bliss, held naked in her arms as she fed me her milk and masturbated me. While I came almost immediately, in my memory it seemed to last forever, and if I ever need to turn myself on or want to come in a hurry I only have to think back to that perfect moment and I'm there. She was very understanding, and gave me a lovely cuddle after I'd come, but she didn't want anything in return and I've always felt a bit guilty, as if I was depriving her baby of his milk, although she had plenty to spare.

By then I'd already read several Nexus books, although the emphasis on sadism wasn't really my thing, but I was delighted to discover Aishling Morgan's weird and wonderful Devonshire fantasies with all those big-breasted, milk-bearing women feeding each other and their younger friends. I only wish I lived in that world.

– *Zoë, London, UK*

Under a Blanket in the Sky

When I dressed for my flight home that morning, I was thinking in terms of comfort. I opted for the short wrap dress – it was a long flight, and the dress was a fitted but stretchy fabric that clung to my curves without being in any way restrictive. The sun proved misleading when I stepped out onto the balcony overlooking London for the last time – the chill immediately caused my nipples to stand at attention.

I had already packed everything else, so another outfit was not an option; I needed to add some stockings to the ensemble to avoid freezing.

I sat on the edge of the bed and watched myself in the mirror as I leisurely drew the stockings up over my smooth legs. There was just something about wearing thigh-highs that always managed to make me feel super sexy. A final glance in the mirror and adjusting of my ample cleavage that seemed to slip out of the wrap dress with the slightest move, and I was off.

I hadn't put that much effort into my appearance so it was a pleasant surprise when the cab driver, so distracted by me, almost ran over an airport security officer!

Standing in the check-in queue proved to be just as great for my ego as a couple of different men attempted to chat me up, though that may have had something to do with my breasts; clad in a black lacy bra, playing peek-a-boo every time I bent to pick up my suitcase. An older gentleman who stood behind me with his wife was the one I opted to speak to. He was a very pleasant and well-spoken man in his late fifties who was tall and dark skinned with very distinguished salt and pepper hair. He told me that he was raised in London but had been born in Sri Lanka in one of the Portuguese colonies, after having seen my last name on my bag tag and realising that I too was Portuguese. He had a couple of interesting stories to tell about his life while his seemingly subservient wife stood quietly behind. By the time it was my turn to check in, I knew that Raj – that was what he insisted I call him – was a retired banker with two sons and three grandchildren, along with what seemed like a hundred other things that I didn't need to know. He was a sweet man, but the deeper he got into conversation, the more bored and agitated I became. With boarding pass finally in hand and luggage checked in, I turned to make my getaway to the duty-free shop only to slam directly into him. He must have been standing barely a couple of inches from me.

'Have a nice flight!' I called out, walking away quickly.

'We'll see you on board.' He smiled excitedly.

I remained in the Skyline bar, sipping an early-afternoon Cosmo until the final boarding call announcement for my flight ran through for the second time. With dirty looks from the crew and annoyed glances from some of the passengers, I made my way to my row, only to find Raj and the missus sitting waiting.

'Oh – what a coincidence!' he gushed.

I faked a smile as I squeezed past his wife and then him over to my window seat, acutely aware of his eyes on my every move. I had thought he must just be lonely or something and that was to blame for his need to be long-winded, but I was beginning to get a different vibe. I struggled to fit my bag under the seat in front of me – even managing to work up a bit of a sweat. Sitting back up, I was immediately bombarded by Raj: 'Why were you so late coming to the plane? I looked for you at the gate.'

'I was at the bar,' I said simply, trying not to give him anything more to go on.

He began to ramble on again and his accent began to ring through my ears like an irritating bell, so I grabbed my blanket and pillow from under me and was about to explain to him that I needed to sleep when I noticed his dark eyes bulging, homing right in on my chest. Following his gaze, I found my lace bra once again exposed for the world to see. When I reached to adjust my dress, Raj placed his hand on mine and whispered: 'Don't worry – you are beautiful. Do not cover them.'

I went on to cover them and felt a rage – or was it disgust – wash over me. 'This man is somebody's grandpa!' I thought to myself. And it was for that very same reason that I couldn't bring myself to be rude to him, so I just smiled.

I leant back into the seat and closed my eyes as the plane took off, figuring that if I slept – or at least looked like I was sleeping – he would leave me alone. The engines roared just outside my window and my ears popped, helping to tune out the sound of the voices around me. While others detest flying, I have always found the feeling of being cocooned in the cabin soothing, so it wasn't long before I really began to drift into sleep. As the plane climbed higher, the temperature lowered in the cabin and the goose bumps began to tingle across my body. I felt something soft brush against my legs and I opened my eyes to find Raj placing a blanket on my lap. His expression was so concentrated and he was gentle as he made sure to spread it over my knees.

'Oh – I am sorry, but you looked like you were feeling cold . . .' he explained.

'Oh no, that's OK. Thank you – I was feeling a little cold,' I said, feeling super guilty for my having misread the old man.

He nodded appreciatively and I closed my eyes and tried to pick up my nap where I had left off, only feeling cosier. I drifted in and out of light sleep, always aware of the fact that I was on a plane. In a place between sleep and waking I felt a familiar stir within me; a mild pleasure bringing me to a deeper state of relaxation. I went with it for a moment, letting it take me farther back into my seat and forgetting about the comfort of the person seated ahead so that I might give in to the urge to extend my legs for a good stretch. My muscles sighed in relief, glad to be drawn out of the curled-up ball of the last few minutes, which caused me to awaken, though ever so slightly. I felt something caressing my thigh under the warmth of the blanket and opened one eye to have a look.

The cabin was now dark apart from the screens flashing the film, and the few heads that I could see had fallen into sleep. Almost afraid to confirm what I suspected – or maybe afraid that my waking would bring it to an end – I glanced to my side with a barely open eye, making certain not to move, and found Raj's arm disappearing under the cheap blue blanket.

My heart began to beat faster and I was infuriated that this old bastard would take advantage of young me in such a lewd way. Only I didn't say a word. Instead I closed my eye and just sat there as his small hand rubbed my thigh, inching its way slowly upwards. My cunt was wet – probably had been since his hand first crept under the blanket. I flinched when I felt his hand leaving the lace edge of my stockings and beginning to explore my bare skin. His hand was hot – dirty old man – yet I found myself becoming moister with each slither in spite of my revulsion. My nipples reacted to his brazen touch and swelled to peaks and immediately he took note of my pleasure; it encouraged him to squeeze my flesh harder between his bony fingers. When he finally reached the edge of my panties I was sure he could already feel the wet. His finger teased me by sliding just under the trim and my clit began to ache to be touched, causing me to open my legs a little more for him. Even though my moves made it obvious, I didn't dare open my eyes and admit that I wanted it and instead continued to play the sleeping beauty. I felt a finger inch its way into my panties and to my slit, but then draw quickly back out as though he was just testing the waters.

My arousal increased as did my impatience and I tilted my pelvis as if offering myself up to him. The finger found its way back in and began to explore the folds of my cunt, revelling in the warm wetness. I could feel him leaning in closer, his breath nearing my neck and then moving downwards until his breath was warming up my left breast – my dress must have opened again. He leant down, his face falling to my bosom, and I am sure that he too was pretending to be asleep and unaware of his position, for anyone who might pass by.

I was so turned on by the way he sloppily used his mouth and nose to push away at the lace demi-cup of my bra until he was suckling on my nipple like a starved baby, that I was caught off guard when his finger pushed into my hole. My whole body reacted with a series of tingles as he pushed his finger carefully in and out of me, at the same time sucking on my tit. Surprising me with his skill, he continued to pump the finger in and out of my pussy while adding a thumb to the mix. The thumb pressed against my clit, pulsing in time with my pleasure until it became overwhelming. His breathing increased and saliva began to dribble into my bra from his disgusting mouth, causing me to feel as repelled as I was excited. Tiny quakes of arousal mixed with contempt made their way through me and he sensed this and pushed his thumb harder against my swollen bud. I couldn't contain my pleasure any longer and I began to shudder, pressing into his hand until he was using all of his fingers to rub the climax out of me. I came and the sharp pangs of pleasure and juices erupted, causing me to gasp.

His hand worked until the trembles subsided then it paused there for a second. I could sense him looking at me as if waiting for acknowledgement, but I didn't budge. My eyes remained closed until I drifted into blissful sleep again, only to be awakened by the thump of the plane's tyres touching down.

In the light of the new day, the entire flight felt like a dream and I addressed him and his wife no differently than before. I could see he looked perplexed, but I didn't care. A man his age really should know better than to do what he did, so why would I justify his misbehaviour? After all, 'I was just the innocent, sleeping victim'. I laughed to myself, adjusting my damp panties as I walked off the plane.

– *Adriana, New York, USA*

He Touched Me

Mistress, since we met my life has taken a definite turn for the better. If it were at all appropriate I'd broach this confession with a simile involving clouds (as in Cloud Nine) or an extended metaphor riffing on trance (as in Hypnotic) or even bliss (as in Transcendental) to describe the last three months. I love to do just that – pour my words like honey all over the Queen Bee that is You.

But it's not appropriate, so I won't. I'll start with the session we had last week. Or rather, the words you spoke when it was over. You said, 'Now, my darling girl, I've completely erased his touch and replaced it with my own.' Your smile was immensely satisfied. I love it when you smile wide enough to show dimples. Your angular face softens and your fierce dark eyes fade to a delightful, dreamy grey. It fills me with pleasure. It *filled* me with pleasure. I smiled back and batted my lashes at you and demurely dropped my glance.

But? But I didn't just drop my glance to be demure, as in sexily so. You know how much mutual pleasure we get from my acting demure right after an act of debauchery such as the one we had just successfully concluded? Well, it wasn't just so I could be demure. I guess, in truth, I was hiding my confusion so I could think about it for a little bit. I know, I am not supposed to think. But we were done at that point and a return to cognitive thought is inevitable. I kept silent. I kept something from you. I have a secret.

The secret is – there remains a place he touched me that you have not. Not in my heart, my love, my Love. Nor my soul nor my mind nor my psyche. But there was something he did to me that you have not. I didn't want to disturb you, not right then, right after you'd taken me from behind like that, so sweetly fucking me, first with your mouth and your fingers and then, when my puckered hole was loosened, with your thick hard black rubber dick. I know you are concerned with anything that has to do with me so it does affect us. I'm getting ahead of myself. May I explain?

You know how he was, a civilised man who unleashed the Beast in the bedroom. You know what that meant I had to be, a modern woman, available to be utterly vanquished at his whim. You know he showed no mercy. You know that the only way out, for me, was completely. I had no 'safe word' save 'Goodbye.'

This is why I said goodbye.

He was transferring planes in town and he'd rearranged his schedule so that we could spend a night together in a hotel near the airport. As usual, I was panicky and terrified and excited to the point of incoherence. But I got all dolled up, groomed and perfumed, and managed to get myself to the door of his hotel room. I knocked. He took over and my mind turned off.

He gallantly got me a drink and nicely *asked* me to remove my dress, just to prove he really was a civilised man capable of restraint. Then he tore my panties off and threw me face down on the bed. He was fully erect. The sight of me always made him hard as steel. He took my ass in one long, painful thrust. He said what he always said at such times: 'You haven't been properly fucked in a while.'

If we'd had more time together I might have become shaped to suit him. But the way it was there was always that difficult first time, where he showed me no mercy and I was not at liberty to ask for it. Anyway, the pain that came with being used like that fed my obsessive adoration and resulted in my extreme pleasure.

It's similar to the way it is now, with you, when I take a dozen stripes across my bottom, biting my lip to hold my safe word back until the pain mingles with your pride and washes over me in waves of pre-orgasmic bliss. But the knowledge that you will keep me even if I break makes me brave and weak with love, a paradox so perfect I know it must be good. I didn't have that with him.

Still I was rather proud of myself when he roared like a caveman and filled my rear passage with the proof of his pent-up need for me. After that he gorged on my pussy until I came. The orgasm was explosive. It was a release I ached for, often for months at a time. Sometimes the relief made me cry. Not this time, though. I was pleased with myself. I'd not only endured the onslaught of his passion without protest, but I'd come in the same shuddering, major way that he had. I was like the cat that ate the canary. He saw my pride and whereas you get a little kick out of it, he always found it evidence of uppityness. He yawned. I knew I was in trouble.

He knelt between my feet and laid the palm of his right hand on my pussy. 'Wider,' he said. I spread wider. He fingered me. It felt good, then it hurt a little and then it hurt a lot. I inched up the bed and he said,

'Stop moving,' so I did. It hurt like hell. My question hung between us, sharp in contrast to the general fogginess that always seemed to shroud our bed. 'I'm fisting your cunt,' he said.

So now I knew what was going on and I chose not to protest. In those days I would always ask myself, 'Would "O" submit to this?' If the answer was yes, which it always was, I'd do it. Which I realise now is sort of asking myself, 'Would Supergirl do it?' and if the answer was yes, jumping off a skyscraper. But my thinking at the time, obviously, was clouded at best.

He fisted me. At first it was excruciating. Then an absolute blizzard of endorphins kicked in. I know my head lolled to one side because I heard him laugh and say, 'You're nodding.'

I was higher than if I'd drunk a magnum of champagne. I could have giggled, believe it or not. There was *intense* pressure and then the pain stopped. Just like that. He said, 'I'm inside you up to my wrist,' and I gingerly looked down to sort of see that it was true.

'Lie back,' he said.

I was full as I'd never been before. There wasn't a breath of air left inside me. Only him. When he turned his hand his knuckles pressed against my insides. When he pumped it was like I was nothing more than my pelvis. Once again I was reduced to this thing that only existed to accommodate his fiendish desires. It freed me to soar. The euphoria was limitless.

'Touch it,' he said. I heard him from a long way away. I carefully reached down to touch his wrist. The rest of him was inside me. My clit was stretched; its hood was flat and wide. I touched it. A spasm shuddered through me, clenching and releasing on his fist. The tiny pressure almost made me scream.

He loved it. The truth is, I did too. I tickled my clit again, dead centre. Another delicate, agonising spasm gripped me, gripped us both. 'Go for it, you slut,' he whispered, so I did. He pumped his fist inside me. I rubbed my clit for maybe a minute, maybe two at the most, before I started coming all over his fist. It was fantastic. This time I did scream, with each fist-grabbing contraction I screamed and soared. I stopped rubbing myself but the orgasm continued, unabated. I'd never experienced anything like it and I never have since.

The force of my climax terrified me. I also knew that even if I could somehow stop the spasms from rocking through me to my centre and grasping his hand so that his knuckles grazed the soft, fleshy glove that was my cunt, if I could stop it I would not, because each paroxysm was immediately followed by another mind-blowing burst of endorphins.

It seemed to go on forever. I was skewered by his hand, helpless to do anything but ride the exultation to its end. Even the sure knowledge that he'd finally managed to ruin me for good made this, my last big orgasm, all the more spectacular.

He urged me on with short, intense statements like, 'More!' and 'Good!' The contractions became tremors; the bursts of endorphins weakened. At last I was motionless. Sated. Spent.

When he dislodged his hand from my body it was covered in cream, thick as Nivea. I felt emptier than I'd ever been. It was as if I, his favourite toy, had been shown to be not real or substantial, but nothing more than a cheap inflatable, now punctured and deflated.

I curled up on my side, my arms between my legs. The bliss began to fade. I ached. I felt misshapen. I wished he would say something nice. I hoped he would spoon me and we would rest. That would give me release from the thoughts that were beginning to form, the usual hot-blooded expletives I always hastened to delete. 'Bastard.' 'Happy now, you prick?' Stuff like that.

If we could just rest I knew that by the time he was ready for more I would be, too. Tomorrow he'd be gone and I'd have plenty of time to recover. I could contemplate my bruises and insanity at my leisure. I could pore over our time together in excessive detail, minute by minute, to try and decide if the end really did justify the means. To try and figure what exactly constituted 'the end', anyway: the part where I climax gloriously, as never before? Or the part after that, where I'm all alone with my aches and my pain?

There's no rest for the wicked, as they say. He pressed a cream-covered fingertip to my anus. The thick hot blood that had so recently coursed with each contraction from the very pit of me to every extremity turned to ice.

'You're nice and open,' he commented, slipping his finger inside me. I was supposed to thank him so I did. No need to rock the boat. I know, I know it's pathetic; please don't feel sorry for me. It's not like I was a child. I entered into it all with my eyes wide open. If they were wide open with addictive, passionate shock, well, how was he to know if I never said so?

You know, Mistress, at the very beginning I told him, 'You can do whatever you want to me.' If I was naïve about how twisted his dark needs really were it's not entirely his fault. Is it?

I had this faint hope that he was just engaging in a little after-play. He'd had his own massive orgasm only an hour before. But he was insatiable for me. At least that's the way I liked to think at the time.

Insatiable for *it* is probably more likely, but that had just begun to dawn on me.

Another finger joined the first. Even it went in easily because he'd already taken my ass. Still there was the slightest discomfort, nothing more than a little internal pressure. It hurt a little. I knew what he had in mind. I knew in a few minutes it was going to hurt a lot.

Maybe if he and I had had more time together, instead of only the odd night here and there, he might have taken more time with me. In the days that followed I liked to think that might have been true. But honestly, if he'd wanted more time with me he could have had it. I would have moved across the world for him, never mind across the country. I don't mean to press the point, Mistress, but it needs to be said.

I must have flinched. 'It'll be easier this way,' he said. 'There's no pelvic cradle to pass through. You'll see, you're going to love it.' He was behind me, whispering in my ear, his two fingers burrowing inside me.

I didn't look at him, I just stayed curled up as I was, my arms still between my legs. What would "O" do? I said, 'What if I don't?' My voice was what You call 'little'. To his ears it likely sounded like a whine.

'You will,' he said. There was a trace of impatience in his voice.

'And then what? After you fist my ass, what next?' It seemed to me that his depravity was fathomless.

'I'll come up with something. Trust me.'

I said, 'No.'

It didn't take me long to get dressed and get out. I had plenty of time to repent, or not, since. Yes, there were times when I wished I'd just done what he'd wanted, just to keep the thing we had, whatever twisted, wild thing that it was, alive. But, really, what *would* he have done to me next? It was always going to end one of two ways, either with me in hospital, or me leaving him, either way alone.

I've loved him and I've hated him. I've been grateful to him for introducing me to the world of BDSM, and I've detested him for muddying the waters of that world to a point where I was afraid to wade back in.

In another man's hands I might have become his happy bi-curious playmate for life. As it is, I've become yours and yours alone. I'm no longer curious about men, which makes me a perfect playmate for you, my Love.

Still, I feel there remains a place where he touched me and you have not. So I humbly ask that you *gently* ready my pussy, with your deft fingers and most delicate, softest mouth, to receive your fine hand.

I want to ride that wave again, my Love. I confess, I ache to be stretched and filled and bruised inside, just a little. The high is intoxicating, I admit. I think you'd like it, too. We both delight in the mingling of pain with pleasure and lust with love. I know I am safe in your hands, in your hand, your hand in me, I know we are safe. Also, I believe you will agree that it must be done. Erase him, please. Replace his imprint with yours. Let there be not even a breath left inside me that lingers from him.

Two things I beg of you, loving Mistress: Please forgive me for keeping a secret. Please Mistress, will you fist me?

– *Lola, Vancouver, Canada*

'Have you got that in a size 16?'

The trouble started when I was transferred from kitchenware to ladies' fashions. I tried to reason with Tubby Tordoff in Human Resources when he gave me the news, but no matter how hard I tried, I couldn't come up with a plausible excuse. It was a done deal.

There's nothing much to get you into trouble in house wares. Jamie Oliver might have helped men like me who love to cook to come out of our closets, but even I find it difficult to get worked up about saucepans and measuring spoons. No matter how sleek or ergonomic the design, essentially they are just objects; mute, inanimate and meaningless.

But ladies' clothes couldn't be more different. They're not practical, mundane or predictable; each seam, fold and dart seems to hold a secret. They're mysterious, magical and potent.

Women's clothes even sound different: the soft susurration of stockings sliding against each other and the clip-clop of stiletto heels against the pavement. They don't have simple, comfortable convenient garments like us, but complex layers of clothing designed to enhance and disguise. Bras that can transform a modest frontage into a spectacular cleavage, panties as insubstantial as a dragonfly's wing and suspender belts with their echoes of bondage and old-fashioned naughtiness.

It's the underwear that gets to me most, I think. Even the word they use – lingerie – with its elongated first syllable and the soft, foreign and slightly lascivious 'g' seems exotic and somehow languid.

There's nothing I enjoy more than looking at a woman and trying to imagine what kind of underpinnings she's wearing. The suited businesswoman whose tailored exterior conceals fishnet tights and a basque. The middle-aged wife whose Laura Ashley covers cheeky Agent Provocateur. Or the punky teenager in manly boxers, tits too small to even need a bra.

There's such variety, from the barely-there thong to the matronly roll-on. And, until she undresses for you, there's no telling if a woman prefers her smalls to be M&S or S&M.

Most of us blokes nurse a secret fondness for nice undies. I bet, if we're honest, we might even admit to having picked up our girlfriend's discarded knickers and given them a quick sniff and rubbing the sheer fabric against our faces, marvelling at their softness and the sheer alien otherness of them. So how can it be so wrong to go that little bit further and slide them over your hips and feel the silky material's snug embrace, like a warm hand cupping your crotch?

I love the way they feel against the skin, the way the gusset's always too small to accommodate a manly crotch. High heels alter your centre of gravity so that when you walk your hips sway like a catwalk model and skirts make you feel half naked and vulnerable.

No matter how you looked at it, anyone with my specialised tastes was bound to run into problems in ladies' fashions. Like putting kleptomaniacs in charge of the bank and still expecting to make a profit, or asking ex-alcoholics to run the brewery without falling off the wagon. I knew it would only be a matter of time before I would be taking more than a professional interest in the stock.

On my first day in the department, Tubby Tordoff introduced me to Ms Walker, the manager. The moment I saw her, my heart flipped over in my chest and my cock grew an inch. She was a statuesque woman, at least an inch taller than my 5′9″. And that was before you took her high heels into account.

Her hair was long and dark. Her skin was porcelain pale and her full lips had been glossed a deep red, giving her the look of a healthy vampire which – ever since my childhood obsession with Morticia Addams – I'd always found strangely appealing.

She was wearing a tailored dress of purple-printed Georgette over a black lining and, while it was perfectly respectable and chaste, there was a hint of the bedroom about it that seemed both erotic and wicked.

I allowed my gaze to slip down to her legs just to see if she was wearing stockings or tights, hoping that I looked casual rather than pervy. Fine black hosiery, definitely stockings, with what's called a harmony point at the heel, tapering into a point that becomes the seam and black suede shoes with a slender stiletto heel. Beneath the stocking, she wore a fine gold ankle chain. The detail seemed exotic and out of place and somehow slutty. My cock was tingling in my pants.

Ms Walker introduced me to Gemma and Kim, the juniors, but one quick glance told me there was nothing to interest me there. The only other male member of staff was Gavin, a spotty, greasy-haired twenty-something who gave me a shrug and a grin when we shook hands as if in solidarity at our misfortune.

The first few weeks were uneventful enough. I was so busy learning the stock and the different routines that there wasn't enough time to misbehave. The store prided itself on old-fashioned service. We wrapped each garment carefully in crackly tissue paper. Handling the flimsy silky items and wrapping them before handing them over seemed like a sacred ritual, as if the ceremony somehow acknowledged the garment's significance and potency. As I slipped them into the store's stiff paper carrier bags and held them out to the customer by the twisted cord handles I'd often notice that my hand was trembling and my heart thumping.

Ms Walker was an ever-present force. Though she never raised her voice or even issued direct orders, she ran the department with the efficiency and organisation of a front-line army unit. When she set you a task, she'd lower her voice and lean close as if she didn't want to be overheard and say, 'I wonder if you'd mind . . .' in a tone so soft and intimate it felt like a caress; as if you'd be doing her an enormous personal favour and hinting that she'd be forever in your debt.

The technique somehow made even the most onerous job seem like an honour. I'd be halfway up a ladder, counting dusty boxes of directoire knickers that had probably been in the storeroom since before I was born, before I even realised I'd been thoroughly manipulated. Yet, somehow, I didn't even resent it. There was something about her manner and the calm, direct and conspiratorial way she spoke that made us all desperate to please her. The department met more of its targets than any other section in the store and it was all down to the magnificent Ms Walker: the heart of Mussolini in the body of Nigella Lawson.

Working with the clothes was both a torture and a delight and I went home most days excited and frustrated in equal measure. In the shower I'd close my eyes and lean against the wall under the steaming water and picture the mysterious garments while my hand expertly provided relief. But the next day it all started again – more titillation, more torment. A never-ending cycle. I began to feel like Tantalus: temptation all around me but eternally denied satisfaction.

Once I got used to the job the days dragged a bit, so I began to concoct little stories about the customers. A bus driver in her mannish, militaristic uniform bought a Lycra mini-dress so tight and clinging that she'd have needed a shoehorn to get into it. I imagined her putting it on for a staff party at the depot, intending to lure a handsome fellow driver she'd had her eye on. She'd totter across the dance floor, her feet aching from the unaccustomed high heels and her heart pounding in trepidation. And, if I closed my eyes, I could imagine the tight dress clinging to my own body as tightly as the embrace of a lover.

An office worker in a smart suit and sensible shoes came in every Friday lunchtime to buy tights, plain cotton briefs and a sports bra. In my fantasies she was a career girl, ambitious and ruthless; a woman competing in a man's world. She worked such long hours that she couldn't even find the time to do her laundry, so once a week she bought new underwear and simply threw the dirty ones away.

A well-heeled wife in her fifties came in to buy an outfit for a wedding, a vivid green affair with a flower-trimmed hat so ornate she ran the risk of being mistaken for one of the floral displays. I imagined she was the mother of the groom, a cherished son she didn't want to lose, marrying a woman she didn't approve of and the outfit was her silent protest.

My favourite customer came in every few weeks to buy underwear. She was beautiful in a wholesome, Women's Institute sort of way; the sort who owned an Aga and drove the kids to ballet in her Range Rover. She bought camiknickers, seamed stockings, French knickers and long-line bras, the kind of thing you associate with 1940s pin-ups or Dita Von Teese. In my mind she was a bored housewife meeting a younger man for illicit assignations.

Occasionally, I allowed myself to imagine myself as her lover, sitting on a bed in some anonymous hotel room as she disrobed, peeling off each garment slowly until she was standing there in her complicated underwear.

I'd drink in every detail. The ruched fabric and the little bow decorating the suspender strap. The tiny, yet perfect silk rose where the bra cups meet and the delicate lace at the hems of knickers. Maybe there would be slight creases at the ankles of her stockings. I'd follow the seam up the back of her leg to where it joined the welt in an 'O' like a surprised human mouth.

Then I'd close my eyes and imagine it was me standing there, displaying myself in all that old-fashioned underwear. What would it feel like against my skin? Would the bra's boning compress my ribs and restrict my breathing? Would the stockings rub together when I moved and would the silk of the knickers feel warm and soft against my crotch?

It might just be a fantasy, but it was all I had and at least it was harmless. Maybe there were women who didn't mind you trying on their knickers and prancing about in their high heels. Perhaps there were even women who got off on it but, in my neighbourhood at least, they were as rare as unicorns. My forays into cross-dressing had always been solo expeditions and, while I'd have loved an understanding woman to share my foible with, I wasn't holding my breath.

Naturally, I made sure that my colleagues never suspected a thing, but it was Ms Walker I worried about most. Somehow she seemed to know every tiny thing that went on in the department, even if she hadn't been there at the time. Though she was never bossy or authoritative, she wasn't a woman you'd want to get on the wrong side of. She left us in no doubt of what was expected of us and she regarded any failure as a personal disappointment. I'd once heard her admonishing Gemma for chewing gum on duty. She'd sounded so hurt and disappointed that the unfortunate girl had burst into tears and promised never to do it again.

Disappointing Ms Walker was unthinkable and I was pretty certain that my unnatural interest in the stock would be just that. I was professional and polite and I handled the garments as briefly as possible and only when strictly necessary. I didn't even look at the stuff unless I had to. I was determined to keep my dirty little secret to myself. And I nearly got away with it.

One lunchtime, I was on the cash desk when Ms Walker was on her break. Instead of heading for the lift as she normally did, she started to wander around the racks. I'd just finished bagging up a customer's purchases and taking her money when I noticed that Ms Walker was next in line. I finished my transaction and smiled at her.

'Can I help you?' We were taught to be polite and just because the customer was a colleague was no reason to let standards slip.

'I'll take these, please, David.' She laid her purchases on the counter. It was all underwear and, as I'd suspected, she favoured the traditional. Half a dozen pairs of fine denier stockings and a suspender belt, three pairs of silk French knickers and two sheer lacy bras. I examined the labels, as we were taught to do to make sure the customer has selected the correct sizes. Though it was part of my job and something I did every day, the intimacy of the act made my heart beat a frantic tattoo in my chest. I had to use every ounce of concentration to prevent my hands from shaking.

'38D, is that right?' I hoped my voice sounded firmer to her ears than it did to mine.

'Yes, thank you.' She was rummaging in her purse and spoke without looking up so at least I was spared the embarrassment of trying to meet her gaze when all I could think of was the size of her boobs.

I wrapped and bagged the items and punched them into the till. The total seemed a small fortune to me but then the knickers were real silk and she probably earned a lot more than I did.

When I handed her the change she leant across the desk and put her face close to mine. I could smell the citrus scent of her shampoo and, beneath it, the hint of a natural, womanly scent that was all her own. I could feel her body heat.

'Thank you, David.' When she turned to leave I realised I'd been holding my breath.

The rest of the afternoon, I could think of nothing else. Something about the intimacy of handling her underwear then the thrilling, private moment when her face was so close to mine that I could easily have kissed her, seemed to have got under my skin.

I found myself wondering if she'd bought the things for a special occasion. Maybe she'd put them on for an evening with a lover knowing that, before the night was over, she'd be undressing for him. Would she allow him the honour of undoing the bra himself and slipping the straps down over her creamy shoulders and then bringing his hands round to cup her breasts?

Would he unclasp her suspenders and then slide her stockings down her legs, rolling them as he pushed them down, then pull them off over her feet as she delicately pointed her toe? And when he pulled down those fluid silk knickers would it reveal a plumply perfect heart-shaped arse with just a glimpse of pussy peeking out underneath?

I spent the rest of the day pressed up against the cash desk, doing my best to control an erection and, while it did go down from time to time, all it took was a glimpse of Ms Walker to resurrect it.

Unfortunately, it was Thursday when the store stayed open until 8 p.m., so my torment was prolonged and painful. At closing time I hung back in the staff room hoping that my obvious arousal would abate sufficiently for me to get on the tube without causing undue attention. By the time I'd composed myself Gavin and the girls had already left and Ms Walker was putting on her coat. I hung about busying myself with taking off my tie and changing my shoes.

I was taking more time than was strictly necessary, fastening my laces in a double bow and then folding my tie carefully and putting it into my locker because just being in her presence was exquisite torture. All I could think of was her exotic lingerie and that all too brief, yet utterly perfect moment when her face was beside mine and I could smell the scent of her skin.

Just thinking about it made my cock throb in response and soon I couldn't have left if I'd wanted to. My erection was painful and obvious, tenting the front of my trousers like a guilty secret. I sat down and fiddled with my shoes, concealing my crotch.

'Goodnight, David. See you tomorrow.' Her voice was soft and sort of slow, as if she was tired or aroused. In all probability, she was exhausted after a hard day in the store, but that didn't stop me imagining that she was secretly wound up with tension and excitement because of me. Well, I could dream, couldn't I? The thought caused an immediate reaction in my already cramped trousers and I let out an involuntary moan of alarm and arousal.

'Are you all right?' She walked over to look at me, her brow creased in concern.

'I'm fine.' My voice came out in a sort of strangled whisper. I bent double to conceal the evidence.

'You don't look fine.' She sat down beside me and laid a hand on my back. I could feel her body heat through the thin material of my shirt. My crotch instantly responded and I bent even lower to cover it.

'I've got a bit of a tummy ache. It happens sometimes. It'll pass in a minute.' In my head I repeated over and over again a mantra I'd developed as a teenager to cope with unwanted erections; the saddest thing to have happened to me in my young life and guaranteed to deflate any hard-on. My dog is dead, my dog is dead . . .

'Can I help? I've got some Paracetamol in my bag.' She rubbed my back through my shirt.

'I'll be fine, thank you. Really.' My dog is dead, my dog is dead.

'Are you sure?'

'Yes, yes . . . it's passing off already.' It was working at last. I straightened up.

'That's good. Don't come in tomorrow if you still feel ill.' She moved her hand away and I felt bereft.

'Thanks, I'll just sit here quietly then make my way home.'

'OK then. I'll get off. Take care, David.' She treated me to one of her heart-stopping smiles then got up and left.

I must have sat there for five minutes after that. My erection might have subsided but I was still a wreck. My heart was thumping, I was dizzy and weak and I honestly didn't trust my legs to hold me up.

When I finally managed to compose myself I was just about to leave when I noticed one of the store's carrier bags on the bench. I walked over and peeped inside; half a dozen tissue-wrapped packages and a receipt. A hot wave of shock and excitement crashed over me like a tsunami. Ms Walker had left her shopping behind. In her concern about me, she'd forgotten to pick up the bag.

How ironic, I thought as I stood gazing at it, that she should leave behind the very thing that had been responsible for my discomfort. I sat down beside the bag. For a long time I just sat there looking at it. I didn't move a muscle. If anyone had seen me they might have mistaken me for one of the mannequins, dressed in my clothes and posed as a joke for colleagues to find in the morning. But on the inside I was a bubbling ferment of conflicting emotions.

Would she come back to retrieve it? I knew that, as a creature of habit, she always caught the same train. I looked at my watch; she'd be long gone by now. Did I dare to unwrap the parcels and touch the flimsy garments? I couldn't risk leaving any evidence behind; I daren't open the stockings, but if I unwrapped a pair of the French knickers who would even know?

I lifted out one of the tissue parcels and laid it on the bench beside me. I opened the package, smoothing out the crinkly paper with the flat of my fingers.

I unfolded them and laid them down on the bench. The knickers inside were black with fine lace detailing around the edge.

I put out a finger and touched the silk. It felt warm and fluid under my fingertip and seemed to gleam in the light. I picked them up and brought them to my face. The material was soft against my skin. My cock was rigid. I longed to strip off my clothes and step into them. No doubt I'd have to rearrange my crotch before I could pull them fully up. Then I'd stroke the tip of my cock through the silky fabric, working myself up to a pitch of arousal and then watch the dark, spreading stain of pre-come desecrate them.

Without thinking about it I slid down the zip of my trousers and slipped my hand inside. I began to rub myself through my boxers. Even though they hadn't been worn, I held the panties to my face, drinking in the alien, almost human and quintessentially feminine smell.

I heard Ms Walker before I saw her. There was a sharp intake of breath behind me and the sound of the door slamming shut. I turned. She seemed to be petrified in mid-stride. Her mouth was open, her eyes round.

With my hand in my pants and her undies against my face there was no way I could claim it was all an innocent mistake. I dropped the knickers onto the bench.

'I'm really sorry . . .'

'Frankly, David, I'd find that easier to believe if you weren't still playing with yourself.'

I pulled my hand out of my fly and zipped up.

'I wasn't . . . I'd stopped. I just forgot to take my hand out . . . This must look awful . . .' I ground to a halt.

'Let's just say I won't be nominating you for

employee of the month.' She walked over to me. 'I'm so disappointed in you, David.'

I could feel shame burning my cheeks. I couldn't meet her gaze.

'It isn't what it looks like.'

'I'm relieved to hear it because what it looks like is that you're a nasty little pervert with a knicker fetish. I bet you're one of those sad men who goes around in a balaclava at the dead of night and steals underwear off washing lines, aren't you?' She was standing with her hands on her hips. Her eyes were blazing with anger, and with the advantage of height and five-inch heels she towered over me. I felt like a naughty schoolboy being put in his place by the headmistress and the thought caused an instantaneous reaction in my crotch. I covered it with my jacket, hoping she wouldn't notice.

'No, it's not like that at all, I promise.' Sweat prickled in my armpits.

'Then perhaps you'd care to explain because, right now, I can't think of a good reason not to march you down to Human Resources and have you fired.' Her voice was hard, her anger obvious.

'Well ... I don't know where to start. This is all such a mess.'

'It certainly is. Your only option now is to tell me the truth otherwise you'll be getting yourself into a lot more trouble. Not just Human Resources but the police as well.'

A hot wave of fear crashed over me.

'Please, I'll tell you everything.' I looked down at the floor, too ashamed to meet her gaze. 'You're right, I do have an underwear fetish, but not in the way you think.'

'I'm listening.'

'This is so difficult for me ... I like to wear the underwear myself.'

I heard her inhale sharply. I was pretty certain that my face was the colour of a baboon's arse. I daren't look up.

'What are you saying? You're a transsexual? A woman in a man's body, that sort of thing?'

'No, I'm straight. I suppose I'm what they call a cross-dresser. I love the way the clothes make me feel. I can't explain it, I just do.' It was agony having to explain my shameful preferences, but I had to convince her I was harmless. I was resigned to getting the sack now, but maybe I could persuade her not to involve the police.

'How does it make you feel? And please do me the courtesy of looking at me when you're talking.'

Reluctantly I looked up and met her gaze. Her expression seemed to have softened a little, but she was clearly still angry.

'It makes me feel ... I don't know ... utterly transformed. Somehow it makes me feel softer, more sensual. More whole in a way. And utterly vulnerable, submissive even. I've never tried to put it into words before.'

Her eyes never left my face, her expression unreadable.

'And do you go out like that?'

'No, never! Not that I haven't wanted to, I just don't have the nerve. It's strictly a private activity.'

'Until tonight ...'

'Yes, I'm sorry about that. When I realised you'd left your stuff behind I just couldn't help myself.'

'So what ... you were planning to put them on?'

'No, I promise. I wanted to but I respect you far too much for that.'

'But you got carried away?'

I nodded.

'I bet you've got a whole wardrobe full at home, haven't you?' Her eyes were shining, and for the first time I thought I saw something other than anger there, curiosity maybe and, perhaps, even interest.

'Yes, I have, a few things anyway.'

'And your girlfriends don't mind?' She took off her coat and leather gloves and put them down on the bench.

'I . . . I've never told any of my girlfriends. I told you, it's strictly a private activity.'

'But you'd like to be able to share it, wouldn't you?'

I nodded.

'And it makes you feel submissive, you said?'

'That's right.'

I looked up at her beautiful face. She began to smile.

'I bet you're the sort of man who fantasises dressing up for a powerful woman, aren't you? Maybe she even forces you to do it? Yes, I can picture it; she makes you put on her undies and with each garment you put on you feel more helpless and vulnerable. By the time you're fully dressed you're utterly in her power.' There was dark dot of colour on the apple of each of her cheeks. I could see her chest rising and falling as she breathed.

'Yes, yes, I do. But I know it's just a fantasy. I bet women like that don't even exist.'

'You think so?' She laughed. She turned and walked over to the door. I watched her perfect arse undulate as she crossed the room. She locked the door.

'I'd like you to undress, please.' She came back over to me and sat down on the bench.

'What?' I stood rooted to the spot.

'Now!'

'Yes, Ms Walker.' I shrugged off my jacket and let it fall on the floor.

58

'And fold your clothes, please. Standards.'

'Yes, Ms Walker.' I picked up the jacket and folded it carefully then laid it down on the bench. I unbuttoned my shirt with trembling fingers, conscious of her eyes drinking in every detail. I pulled the tails out of my trousers and fiddled with the cuff buttons.

'You're quite slender for a man, aren't you? And there's no hair on your chest. Do you shave?'

'No, it's natural.' I folded my shirt.

'Mmmm, it suits you. I bet you make quite a good woman.' Her voice was deep and dreamy.

'Thank you, Ms Walker.' For some reason I was filled with irrational pride. I sat down on the bench to undo my laces. I took off my trainers and socks. I stood up and undid my trousers and slid them down. Already, I had the beginnings of an erection and my instinct was to cover my crotch, but I wanted to obey her and to obey her completely. I removed my trousers, trying to pretend that doing so in front of your manager was the most normal thing in the world and my burgeoning erection was of no consequence.

When I'd finished folding my trousers I straightened up, reluctant to remove the last garment but fairly certain that she expected me to. Seeing my hesitation she gestured with a fingertip for me to remove them. As I slid my boxers down over my hips my face burned from a combination of shame and arousal.

Ms Walker reached into the carrier bag and began to shake out the parcels, tearing the crinkly paper. She found the suspender belt and held it out to me. When I took the filmy garment from her I noticed that her hand was shaking.

'Put it on.'

I obeyed. The suspender belt was deep and boned and, as I fastened it, I realised that it had the same effect as a waspie corset, pinching and shaping my waist. My chest was heaving. My armpits prickled with sweat. My cock swelled.

She picked up a pair of stockings and opened the packet, slitting the Sellotape with her long red fingernails. She handed me a stocking and I sat down to put it on, rolling it down to the foot and then pulling it up my leg slowly, as I had seen women do.

'You've obviously done that before.' Her voice was throaty and deep.

'Once or twice.'

'What size are your feet?'

'Nine.'

'Good, same as me. Hang on . . .' She bent down and removed her shoes. She pushed them across the floor to me and I put them on. They were still warm and, for some reason, stepping into them seemed like the most intimate act. My cock lengthened. Silently she handed me a pair of knickers and I stood up to put them on. I held onto the bench with one hand and stepped into them feeling unstable but wonderful in her high heels. The knickers felt warm and sensuous against my crotch. I had to do quite a bit of repositioning to get my excited cock completely covered but there was nothing I could do to conceal my erection.

She rummaged through the packages and handed me a black bra. When I'd got it on the cups bagged and drooped, and for a moment I was utterly ashamed of having nothing to fill them. Ms Walker picked up a pair of French knickers and rolled them into a ball then stood up and fitted it inside one of the cups, fiddling with it until she was satisfied. The physical contact, though utterly practical and perfunctory, was divine. My cock tingled. She repeated the process on the other side then stepped back to look at me. She smiled.

Ms Walker began to unbutton her dress. She was wearing a lilac dress in a fine floral print, which was one of my favourites. It buttoned all the way down the front and clung to her figure so perfectly that I could see the outline of each individual breast and the womanly curve of her belly. It took me a second to register that she was taking off her dress because she wanted me to put it on and another second to realise that would mean I'd get to see her in her underwear.

When she'd finally got it undone she slid it off like a coat and held it out to me. I reached out to take it but the sight of her underwear seemed to paralyse me and my hand hung in the air, halfway to its destination, as if I'd been petrified. She was wearing a burgundy lace bra much like my own except that I could clearly see her nipples, dark and hard through the sheer fabric. Her suspender belt reached from her waist to the bottom of her hips and was the same colour as her bra. Over it, she wore a pair of transparent French knickers. I could clearly see her pubic hair, neatly trimmed into a small triangle above her slit. I took the dress and put it on. It took ages to do up the buttons because my fingers were trembling and clumsy.

When I'd finished Ms Walker opened her handbag and took out her make-up. I stood motionless as she applied lipstick and blusher to my face, hardly daring to breathe.

'Now, let me look at you.' She took a step back. 'Well, your eyebrows need plucking, but you'll do. In fact you make a very passable woman. Davina.'

The use of the feminine version of my name filled me with shame and pride. My cock was rigid, making the front of my dress stick out. She walked over to me and flicked its tip then laughed as it wobbled. I was tingling all over. The hairs on the back of my neck were standing to attention. Liquid shivers of excitement slid up and down my spine.

I could see her chest heaving. A dark flush of arousal stained her throat and décolletage. Her lips were berry-dark.

'I want you to get on your knees and take off my knickers.' I didn't need telling twice though it took me a second to work out how to bend in my high heels. When I was finally on my knees, looking up at her, I knew this was what I had been born for. I gazed up at her, so full of tenderness and surrender that I didn't want to break the spell.

'Take them off, I said.' Her voice was full of urgency and hunger with an edge of irritation that made me immediately ashamed for not obeying instantly. I reached up and hooked my fingers under the waistband of her sheer panties and slid them over her hips. I inhaled sharply when the full glory of her pussy came into view. Her plump lips were bare – waxed or shaved, I wondered? I could see the slit between them disappearing down between her legs like the road to paradise.

'Now sit down here, on the end of the bench.'

I instantly complied. She leant forwards and unbuttoned my dress from the waist down. She pulled the front of my knickers down and lifted out my cock and balls, delicately, as if handling an heirloom. She straddled me and lowered herself onto my lap, reaching down with one hand to position my cock. I felt its tip up against her moist pussy then she sat down on it and I slid into her millimetre by delicious millimetre.

She put a hand on each of my shoulders and bent her head to kiss me. Her lips were soft, her mouth tasted sweet. I could feel her breasts pressing up against my chest and her hair brushing my skin. She slid her mouth down my neck and kissed my throat. I shivered all over.

'Take off my bra.'

I reached round behind her and unhooked it then slid it down over her arms. I bent my head to kiss her nipples. She gasped as my mouth made contact. Her nipple was hard in my mouth. I gripped it with my teeth and ran my tongue across the tip. Every time I did it, I felt her body shudder and she let out a low, deep moan of appreciation.

Her cunt was hot and wet and tight. I was in up to the balls. She bounced up and down on my lap, sliding up and down my cock. The bones in the suspender belt were digging into my waist. I was beginning to sweat. The dress clung to my back. I was covered in goose pimples. Blood pounded in my ears.

She grabbed my face with both hands and tilted back my head for another kiss. I surrendered, opening my mouth and closing my eyes. Her hair fell in my face, scented and warm. I slid my hands down to her hips. I could feel her muscles contracting as she used her thigh muscles to move up and down on my cock.

Her skin was warm against mine. There was a soft little hiss of friction as our stockings rubbed together. I was tingling all over. Tension built in my groin. She used her muscles to squeeze my cock and I shivered all over at the delicious surprise of it.

She was rolling her hips back and forth. Arching and then rounding her back to rub her clit against my pubes. Her breathing had grown noisy and erratic. Her lips were swollen and dark. Her face was filmed with sweat. Her hair was damp and clinging to her forehead.

I held onto her hips and rocked my pelvis, meeting her thrusts. I could feel her round, creamy arse against my thighs. She was heavy, solid and powerful. There was nothing fragile or delicate about her. I didn't have to worry about hurting her. This was raw, urgent, animal sex. No holds barred.

I looked into her eyes. They were shining with intensity and arousal. Her lips were slightly parted and I could feel warm breath rushing out between her teeth. Her cheeks were pink. The flushing on her throat and chest had developed into a vivid red rash. Somehow it seemed to symbolise her loss of control and seeing it made my cock tingle and my arousal rocket into a higher gear.

Sweat ran down my face and into my eyes. The bra wires were stabbing me in the chest. Beneath my stockings my legs felt clammy and prickly. Her hair fell around her face and shoulders, like Medusa's serpents. A strand clung to her lips. She bent back her head and moaned at the ceiling.

Her breasts bounced and shook as she rode me. Her thighs were slippery against mine. She ground her crotch against mine. She pushed down hard on my shoulders for leverage. Delicious, watery shivers slid down my spine. My crotch was on fire. Heat and excitement spread through me in a rush.

She was sobbing and groaning, bouncing on my cock like a woman possessed. I could feel her muscles growing tighter as her orgasm approached. A trickle of sweat ran down between her breasts and disappeared into the thumbprint of her belly button. Her make-up had softened and smudged. She'd never looked more beautiful.

I ran my hands up and down the curve of her back. Her skin was hot and damp under my fingers and silky soft. I could hear obscene squelching noises as her crotch moved against mine. I kissed her neck, sliding my lips along her throat, sucking and licking her hot skin. My breath gushed out in short, noisy bursts. I could feel the insistent beat of arousal thumping in my groin. My balls were hard and tight. My cock was rigid. My nipples were erect and sensitive beneath my bra. The silky knickers padding out the cups felt warm and damp against my skin.

Ms Walker was practically screaming now. Her breasts swung. Her arse banged against my thighs. Her throat was stained scarlet from my lipstick. Her hair was wild and damp.

I put my arms around her then brought my hands up to grip her shoulders, pulling her close. I pulled down on her shoulders, bringing up my hips to meet her thrusts. I could feel her warm breath on my neck. She was shouting so loud it hurt my ears.

I was fit to burst but I held back, willing myself not to come until she had. She was riding me hard, hips pistoning rhythmically. Her thighs slapped loudly against mine as she fucked me. Her whole body was quivering. She pressed down on my shoulders. Her fingernails dug into me, but I didn't care.

All that mattered to me, all that existed for me, was her cunt and her orgasm. She was howling, a high, animal wail of pleasure in extremis. She began to rock her hips back and forth, rubbing her crotch against mine. Her hair tickled my skin. She arched her back and extended her neck and I knew she was coming at last. She trembled in my arms. She let out a single high note of satisfaction.

That was all it took for me to tip over the edge into my own climax. I curled my spine, thrusting my cock deep into her cunt. Pleasure flooded over me like a tidal wave, knocking the breath out of me.

I held onto her, pressing her body against mine as I pumped out spunk inside her. I was breathless and sweating. Hot coils of exquisite pleasure spread out from my groin, coursing through my body like a drug.

We sat like that long after it was over, our hot bodies pressed up against each other and her damp hair falling over us both. It wasn't until we heard the cleaner pushing the Hoover about outside that we got up and hurriedly got into our own clothes. We tossed her new undies, now somewhat the worse for wear, back into the carrier bag then said goodbye and went our separate ways.

The next day at work she behaved as if it had never happened. I kept waiting for a summons from Human Resources or, worse, to feel the hand at the end of the long arm of the law coming down on my shoulder, but it never did.

A week later she invited me to her house for a repeat performance. After that we were colleagues at work and lovers in private and, though we never repeated our session in the staff room, every Friday she invites me round to her place for a private fitting.

– Silklover, London, UK

Effing Mablethorpe

Last summer we holidayed in the UK. Part of it was down to John: fretting about flights, terrorists and some airport safety scandal he'd seen on Trevor McDonald. Part of it was me: too prone to seasickness to consider a cruise, and unwilling to take the Chunnel just so we could drive on the wrong side of the road and get insulted by the French. Arguments are rare in our marriage and, like most of the others, this one had ended before it properly began.

'If we can't go abroad why don't we just go to effing Mablethorpe?' John demanded.

'Then *effing* Mablethorpe it is,' I returned.

The decision was made as simply as that. Neither of us realised how prophetic those words could be. Not that there's anything wrong with holidaying in the UK. Or effing Mablethorpe. Admittedly, we would both have preferred somewhere with sun and entertainment but the chance to unwind for a fortnight and recharge our batteries was enough for me and John. When we arrived in the quaint little seaside town, we resolved to make the best of our holiday. A light supper, a couple of drinks, and then a walk along the beach helped us relax. It was a warm evening, the weather promised to be fine for the next two weeks, and we enjoyed the sound of lapping waves on the shore and the haze of twilight as night approached.

John whispered, 'Did you see that?'

I nodded. You reach a stage in married life where you understand your partner on a psychic level. I knew what John had seen and I understood from his whisper that it had aroused him. I figured we were both enjoying a mild thrill of excitement. John was certainly walking as though he was trying to hide his hard-on. My legs trembled, the way they always do when I get that tingle. 'Just keep walking,' I hissed. 'Pretend you didn't see them.' As soon as we had a chance to talk we fell into each other's arms, giggling like adolescents.

A woman and two men had been sitting together on the beach as we passed. She was striking. The swarthy complexion, dark curls and dark eyes gave her a gypsy-like appearance. The man on her left had his hand inside her blouse as he kissed her. The man on her right had his hand beneath her skirt. The woman had a hand on each man's lap. After comparing notes from our half-glimpsed glances, John confirmed we had seen exactly the same thing. The gypsy woman was making out with two men.

'I didn't know they did that in Mablethorpe,' I laughed.

'Now, aren't you glad you came?' John grinned.

I sniffed. 'As if you'd let me do anything like that.'

He raised an eyebrow and, although the conversation had started off as light banter, I realised we were no longer joking. After ten years of marriage, and neither of us ever straying from the marital bed, it came as a shock to contemplate doing something sexual with someone else. The idea had me more flustered than the sight of the gypsy woman being fondled by her two men.

John asked, 'Would you want to?'

I didn't answer. I couldn't answer. But the idea wouldn't leave my thoughts. When we got back to our hotel room I dragged John into bed before he had a chance to properly close the door. The sex was magnificent and urgent. I was dripping for him as soon as he was naked. I don't know how long we screwed that night, or how many times I coaxed John hard after I'd ridden him dry. But I do remember, whenever I closed my eyes, I was with someone else instead of my husband. The fantasy made me wetter and more responsive. Each time I came, it was harder than the time before.

John didn't complain about this unexpected bonus to the holiday. The following morning, at breakfast, he joked that we should again examine the beach in search of anything else that might get me so horny. I hadn't realised my reason for the previous night's passion had been so transparent but I began to see that John found the idea equally exciting.

'Wouldn't you be jealous?' I asked. The conversation made my entire body tingle. We were talking about having sex with other people. It wasn't something we'd ever discussed before. 'Wouldn't you think less of me?' I asked.

He treated me to a kiss. Because we were at the breakfast table I understood it was one of his rare displays of public affection. The tenderness reminded me why we had been able to stay happily married for so long. 'If I get jealous, I'll tell you about it,' he promised. 'And I'd only think less of you if you shied away from doing something you wanted.'

I didn't know where the conversation was going. My heart raced and my immediate instinct was to drag John back upstairs and ride him again and again until I'd finally banished the lust from my system. I was so wet and hungry for him my hands shook and my teacup clattered against the saucer when I tried to drink.

And then the gypsy woman entered the dining room.

She was followed by the two men who had been with her on the beach. While she took a table in the smoking section of the dining room, her men went to the breakfast bar and filled two trays. The gypsy woman sat down, folded one leg over the other to reveal a gorgeous expanse of sun-bronzed thigh from beneath her summer frock, lit a cigarette and snatched a drink of orange juice from the table. She leant back in her chair, thrusting her full breasts out, and exhaled a plume of smoke towards the smoking section's ceiling fans.

'You're staring at her, darling,' John observed.

I wrenched my gaze away and almost spilled my cup of tea. 'It's her.'

'It's all three of them,' John replied. He stood up and asked, 'Should I go over and say hello? Maybe ask if there'll be another performance on the beach tonight?'

I almost screeched at the suggestion. 'Don't you dare!' Shaking my head, telling him to shut up, sit down and be quiet I was blushing ferociously at his absurd idea. Arousal still held a tight grip on my emotions but now it was muffled by a hot blanket of embarrassment. Not unkindly, John laughed at my discomfort and told me he was only going to get another coffee from the breakfast buffet bar.

Relieved, I settled back to finish my cup of tea. It was only when I heard John's voice that I realised he hadn't been entirely honest about only going for a coffee. I glanced towards the breakfast bar and saw he stood between the gypsy woman's two men. He laughed loudly and fell easily into their company. Ten minutes later, when he came back to our table, he explained the five of us would be driving out together for a pub lunch in the nearby town of Louth.

I struggled to digest the news without showing panic, aware that the gypsy woman and her men might be watching. Feeling too numb to know what to do, I waved at the trio and flexed them a grin that felt terribly false. I told John to take me back to our bedroom and, when we got there, I ravaged him again.

In all the years of our marriage I have never known myself to be so wet or so eager for my husband. The muscles inside my sex were in a constant state of frenzy that needed to be filled by his hard-on.

Fortunately he was able to satisfy my demands and allowed me to indulge the coarsest of my appetites. In my fantasies I was the gypsy woman. Each time I closed my eyes I was either with her blond pretty-boy lover or I was with her muscular dark-haired man. It was only when I opened my eyes that I acknowledged my beloved John. He pumped in and out of me for an age and I think we might have spent the entire day in our room if the bedroom assistants hadn't repeatedly knocked at the door and asked if they could come in and change our sheets.

'We can't really go to Louth with them,' I said later.

'It's arranged,' John replied. His voice left no room for argument. 'They've been here a week, and Ricky says the three of them are bored with the town. Ronnie wants to take Carla somewhere different and, when I suggested we make up a fivesome and head to Louth, the three of them jumped at the idea.' Giving me a reassuring kiss, promising me that nothing would happen unless it met with my approval, he told me to relax and enjoy our holiday. There was no chance to argue with him.

And, while I told myself there was no likelihood of anything happening between the five of us, my heart still raced when the trio piled into our car. John and I sat in the front seats with Ricky, Carla and Ronnie squashed in the back. They were cheerful and good company, grateful for the chance to escape Mablethorpe for a few hours, and infuriatingly normal. I don't know how I had expected them to behave, or what I had thought they would be like. But their conversation was so pleasant and inoffensive I quietly chastised myself for imagining the three of them to be anything different.

The banter between us thinned as John drove away from the coast and negotiated the meandering Lincolnshire roads connecting Mablethorpe and Louth. I navigated from an out-of-date map and, eventually, we worked out a route that might get us where we wanted to go. I glanced into the back of the car, about to apologise for the unexpected delay.

My eyes opened wide and I couldn't speak.

Carla was squashed between Ricky and Ronnie while the two men fondled her. Carla's T-shirt had been pushed up to expose her bare breasts, although they were hidden as Ronnie cupped her left and Ricky held her right. She had an arm around the shoulders of each man and her legs were draped over their knees. From my position at the front of the car I could see directly under her frock. Ronnie had a hand at the top of her thigh. But Ricky's fingers had punched inside the lips of her sex.

Carla's gaze met mine. The air inside the car throbbed with electric tension. 'The boys were just distracting me from the monotony of the journey,' Carla explained. She spoke evenly, with only a suggestion of arousal in her tone. Neither Ricky nor Ronnie made any attempt to stop what they were doing while we talked. They fixed their efforts on pleasing Carla. 'This doesn't make you uncomfortable, does it?'

I wished I could be as confident and cool and struggled not to show how flustered I felt. It was difficult to tear my gaze from the sight of Ricky's fingers slipping in and out of her sex. The dark curls around the lips had turned black with wetness. 'It doesn't make me uncomfortable,' I said, as calmly as I could. 'Only jealous.'

'Good Lord!' John cried. I glanced at him and saw he was looking in the rear-view mirror. I doubted he could see as much I had seen but I figured he had noticed enough to get the general idea of what was going on. 'You three don't waste much time, do you?' he laughed.

Carla ignored him. 'There's no need to be jealous,' she assured me. 'We have three men here and two women. I'm sure we can come to some arrangement where everybody is happy.'

I squashed a hand into my lap.

I barely remember what happened when we stopped in Louth. John found us a pub that served food. The five of us enjoyed a meal and a couple of drinks together, and the conversation was a stumbling exchange to which I barely contributed. Ronnie and Carla explained they had been married for six years. Ricky was a close friend to them both. They returned to Mablethorpe most years: it was the place where Carla and Ronnie had met as childhood sweethearts. Ricky had been accompanying them for the past two years. Carla said, whenever the three of them got together, 'We fuck.' She used the word in a way that made it sound like she was describing something magical and special. Her quiet revelation hit me with such a strong arousal I quivered in my seat.

I said very little during that exchange. John talked for the both of us. 'What do you fancy doing while we're here in Louth?' he asked cheerfully.

Carla glanced around the pleasant pub and stretched out her arms to caress Ronnie and Ricky. 'The town looks pretty dull,' she confided. 'I can't be bothered looking round breweries and antiques shops. Why don't we drive somewhere pleasant and fuck?'

Everyone stared at me, as though waiting for my approval to this suggestion. 'That sounds like a fun idea,' I said, forcing myself to sound casual. 'Do you know anywhere in the Wolds that would be appropriate?'

Carla treated me to a wicked smile.

I don't know what I was anticipating but, as I visited the ladies room before we set off, I told myself I had plenty of time to make up my mind about whether or not this was something I wanted. However, when I went out to the car park and saw Carla sitting beside John in the front, and Ronnie and Ricky waiting for me in the back, I realised the chance to back out had already slipped past me. I swallowed the lump that had risen in my throat.

'I know a lovely beauty spot not far from here,' Carla explained from the passenger seat. 'I thought I'd be better able to give your husband directions if I sat here in the front with him.' She flashed her wicked grin at me again and said, 'You don't mind, do you?'

I couldn't speak. I just shook my head.

'Ricky and Ronnie will take care of you in the back,' she grinned. 'They're marvellous travelling companions.'

I felt sick with excitement as I squeezed into the back seat between the two men. I wished I had been given more time; time to make sure John was comfortable with what we were doing; time to make sure I was comfortable with what we were doing; and a chance to decide if it was what I really wanted. But, by the time John had pulled out of the pub's car park, Ricky's hand rested on my right leg and Ronnie's was on my left. The decision had been made for me.

'John was right,' I breathed. 'You two don't waste any time, do you?'

Ricky's hand stroked my right cheek, drawing my face to look at him. To my left I could feel Ronnie stroking at my left breast through the fabric of my blouse. 'Holidays go by too quick,' Ricky whispered. His fingers fell lower, heading towards my right breast. His pretty-boy smile was an invitation to kiss. 'Why would anyone want to waste a moment of their holiday?'

I couldn't think of an answer. And because my mouth was locked against his, with our tongues meeting and touching, I didn't have to reply. I could feel Ronnie's fingers working swiftly to unfasten my buttons and, with Ricky's hand creeping higher up my leg, my arousal soared.

The scenery sped past us in a blur.

The only time I broke my concentration from Ricky and Ronnie was when I glanced into the rear-view mirror and met John's eyes. I could see he had been watching me, and I knew the broad grin in his smile was fifty per cent excitement and one hundred per cent encouragement.

I reached into the laps of both men on the back seat and stroked the lumps that nestled at the fronts of their jeans. They were both hard. Without breaking from Ricky's kiss, and without disturbing Ronnie as he fondled my left breast and teased the stiff nipple, I was able to release both their hard-ons.

It was the first time I had ever touched another man's penis in more than a decade. It was the first time *ever* I had held two hard-ons at the same time. Ricky's length was long, slender and beautifully smooth. Ronnie's erection felt shorter, but thick and with a base that was coarsely coated with hairs. I slipped my fingers around each hard-on and stroked up and down.

Ricky's fingers pushed my panties aside and found my sex.

Ronnie's hands stroked at the tops of my thighs, and then he was teasing my pussy lips as Ricky pushed in and out of me. The tingles of pleasure that had nestled in my sex were now tremors that rocked my body. I was breathless, excited, and desperate for orgasm. I kissed Ricky with more urgency and stroked Ronnie faster.

'Is this OK for you?' Ronnie asked.

I pulled away from Ricky's face and turned to smile at him. 'It's not what I expected to be doing on this holiday,' I admitted. 'But I'm not complaining.' He laughed, and didn't stop chuckling until I'd lowered my face over the thick head of his hard-on and sucked against the purple end.

'No fair,' Ricky complained. It wasn't genuine upset in his voice: only playful teasing. 'How come Ronnie gets head and I'm left with a wrist-job?'

I lifted my face and turned to grin at him. 'Since you asked so nicely,' I began. And then I pushed my mouth over his hard-on. If I had taken a moment to think about what I was doing I'm sure I would have leapt from the moving car. I had never behaved with such abandon but, with these three people, and because of John's encouragement, it felt like the natural thing to do.

'Poor John,' Carla murmured. She wasn't looking at my husband. Instead, when I glanced up, I saw her staring at me. Now that I had shifted position I wondered what sort of sight I presented. I had my mouth around Ricky's erection while my bare buttocks were shoved in her husband's face. Fingers and a tongue fluttered inside my sex and I could never remember feeling so wanton. 'John's being neglected here,' Carla declared. 'And he's doing all the work for us.' There was the sound of a zipper being pulled down before she said, 'I'll have to make sure he's amply rewarded.' She winked at me before turning away and lowering her face over my husband's lap.

It was a car journey that set the tone for the remainder of the holiday.

When we arrived at the isolated beauty spot the five of us staggered from the car and fell together as though it was the way we were meant to be. John and Carla lay across a picnic table as she sucked his penis and he licked her sex. Their clothes were already loose and quickly discarded. But this was a detail I only noticed from the corner of my eye. Ronnie had been aroused as he tongued me on the journey and I was equally desperate to have his thick erection in the eager wetness of my sex. I knelt between the two men as Ronnie took me from behind and I sucked and licked Ricky's hard-on.

We repeatedly shifted positions.

I watched my husband plunge his penis inside Carla. And I was able to stroke his balls as he slipped in and out of her tight pussy. Both Ricky and Ronnie climbed between my legs during that afternoon. And I sucked both their cocks while John took me from behind and Carla pressed her tongue against my sex.

The sun was glorious. A light breeze dried the sweat on our naked bodies. The picnic spot remained

77

wonderfully isolated. And our climaxes came in glorious waves that had us all panting, laughing and exhausted. It was an afternoon where we did so much. It was an afternoon where we simply fucked.

When we got back to the hotel that evening, and returned to our separate rooms, the sex was better than ever. It had been incredible to be with Carla, Ricky and Ronnie. But it was even more rewarding to relive that thrill while it was just me and John. I felt sore after all the pleasure I'd had through the day. But that didn't stop me from wanting every inch that John could drive into me. When we eventually fell asleep, we were wrapped in each other's arms and completely drained and satisfied.

We met up with Carla, Ricky and Ronnie each day for the rest of that week. Although they were scheduled to leave on the Saturday morning, Ronnie extended their stay for another week and we were able to spend the remainder of the holiday together. It truly was a memorable fortnight. We exchanged names, addresses and telephone numbers and have seen the three of them several times since. Those experiences, too, have been incredible. And this year, when it comes to booking our holidays, I feel sure that John and I will be going back to effing Mablethorpe.

– *Tanya, St Albans, UK*

Stranger on a Ten-Speed

I watched as a group of girls my age walked by. They were carrying shopping bags and all looked so pretty with their stylish clothes and make-up. They were laughing and seemed to be having so much fun, and as they walked away I noticed a group of guys from across the street watching them and whistling out. How I had wished that it was me that they were looking at.

I continued down the street alone towards the park where I usually went with my best friend, only she was away on a family vacation so I had spent most of the summer on my own, sitting and reading in the park. I had other people that I had been friends with through high school, but most of them moved away as soon as they were eighteen, in hopes of a life more exciting than our small town could ever provide and, being as shy as I was, it was hard to make new friends.

Guess I had lived a pretty sheltered life; here I was at nineteen years of age, never having had a boyfriend – not even so much as a real kiss with tongue! My parents were kind of old school and quite religious, so growing up, my socialising was limited to other kids from the church. I didn't really think much about make-up and clothes then, but now that I was older, being plain was something that bothered me. I wasn't ugly or anything, but my hair, which had been the same since elementary school, was plain, short and brown – easy to take care of – and my clothes were pretty conservative, with my summer uniform, if you will, consisting of a basic pink T-shirt and a knee-length cotton skirt and sandals.

As I turned the corner, a leaf came floating down to my feet, brushing past my face on the way – the first indication that summer was coming to an end. I bent to pick it up when a bike tyre zoomed past, almost knocking me over.

'Oh – sorry about that, sweetie,' said a frazzled voice.

'Whatever,' I mumbled, feeling more invisible than ever and resuming my walk.

I could hear the clicking of the wheels of his ten-speed behind me and looked back. He was at least in his late twenties, with dishevelled curly hair – one of those red-haired freckly guys. He sped up until he was riding at my side and I tried not to look at him.

'You mad at me? Come on, don't be mad,' he mocked.

'I'm not mad. Don't worry about it, I'm fine,' I said while picking up the pace.

'No, I can see yer' mad,' he insisted. 'Let me make it up to you. Just stop for one second – please?'

I stopped and just looked at him impatiently as he rested one foot on the ground to hold the bike steady. I immediately noticed something bulging in his tight black biker shorts and felt my cheeks go red. He homed right in on my accidental gaze which embarrassed me further.

'See something you like?' He grinned, showing his less than perfect teeth.

'Eeew! No!' I cried out, looking away.

'Saw you lookin',' he said.

'Why are you even wearing those shorts? You're not even a real cyclist! And they're too tight and look silly!' I said, turning to walk away.

'I'm sorry. I didn't mean to embarrass you. You seem like a sweet girl and yer' real pretty . . .' he said, changing to a softer tone.

I immediately took note; he was the first person of the opposite sex to ever call me pretty and I was blown away. He could see the effect it had on me and grinned.

'Mind if I walk with you? Where are you going?' he asked, getting back on the bike.

'Just over to the park. I guess you can come if you like,' I replied, feeling a bit nervous.

'I would love to go some place more private so maybe we could talk a bit. I really like you,' he cooed.

'Sure,' I replied, excited at the prospect of my first 'date', even if it was with someone older and not so cute.

'Follow me,' he said, opting to walk his bike instead.

We quickly turned off the road and up a driveway to a building, but instead of going in the door, he began to walk down the ramp to the underground parking. I hesitated for a moment, but then went on after he flashed a smile that put me at ease. Inside, it was dim and what little light was in there glowed almost pink.

It felt chilly compared to out in the sun and the air was almost damp – certainly not the most romantic place to talk. We finally stopped at the end in a little alcove with some sunlight peeking through the grid above.

'Sit down, relax,' he said, pointing to a concrete stump. He took a seat next to me, paused and asked:

'Have you ever been with a guy? Or even seen one naked before?'

I was stunned and excited at the same time. I felt my cheeks flush and a tingle between my thighs, and was a little scared, but somehow liked it. I didn't dare reply – I was too embarrassed.

'It's nothin' to be scared of. You're pretty, so I would love to see you naked . . .' he said, leaning in to me.

He pressed his open lips to mine and gave me a wet and sloppy kiss, causing my entire body to feel warm. He looked at me for approval and then moved my arms to my sides and raised my T-shirt, revealing my bra.

I just watched him, not knowing what to say or do. His fingers worked to pull my cotton bra down, exposing my milky-white breasts. My nipples were harder than I had ever seen them and I worried if that was even normal. He squeezed hard, kneading the flesh with his entire hand, stopping to pinch the nipples till it hurt and I felt myself getting moist between the legs. He leant in, taking a tit in his mouth, slobbering all over it the way he had my lips earlier. The arousal washed over me and I knew I wanted to do something more, but I didn't know what or how, so I just stood there, my arms still at my sides, letting him do as he pleased.

'Take off your skirt. I want to see you,' he said as his face remained expressionless.

'But . . .' I stammered.

'Now!' he commanded.

I reached around the back and undid the zipper and watched as the skirt made its way to the floor around my ankles. There I stood, in my panties and bra with my tits – wet with saliva – resting outside the cups, while he began to pull down his shorts. His tank top, though long, rested just above his pubic hair. When he stood up, tossing his shorts off to the side, his cock stuck out and was hard and swollen. I had never even realised that they could be so big! His balls were long and hung down pretty low, and the curly hair, though darker, was also red like the hair on his head.

'Your underwear too,' he said.

When I lowered my panties, I could see the wet spot on the crotch and hoped he wouldn't notice. He bent to push the skirt and panties away from around my feet and pressed his hands to my legs, motioning for me to spread them apart. The cool air in the garage gave me goose bumps and felt good against my wet pussy.

'I know you've never done this before, so I'll try to be nice,' he said, sounding almost annoyed. He stood closer; his cock brushed against my leg and he reached down to my cunt and began rubbing it with the palm of his hand. He smiled as he felt the wet and slowly ran one finger down and around my slit until reaching the bottom when he started to push it inside. I flinched and he paused for a second and then used his other hand to take mine and bring it down to his dick. 'Stroke it up and down, but not too hard,' he commanded.

I did as he said, taking a hold of it and feeling the ridges of his veins and skin as I ran my hand along it while it grew even more inside my grip.

His finger began to ease its way inside me again and I tried to relax – I was horny and felt like I needed something inside of me. Once his finger was inside, it felt good having it move in and out of the wet, so when he began to force a second one inside I tried to welcome it. My knees felt weak and I leant into him for balance. I tried to kiss him, but he turned his face and continued pushing two, maybe three fingers in and out of me while I continued to stroke his cock. As I was really beginning to enjoy it, he grabbed my shoulders and pushed me down onto my knees. He didn't look angry or mean, so I wasn't scared.

As I kneeled there on the cold dirty floor, his cock dangled right in front of my face. He took it in his hand and pressed it to my lips. I could feel something wet and a bit sticky on it and tried to move it away, but he persisted.

'Open your mouth. Come on, just lick it a little – you'll like it,' he said.

I opened my mouth and he pushed it deep inside while I tried not to gag. He began pumping it in and out of my mouth and I used my tongue to keep it from going in too far as he grunted out loud. When we heard a car horn echoing through the garage he pulled out, his cock hitting me across the face.

'Lay down!' he said with urgency.

I lay on the floor which was freezing against my bare back, with little pebbles digging into my skin. He spread my legs apart and kneeled on the floor between them, leaning forwards until he was hovering over me.

'Just relax,' he whispered.

He watched me, looking into my eyes as his hands shuffled around between my legs, before taking his cock and pressing it against my wet slit. He pushed it around, looking for a way in, and my cunt ached to be filled.

I could only describe it as a strong itch that needed to be worked and I spread my legs farther apart, hoping to make it easier. He was pushing so hard that when he finally got to the right spot, his cock drove hard into me, causing me to yelp. He shushed me and pulled out a little, only to keep going back in and out harder and faster.

It didn't take long before the pain stopped and was replaced by a feeling so good that I just wanted him to go deeper and deeper. Drops of sweat from his brow dripped onto my face and neck and I could feel every inch of him pumping in and out of my tight hole. Something warm and wet trickled out of me and down my ass and I wondered if I had peed myself. I had felt myself get wet before when I would see sex on TV, but had never felt it quite that wet!

I noticed the shadow of two people walk past, but they had not seen us. He began to fuck me even faster and the skin of my back and ass stung from the scrapes against the rough floor. His grunts grew louder and his thrusts harder until he pulled out of me and practically trampled me, bringing his cock to my face.

He stroked it until I began to feel hot cum dropping onto my mouth and chin and I squinted to keep it from getting into my eyes. With a final moan, he rubbed his moist and sticky head over my lips and I could taste the salty milk on my tongue.

'Thanks, sweetie. That was great,' he said, getting up and quickly getting dressed.

He tossed my clothes to me and he used my panties to wipe my face. I quickly put my clothes on and remained quiet. I really didn't know what to say as I followed behind him back through the garage.

'Pick up the pace – I have to go,' he said, looking back at me.

'So go,' I said quietly.

He continued to walk with me up the ramp towards the daylight and said, 'Well, I'm not lettin' you walk through here alone – it could be dangerous for a girl.'

Once outside the garage, he grinned at me one last time and rode away on his bike.

– *Dianne, Toronto, Canada*

Jan's Buyer

I thought I would tell you about how my fetish was revealed to me recently and has completely changed my outlook on sex.

I was a pretty ordinary girl, originally. I would regularly go out with guys, but without being promiscuous or easy to catch. I even had a wee rule: no sex in the first month. I found this tended to root out the ones who were only interested in shagging me before they moved on to their next conquest, but it also gave me a little feeling of power sometimes: when things were getting hot I always found amusement in how agitated my suitors would become with an erection in their underpants that was going nowhere. I used to let them finger me or lick me, they were all too keen to do that since they imagined it would lead somewhere else, especially if they made a good job of it, but I never touched them, save to rub their aching rods through their jeans, to egg them on a bit more, until the four weeks were up.

Some of the tongue and finger work on my fanny and clit, during what I suppose was essentially a trial period, was fantastic. Those that got fed up with me after a fruitless week or so were useless at it anyway, but those patient enough to stay on through weeks two and three seemed to be more studious and dedicated. I even wondered if some of them had gone home to study or read up on pleasuring a woman in an attempt to persuade me to give it up, because they seemed to get better at it as the month wore on.

I used to encourage them with comments like 'I'll be worth the wait', or 'Not long now, baby', to try and egg them on for as long as possible. It gave me another wee power thrill to string them along like that. I held out as long as I could, but the truth was I did want to fuck, and if a guy got close to the month mark I became tempted on many occasions to give him time off for good behaviour. But I kept my resolve and never broke my one-month rule before humping anyone's brains out.

The latest candidate for fucking my auburn-haired pussy was Alec. He was your typical Lanarkshire local boy: pale skin, dark hair, friendly as anything. He lived in the neighbourhood adjacent to mine and used to catch the same bus from his work (at a bank in town), getting off at the same stop every day but walking off in the opposite direction. I knew he was glancing at me every now and then, which is always pleasing, as long as they don't get leery about it. Eventually after a few weeks, he gave me a hello as he walked past me on the bus and, of course, having been brought up to be nice, I returned the hello the next time. After a week or two of this, I think Alec felt he had built up a foundation of familiarity and was confident enough to ask me out without it looking too forward. He chose his moment as I stepped off the bus, and I let him walk me home.

I first kissed him in his car, as he dropped me off from a trip to the flicks one evening. It was certainly a lustful kiss, but he didn't let things get carried away; I felt his hand on the inside of my leg and certainly under my skirt hem, but not so high that he would have felt the tops of my hold-ups. He seemed to be well behaved therefore and I predicted that he might very well stay the one-month course.

On our second date I went back to his house and he got a little bit braver as we clinched, feeling my breasts through my dress and then allowing his hands to wander up past my stocking tops, which he discovered without any apparent reaction, and onto the gusset of my knickers. I let him tickle and press through the thin white fabric on my glowing clitty and moist pussy, but grunted in discouragement when I felt his fingers feeling their way underneath them; he retreated back to the good work he was doing on the gusset. He pulled my auburn hair to one side and licked and munched on my ear as he softly rubbed me and I lay back doing my best to cope with, and enjoy, the arousal and the pleasure I was getting from his efforts. But I allowed him no further. He was hard as a rock when I left him to get into my taxi and I thought about how he would be pumping a lonely tribute to me as I was driven home. It made me feel wonderfully in charge of him and the relationship.

In the middle of the third week I invited him to mine, and dressed to tease him horribly as we ate dinner, knowing this would make him work harder to please me once we had retired to the couch. I wore another light dress, flesh-coloured hold-ups, which are the only leg coverings I will ever wear, and light-tan high heels with an ankle strap. I put on the same pair of knickers I had on a few days before, unwashed and ripe with my juice.

This time, once I was satisfied with the stimulation he had given me through the dirty knickers, I let him peel them off me. Then, pushing his hand away from my crotch, I whispered to him to suck the gusset. He was so desperate to get further with me that he did it without hesitation; at first the tasty cocktail of new and old juice overloaded his senses, but after a second or two I knew he was enjoying every last molecule he could suck from the weave.

I was most definitely in command; I think I had him so teased and entranced that he would have sampled other of my bodily concoctions quite willingly, had I made him. The sex-starved man will perform like a monkey on an organ if you play a tune that implies imminent intercourse, I've found, and he'll certainly lap at your clit until his neck aches, which is what I had him do on this occasion.

I coached him on cunnilingus in the same way I coached previous lovers, with appreciative moans when he was getting it right, and silence when he was getting it wrong. Soon the pressure and frequency of tongue movements was perfect and I placed my hands on the back of his head to keep him in situ while I made my way to an intense climax.

We kissed a little more, writhing a little as our legs and arms entangled. I could taste my sap on his lips and tongue. I rubbed his hard penis through his trousers and massaged his balls as reward for his fine work, but shortly thereafter I announced that he would need to call himself a taxi. He was such a docile gent, apart from the look of sweet regret on his face at leaving my company there was no real show of frustration. Up to now he had not even mentioned the idea of us having sex, he seemed quite willing to let me go at my own pace, which made teasing all the easier.

So it was with a mere ten days to go before the expiry of my one-month trial period, and Alec's big lucky evening, that I met Wil. I work for an Estate Agency in town, and one of my main duties is to escort prospective buyers around available properties.

I was booked in to show a gentleman around a new complex near to the racecourse in the afternoon and I went along without the slightest inkling that the encounter would turn out to be a little unusual. Actually, there was a slight inkling: the gentleman had come into the office to ask for a viewing during my lunch hour, so I had not seen him at all, but Elaine, who booked the appointment, winked at me as she handed me a note of the arrangement. I did wonder why, I must admit.

I knew why when I saw him. He was standing outside waiting for me, in a pair of loose canvas-coloured trousers and a navy-blue short-sleeved shirt, open to two buttons at the collar, which wafted in the strong breeze. He was dark, very dark, of skin and hair, and I reckoned was probably of West Indian lineage. He had smooth-looking lips and clear white eyes with deep brown pupils and now I knew why Elaine had winked. He was quite sexy.

'Hello, Wil Simms?' I asked, hoping he would say yes.

'That's right,' he said.

'Shall we step inside?'

I led the way.

'There is a variety of different apartments available in this complex, over a range of size and price. Was it one in particular you were interested in?' I asked him, trying my hardest to get as much eye contact with the handsome buck as I could.

'It was the top flat with the roof and balcony I was interested in,' he said, responding to my eye contact with some of his own. This pleased me immensely.

'Oh yes, the most expensive,' I commented jovially.

'Only the best for me.' He laughed.

I called the lift down and we stepped inside. I deliberately stood right next to him, trying to brush

91

against his vein-covered forearm with my elbow. His strong-looking body was really attracting me, I couldn't help it. I reached over and pressed the button for the top floor.

'What is it that you do, Wil?' I asked. It's always good to know what a client does as it may help you find a selling point in the property.

'I just started a job at a local solicitors. I'm their new consultant on English law, so I'm looking for a place nearby.'

That explains the absence of a local accent, and the interest in expensive realty, I thought to myself.

'Oh, interesting,' I said, keenly.

We reached the top and I deliberately stepped forwards too early so that we rubbed against each other as we emerged onto the landing. I was flirting with him and trying to enjoy myself at this stage, but I should say that was all I was doing; I had no realistic plans on actually getting together with him.

'This way,' I said.

He seemed very interested in the flat itself, and I don't blame him, I wish I could have afforded such a home. It was unfurnished at present and not particularly homely, but it was some living space nonetheless.

'Care to check out the roof?' I asked him, once he had seen all the rooms. We were in the living room now where two glass screen doors led out onto a walkway around the roof.

'Yes, sure, but do you mind if I just go to the toilet before we go out there?' he asked, slightly embarrassed at his lack of bladder control.

'Aye, of course.' I laughed: I did not really think he had too much to be embarrassed about and, provided he put the seat down after him and flushed, it was no problem if he wanted to use the toilet. I had just shown him that room so there was no need to give him directions. 'I'll wait here,' I told him.

I waited that is until I heard the sound of Wil peeing into the toilet: it was a surprising sound to me; of course I'd heard a man peeing before, but this was very loud, and I concluded, with some puzzlement, that he must be peeing with the door open. That did seem rather strange behaviour.

I did not ruminate on this for long, however, as the mischievous little pixies put another thought in my head at that time, that I really couldn't get rid of: I began to think, with some regret, on the fact that I had never seen a black cock in the flesh.

A silly thought I know, and I don't know how it got there, and I'm not really sure how I reached the conclusion that it would be a good idea to try and take a look at Wil's cock, but I found myself creeping up to the bathroom and poking my head around the open door with just that aim.

'Everything all right?' I asked, by way of a ruse for my nosiness.

'Yes, fine,' he reported as he shook the last drops of dew from the end of the branch and zipped himself up. He did not seem in the least bit embarrassed that I might have seen his penis, nor bothered that I had invaded his privacy.

I had got myself quite a good look. The first thing that surprised me was the darkness of his shaft; it was much darker than the rest of him. Thinking back I suppose I should have expected this; after all, all the penises I had seen up to then were darker than the general skin tone of their owners. Why should Wil's have been different?

The second observation was the colour of the head of his penis – I was expecting it to be a standard purple-pink colour, but it was not, more a mouth-watering chocolate-cherry colour if truth be known.

I also noted that it was a good size, just big enough, I imagined, fully engorged, to stimulate a woman comfortably and thick enough to feel good.

I took him out onto the balcony to enjoy the view of the country park and racecourse. He liked it, I think, and despite the stiffening breeze at our slightly higher altitude I'm sure his head was full of thoughts of relaxing summer evenings.

'I hope you're going to invite me if you have any barbecues up here,' I suggested.

'Of course,' he agreed, smiling.

'Can I show you anything else?' I asked. It was a question full of ambiguity on this occasion, and in hindsight the timing could have been better: at that second, a stronger gust of that beautifully warm air caught my light dress and blew the hem up over my waist. I gave a girly shriek and fought it down with my hands, but it was too late to save my knickers and hold-ups from being exposed.

'I'm sorry about that.' I smiled awkwardly at Wil as I pulled my dress down again. I have no idea why we tend to apologise when such things happen to us, but I did.

'Now we're even,' he smirked.

On my return to the office, Elaine was waiting eagerly to rib me about the customer and to cause me great embarrassment by accusing me, in front of our colleagues, of humping the handsome hunk in the show-flat. My redness gave away my interest in him, I think, but I hoped they were not so gullible as to think I had actually been so unprofessional.

Nonetheless, Wil entered my thoughts a lot over the next few days, and especially when I was with Alec. I found myself lying back in my armchair as Alec knelt on the carpet between my legs, trying his best to give an oral performance worthy of being granted intercourse with me. I kept Alec sort of happy by rubbing my stockinged foot on his twitching penis as it poked up from his crotch. He still didn't have the nerve to ask for sex, bless him.

I satisfied myself by thinking of Wil as the wet tongue vibrated over my clitoris and those delicately curling fingers sought out more hidden pleasure centres. For one moment they did not belong to Alec, but to Wil, bending me over the balcony of that flat and finger-fucking me from behind. I shut my eyes and took myself away to that fantasy, soon coming with the thought of it as my thighs jolted and I nearly squeezed Alec's head from his shoulders.

He seemed pretty pleased with his handiwork as he smiled up at me, and I can't deny he had done very well over the few weeks that I had known him. If my mind was not elsewhere I'm sure I would have decided then and there to keep him for the full month.

But my mind was elsewhere: I was desperate to meet with Wil again and, as I kissed and cuddled Alec while he waited for his taxi, I came to the conclusion that I would most certainly have to take steps to meet Wil again. He deserved his chance as well, did he not? I could always drop him if things went really well with Alec, I said to myself, justifying my decision.

I must have been feeling so in charge of this relationship with Alec to think such selfish things, to give such little consideration for the feelings of my current, well, boyfriend, I suppose. If these thoughts weren't high-handed enough, then the question that blurted out next was:

'Alec, it's all right if we see other people, isn't it? I mean, you were aware of that all along, weren't you?'

I could see from the reddening of his cheeks that he was disappointed with the tenor of the question;

he was clearly secretly hoping that we were now exclusive, I think, but yet again he gave the quiet, grey, compliant, accommodating answer.

'Yes, yes of course,' he said hesitantly, trying to hide his pangs of disenchantment.

'I mean, don't worry, it's not like I have anyone in mind or anything,' I reassured him, 'I just wanted us to be clear where we stood.'

'No, no that's fine, of course, you should – we should,' he replied, zipping his semi-hard cock away into his trousers.

A horn sounded outside. The taxi had arrived.

I spent the next morning searching through our office database for properties on our books that might suit Wil's tastes. This, I thought, would give me a believable pretext for contacting him and inviting him to meet me for another viewing. I could then make my move, whether that be a kiss, a date proposal or what, I did not know, I just knew that some sort of positive action was imperative.

I found a little something that might suit him, I thought, in a nearby suburb, well known for its grand residential homes. An attempt was being made to bring new blood into the area and this included construction of a complex very similar to the one near the racecourse where I had met Wil. I hoped he would be tempted by it.

I picked up the phone and called the number he had left with us.

'Oh aye, ringing your new fancy-man then,' taunted Elaine. She had been spying on me and noted that I had called his personal details up onto my screen. I just ignored her. I knew she didn't really suspect anything, as far as she knew I was just pursuing a genuine sales lead with him.

'Hello?' Wil answered.

'Hi, Wil, it's Jan, from Stewart & Son Estate Agents, I took you around the flats at the racecourse recently?' I don't know why I posed it as a question, I think I was nervous.

'Oh yes, how could I forget? What can I do for you?' he said, a little cheekily. He seemed pleased to hear from me anyway, which calmed me a bit.

'I was wondering what your feelings were about the property we saw? Are you thinking of having a survey done, making an offer?'

'I liked it, I liked it, but I want to see a few more flats before I pick one or two to pursue further.' A smile of satisfaction spread over my face – that was exactly what I wanted to hear.

'Perhaps I can help you out with that side of things too. I was looking over some of the properties on our books at the moment and I noticed another modern flat that really might suit you. Would you like to meet for a viewing?'

I could hear him considering it.

'Yes, yes, sure,' he agreed.

We made the arrangements to meet there the following afternoon, so I'm afraid I had to endure an entire afternoon of silly teasing from Elaine, but I comforted myself it would be worth it come the following day.

I found myself carefully considering my outfit, something I never really tended to do usually. I'm not a scruffy dresser as you may have gathered, but I do tend to be able to grab the first thing that looks right on the rack and then just go with it. Not so that day. I dithered over it a bit and in the end went with a white blouse, a black pencil skirt and the ever-faithful light-coloured hold-ups I never go anywhere without.

It was an impatient morning of nervous anticipation for me as I watched the clock. Having seen my first black cock, I was now desperate to get my hands on it and could barely think about anything else.

My excitability reached a peak at lunchtime, when I was absolutely bursting to meet up with Wil. So distracted was I that I barely heard Elaine calling at me from her desk.

'Jan, that's your hunky client on the phone for you,' she said.

I didn't even hear it. I was thinking about him at that very moment, and her words fitted so seamlessly into my daydream that I barely noticed them.

'Jan! I said, that's your hunky client on the phone for you.'

Her raised voice woke me from my reverie and I gestured her to put the call through.

'Hello, Jan?'

'Hello,' I said and hoped he could hear my smile.

'Jan, I'm sorry. I've been thinking, I don't think I want to see any more flats, I want to maybe get something more homely, a house, maybe in Earnock or somewhere like that? Could we cancel today's viewing?'

I tried my hardest to hide my disappointment.

'Of course, that's fine.'

'Do you have anything else I could view that might meet the description?'

I thought for a moment to try and recall anything from our files that would meet the case, but nothing sprang to my racing mind. I was sure we had something, but I was too flustered and worried about losing my chance to meet Wil again and I couldn't think of anything.

The only thought that entered my head was that Alec's house would have been perfect, if only it were for sale. I tried to keep Wil talking, for more thinking time.

'Yes, there is something actually, when would you like to view it? I'll see if I can arrange it.'

'Soon as possible really, later this afternoon?'

I was so desperate to see him I could not face the ordeal of waiting again for any later appointment to come by. I agreed to meet at three o'clock that very afternoon.

'What's the address?' he asked.

I felt a lump come to my throat, silencing me. I hadn't thought of that; my plan had been to agree a meeting for later today and then rummage through our database for a suitable property, in time for three. But it was a rubbish plan: he had to know the address now, I did not have time to search for a property. I was stuck, and I was desperate to see him. I was dying to feel his dark cock in my hands, taste it even. So desperate was I, in fact, that I did something rather questionable: I gave him Alec's address.

'See you later,' he said, and I heard the line click dead.

I sat motionless with the phone in my hand for a length of time indefinable to my own perception – a second? A minute? – as I thought about what I had said, and where it left me. One thing was for sure, I could not afford to sit about. I made my excuses to the smirking Elaine, and left for lunch, advising her I would not be back until after four, as I had a number of buyers to escort.

Round the corner, out of sight and sound of my colleagues, I called Alec on my mobile.

'Hello, Jan,' he said in a very happy tone; he was pleased to hear from me, that might help.

'Hi, Alec. Look, I've got a problem at work, I need you to help me keep a client,' I said to him.

'How?' he asked. There was genuine interest in his

voice, and I knew that he was keen to assist if he could. I breathed a little easier.

'I know it sounds weird, but I need to pretend your house is for sale and show a client around it this afternoon. Can you meet me at about two o'clock to let me in?' I explained. 'I'll make it worth your while,' I added in a more suggestive tone.

He coughed and tried to turn it into a laugh, but I could tell the chance of a bonus get-together was exciting him. 'No, it doesn't sound weird, Jan. I'll try and get away from work. See you later.'

I hung up and gave a sigh of relief. There was a lot for me still to do, but it looked like my horny little doormat would save the day.

He was waiting outside for me as I arrived, a look of needy supplication on his face. I wondered if he thought my promise of recompense would include penetration.

I handed him one of those FOR SALE boards that stick to the window (it would have been too draining on a warm day to carry the more classic sign-on-a-pole over to the address) and asked him to affix it.

'Then come inside and I'll help you get the place looking neat,' I said.

He agreed wordlessly, which I did find a bit eerie, however empowering.

Inside I did a modicum of dusting and a sinkful of dishes while he fixed the board to the window. When he came inside, though, I left it all to him.

'It's a really good client, but we don't have anything suitable for him just now. I want a property to show him to keep him hooked for a week or two while I find something else for him,' I explained.

'I see,' said Alec.

The place was looking presentable soon enough; Alec could hardly be described as a slob, admittedly, so there wasn't all that much to do. I beckoned him over to the sofa. As he sat I slowly pulled my hem up to reveal my stocking tops and kissed him. His hands wandered up the sheer nylon on my legs to the lacy bands and even my tender thigh flesh. I did not discourage him, allowing his fingers to rise higher and higher to my knickers, which were peeled off in no time. By now he had learned the steps to this dance and had his head stuffed up my dress and his tongue working hard on my bud in no time.

I lay back and tried to savour the pleasure as best I could. I hoped he was doing the same, as I considered this was the reward I had promised him.

The sound of a car pulling up outside reached my ears and I gave Alec a tap on the shoulder to disengage him from his eager cunnilingus.

'He's here. Hide somewhere,' I instructed him as I adjusted myself. I put my knickers back on over my sopping wet pussy. Alec had disappeared and I did not think to see where he had gone.

'Hello!' I called to Wil across the front garden. 'What do you think?'

'Nice,' he commented. 'Quite a nice area too.'

'Want to come inside and check it out?' I asked.

'Sure.' He smiled a bright white smile.

I showed Wil around the house, giving it all the usual Estate Agency stuff, but without the hard sell. After all, I wanted him to be impressed, but not too impressed: it would get complicated if he tried to make an offer.

I tried my best to touch him and brush past him in the corridors and gave him plenty of eye contact whenever I could. I even allowed my hand to brush along his back and ever-so-lightly touch a buttock as I motioned him from the kitchen to the dining room.

Going up the stairs I skipped in front of him and wiggled like a slut as he followed me; I knew my dress hem would dance enticingly, and that he would be feasting his eyes on the back of my shiny legs. I did not notice Alec anywhere, so good was his hiding place, and indeed, I forgot about him really. It is hard to give a tour of a house and think about how to make a move on a sexy guy and also think about where your boyfriend is hiding, all at the same time.

'There's no balcony, I'm afraid,' I joked as we concluded the tour, upstairs in Alec's bedroom.

'Shame,' commented Wil; I noticed him eyeing my legs blatantly, trying his best to recall the thrill of my wee mishap in the wind. We laughed.

Wil stepped nearer to me.

I wanted to tell him how I felt, to reach out for his hand, ask him about his 'situation' as they say, but I had the very real problem that I did not know where Alec was hiding, and the last thing I wanted was for him to hear me asking another young man for a date. My face creased with a combination of lust and frustration.

Wil stepped nearer again, and it suddenly dawned on me that he might be having similar thoughts to mine – only as far as he was concerned, we were alone in the house and had no reason to hold back. Involuntarily, my eyes searched the V shape at the neck of his shirt, open to two buttons, and I admired the exposed part of his copper-coloured chest; I felt like running my fingers across it.

'Do you have to be back in the office by any particular time?' he asked, fixing my gaze with two huge ebony pupils. I melted in their intensity and my lips parted slightly as though to kiss. I felt a thrill run through my pussy and clitoris that I could not ignore. I was itching to let him know I was interested, and I leant in to whisper a warning that we were not alone.

I never got to speak – managing only a gasp as I felt two clamp-like hands close around my arms and draw me in. I felt the warmth of his torso on my breasts as they squashed against him and I gasped as he kissed me roughly on my neck.

'I must have you, now,' he whispered passionately.

My pussy ran with dampness and I was overcome with lust; without thinking, I allowed my head to loll back submissively. Wil devoured my exposed neck with hungry kisses and nibbles of his teeth.

'No, we can't, not here.' My voice was barely a wheeze in the excitement.

'I am fucking you now,' he said confidently. I wanted to protest, I wanted to struggle, and I knew that these would have been the right things to do. But so much was making me want him: the closeness of his firm body, the pressure of his engorging penis against my belly, and, most of all, his uncompromising, commanding attitude. I knew if I stopped him now, we would only end up fucking somewhere else by teatime, but I would have lost the raw animal exhilaration of being taken at this moment. I could not, I knew, recreate the tingling pleasure on my tongue, in my anus and on my clitoris, or hope to orgasm as deeply and fully as I anticipated I would now with Wil's cock hammering my pussy as hard as he was likely to in this mood. A slave to the signals ringing off in each of the erogenous zones of my body, I damned the consequences and let it happen.

My knickers were yanked down to my knees as Wil continued to feast on my neck, earlobes and mouth. I was being forced backwards in the rush and I felt Alec's bed on the back of my legs and a feeling of entrapment overcame me: I could back away no more.

Wil finally planted his mouth on my own and I was able to return his passionate kiss, pressing my tongue against his. But the kiss was a mere distraction as Wil's real attention was on his hand, which crept up my skirt, past my hold-ups to my dripping pussy. I felt two fingers part my lips and press inside. I grabbed the back of Wil's neck as I kissed him.

Wil was like a tidal wave, relentless and unstoppable, as he progressed towards his ultimate goal. He was not pleasuring me with his fingers, he gave that no thought, he was testing and preparing my pussy for penetration, and the single-mindedness of the action thrilled me further. I was now sufficiently dilated and lubricated for cock, and I felt Wil push his two fingers all the way inside me, to confirm this for himself.

He spun me round and I faced the bed. I felt his strong black arm encircle my waist and tighten around me, followed by the impetus of a firm hand against my back. I bent over and put my hands on the bed.

'Are you ready for your first black dick, you little cock-teaser?' he asked. I didn't answer because the question was completely rhetorical; he was going to fuck me anyway, ready or not. I had no idea how, or if, he knew that this was my first black dick; I guessed I wasn't the first white girl to pursue his cock and that he was used to helplessly horny girls like me turning to utter whores in his hands. That would certainly explain his confidence and authority; he just took girls the way he wanted them, knowing they would not object.

I felt my hair being gathered into his fist and I heard his trousers being unfastened. I would have liked to take another look at the black hose that was about to drill me, but he would not let me turn my head. I shut my eyes and pictured it in my mind as I felt it press to me and slip inside. A moan of utter contentment accompanied two slow, explorative thrusts into me, as Wil used his hard cock to open me fully.

Then the real fucking started, hard and fast, reaming my cunt in selfish pursuit of satisfaction. I felt like my pussy was on fire, so intense were the feelings, and the sensations from each thrust began to run into each other, until they became one constant burning inferno inside me. Moaning through gritted teeth, I came so quickly that I was almost ashamed of myself.

Then the journey started again: Wil had not adjusted his rhythm or stance, even throughout my orgasm, and just continued, allowing me no respite.

A second time, my pussy combusted in the same fashion and I whimpered my way through another orgasm. Wil carried on regardless and I wondered if I would even survive another climax.

Fortunately the only climax I had to survive was Wil's. It was building for him too and, overcome with pleasure, his thrusts became more choppy until, at the point of release, I felt him grab my shoulders and hammer his cock, and semen, home.

I savoured his cock as he slowly pulled in and out of me, catching his breath. I was greatly disappointed when he finally withdrew, cheekily wiping his cock clean on my buttocks. This time I was able to turn and admire it one more time, black and glistening. He began to dress himself once more.

'That was good,' he said. 'Listen, I got to go, but call me, OK?'

I said I would, and stood to readjust myself. Only at that moment did my thoughts begin to return to

Alec, and now my face was burning with shame for I could not even begin to imagine that he had not heard us. Why had he not interrupted us?

Wil did not even stop to let me see him out, but kissed me on the cheek and left me in the bedroom. I sat on the bed and listened for the sound of the front door.

'Alec?' I shouted, hoping he would answer from downstairs or further down the hall – the further away, the better. There was no reply.

'Alec!?' I shouted again. There was only silence.

Then, by just a crack at first, the wardrobe door creaked open, and I saw four fingers creep around it before it was flung open, revealing Alec. My heart stopped. He would have heard, and possibly even seen the whole thing from just feet away. I was scared: why had he not emerged to stop us? Confronted us? Was he about to explode in jealous anger now? I had teased him for nigh on a month and then just let myself be taken by a comparative stranger.

Alec emerged from the closet, crawling, a serene look on his face that soothed my fears a little. I said nothing, watching him come nearer. His cock was bulging in his trousers and he looked surprisingly amorous. Wordlessly, he pushed his head up my skirt and began to do what he still does best to this day . . .

– *Janice Bell, Lanarkshire, Scotland*

Word of Foot

My fetish is women's feet. I work at a women's shoe store. Who says business and pleasure don't mix? Not me. I've been mixing them footloose and fancy-free for two high-stepping years now. And getting quite the reputation for it, as I found out the hot way not so long ago.

The sultry sight, feel, smell and taste of girl peds have thrilled me ever since I was old enough to wet myself – the good way. The sculpted, arched elegance, the shapely, playfully plump toes and smooth, contoured soles, all the delicate curves and complexities of the female foot have been feeding my sexual appetite going back to the day when I first became fully aware of my best friend's cute little feet.

She was innocently applying sparkly toenail polish to her separated and extended piggies, and as I stared at her curvy peds, my hands suddenly went damp and my fingers shaky, my throat dry and my pussy dewy. She asked me to help her, and I fumbled polish all over her outstretched toe-tips, then abandoned the brush for good and openly petted her smooth arches and supple soles. She thought I was crazy, but I knew I'd found the love of my life.

From that first awkward experience was born my craving for female feet. I studied shoe catalogues, took in swimming and diving events, sat on park benches and watched the girls go by in their summer sandals. The beach became my second home when it was hot, the bowling-alley shoe concession when it was cold. I devoured foot-fetish speciality books and magazines by the yard, girl-girl ped-porn videotapes by the shopping cart. By the age of eighteen, I was a fully fledged foot-whore.

And it was in college that I had my first honest-to-goodness full-on foot sexual encounter with another woman – my size-eight psychology professor, Anne. She had the longest legs showcased in the shortest skirts, shapely, toenail-painted feet openly displayed in swaybacks, sandals and pumps. We played bare-ped footsies on top of her office desk after class one day. Then she handled my feet as only a fellow fetisher can – gently rubbing them, stroking them, licking and sucking them – till I came in a heated gush, with a whoop and a holler, which brought the department head barging through the door, catching the two of us in flagrante foot delicto.

I've been selling shoes to my soul's content ever since. Women's feet are my beat, an endless parade of lady limbs and peds to be hand-fitted into hand-tooled coverings. Work is a joy, rather than a labour. The rich, musky scent of the leather and suede and the slick feel of the beautifully crafted, vibrantly coloured ped-holders is enough to get me misty where it counts most. And when a sexy customer sashays in and takes a seat, and I lovingly cradle her tapered leg-tips in my hands, dress them up in a pair of stilettos that blazingly enhance the natural sensuousness of the female-formed foot, it's all I can do to control myself.

Sometimes, I don't.

Like when stunning Melinda strutted into my store in a whisper of silk, and a pair of four-inch heels.

It was 9.20 on a Monday night, ten minutes before mall closing. I'd been working the full twelve-hour shift, as usual, but it had been quiet enough up to that point to hear a stocking drop – only a handful of heavy-footed housewives and retirees. Until tall, leggy, ped-perfect Melinda strolled into my life, and heart.

The dark-haired, brown-eyed beauty with the moist scarlet lips and pale oval face seemed somehow familiar to me. But I couldn't place her, and I didn't waste much time studying her face anyway. I briefly glanced over her tailored black jacket and pearl-white blouse, her thigh-high black leather skirt, and then my eyes plunged downwards. They slowly slid down her long black-stockinged legs and came fully to rest, wide and wondering, on her sheer-stockinged feet, delectably packaged in a pair of shiny black pumps, a shiny gold anklet adorning her slender right ankle.

She did a quick walkthrough of the store, fingering this and studying that, my gleaming orbs following her every step of the way. Then I remembered that the clock was ticking, and I leapt into action.

'Anything I can help you with? Anything at all?' I asked, rushing up to the statuesque goddess with the spectacularly moulded base.

She looked at me, looked down where I was looking. 'I want the sexiest pair of stilettos you have,' she stated, sending shivers racing down my spine and into my pussy.

I glanced up, gazing in awe at the sly smile that spread across her full lips. And I resolved right then and there to find out where the gorgeous lady stood on the issue of female foot worship.

'Gimme a minute,' I yelped.

I dashed around the store like a woman possessed, loading up on the sluttiest spike-heels I had on hand, including some from my own private stock. I could've shod a platoon of streetwalkers in guaranteed sales with the armful of sexy footwear I gathered up and tumbled down onto the chair next to Melinda.

Her slim silk-sheathed limbs were crossed in a symphony of casual elegance, her right foot dangling, dancing under the lights. A voice on the mall loudspeakers shattered my google-eyed reverie, however, informing one and all that it was 9.30, mall closing time.

'Oh, I'm sorry,' Melinda said, rising to her feet. 'I guess I left it a little too late. Perhaps I'll come back some other night.'

'No,' I protested. 'It's – it's OK. I – I have a key. I can let you out the back way – when we're . . . done.' I scampered to the front of the store before she could say anything and yanked out and locked the transparent security shutters. In two shakes of a lady's tail, I was back at her feet.

'You sure you don't mind?' she asked.

'No – no, not at all,' I gasped. 'Please, sit down.'

She sat down, folding her exquisite limbs one over the other as before, a soft smile on her face.

'We have all the leading brands,' I babbled, pulling up a stool and plopping down. 'Anne Klein, Prada, Franco Sarto –'

'Let's try those red ones first – the ones with the golden heels and arches.'

'Good choice,' I exhaled, grabbing up the shoes by their seven-inch spikes and presenting them to Melinda.

She started to remove her own heels. I stopped her. 'Allow me.'

She smiled, extended her right foot to me, and I captured it in my hands, electricity arcing from it into my body. I held her by the ankle, the toe of her shoe, feeling the thin gold anklet, the very pulse of the lovely lady. Then, shivering with delight, I slid the shoe off, heel to toe, exposing her ped.

The warm moist leather and silk scent of her shoe and foot flooded my senses, leaving me momentarily dizzy, the breathless sight of her sheer-stockinged foot with gloss-painted nails dazzling my eyes. I took a deep breath, inhaling everything, and Melinda slipped her right foot down and her left up. I tenderly freed the other high-arched ped from its highly polished covering.

Then I slid off my stool and onto my knees, and she placed a foot in my lap. I gazed at the erotic hour-glass figure, but somehow managed to slip one of the shaking stilettos over her toes, lift her ankle and fit her snugly inside the wicked shoe.

She withdrew her erotically costumed foot from my lap and asked, 'How did you know my size?'

'I knew,' I breathed.

I dressed her other foot, and she stood up and walked back and forth in front of me. I stared down at her feet, up, up the soft shining contours of her legs. 'How d-do they feel?' I mumbled.

'How do they look?' she countered.

My eyes flashed crimson and gold. 'Like heaven.'

She laughed. 'Let me try on another pair.'

She was a finicky shopper – just the kind I like. We tried on every pair I'd brought her, me surreptitiously stroking her feet and ankles and calves as I shod and unshod her, she putting on a scorching footwear runway fashion show that had me gasping in the aisle. My face burned hot and bright and my whole body shook, my pussy soaked to unsatisfaction beneath my skimpy skirt and panties. It was too much to take, without giving something back.

'My, it's getting late, isn't it?' Melinda spoke, glancing at her watch.

Time has no meaning for the dedicated shoe saleswoman – customer service is her *raison d'être*. And I was darned well going to service this customer the best and wickedest way I knew how, or be told off trying.

She sat back down and extended her right leg for shoe removal. I caught her by the anklet and the toe of the wild leopard-print stiletto. I squeezed her ankle and toes in a meaningful manner and stared deeply into her soulful eyes, willing her, begging her to allow me to truly fall at her feet and worship them for the erotic *objets d'art* that they were.

She stared back at me. I slipped the exotic slutwear off and let the shoe drop. Then I gripped her bare foot and pressed my thumbs into her vulnerable sole. I rotated my thumbs, massaging her soft foot-bottom, and she smiled. My world lit up with a thousand suns.

I traced my thumbnails from the rounded ball of her ped down into the depths of her arch. Her skin was warm and supple. She bit her lip and her foot quivered slightly, and I hastened to take advantage. I lifted her foot higher and boldly thrust out my tongue, licked at her heel.

'Oh,' she murmured, sinking back into the chair.

I was brimming with sexual energy, but I managed to oh-so-slowly run my wet tongue over her heel, across her sole, up into her toes. Then I did it again. And again. Slow and sensuous, dragging my tongue over her sensitive foot-bottom. It took a monumental effort to stop myself from just devouring that incredibly edible foot, but I made it. I didn't want to frighten that trembling ped back into its shoe.

I licked and licked at Melinda's silky sole, and her hands strayed onto her braless breasts. She gently cupped and squeezed her large breasts as she watched me lap at her sole. I swirled my tongue all over the tender flesh, and her body jerked and her foot-bottom crinkled. She moaned when I plugged my tongue into her toes, swept it back and forth across their curvaceous undersides. Then she out and out shrieked when I tilted her foot down and swallowed her toes.

'God, that feels so . . . strange,' she breathed, eyes half closed, hands kneading her breasts.

I inched my lips forwards on her ped, taking in as much as I could, then slid her foot back out of my mouth until her toes reappeared, glistening with my wetness. I sucked on them, pulled on them, all at once, then individually, revelling in the sweet taste of them, their shapely plumpness.

Melinda closed her eyes and pinched the stiffened imprints of her nipples, her chest heaving. I tugged on her big toe with my mouth, then moved down and bit into the slick material between her big toe and the next in line, tearing at the fabric with my teeth.

'Jesus,' she gasped, eyes open and staring, fingers frozen on her nipples.

I ripped the stocking tip open, baring the woman's pale, gloss-painted big toe. I shook the stocking like a dog shakes a bone, until the run widened to reveal all of her toes. Then I captured the five of them in my mouth again, skin-on-skin this time, hot and wet.

Melinda rolled her nipples between her fingers and groaned as I sucked on her naked toes, squirmed my tongue around underneath them. She urged me on, wriggling her toes in my mouth, lifting her other foot and crossing it over the one I was sucking on, presenting it to me.

I disgorged her foot-digits and dropped the gleaming threadbare ped in my lap and anxiously attacked her other stiletto-clad foot. I pulled away the tease-shoe and placed it on the carpet. Then I inhaled the heady fragrance of her spectacular foot for a moment before gorging on it, devouring her stockinged toes, sucking on them.

She squirmed around in the warmth of my mouth-embrace, the blowtorch heat given off by my fondling hands and tongue. I encircled her ankles with my fingers and caressed them, rubbed her muscled calves, wagging my tongue back and forth across the ball of her foot as I tugged on her toes.

'Oh my God,' she exclaimed, jerking her foot away as a thought suddenly struck her. 'Somebody could see us.' She stared at the plastic security shutters draping the front of the store.

'So?' I replied, rubbing her feet together, catching my breath.

She looked at me, perhaps now fully realising the awesome power of my foot need. 'Well, uh, is there someplace a little more private . . . where we can continue . . . this?'

I lowered the woman's saliva-slick feet to the floor, then jumped up and pulled her out of her chair. I led her by the hand into the back of the store, into the break room, watching as she tip-toed after me like my own private ballerina.

The break room's small – a sink, a counter and a couple of cupboards; a small white fridge and brown couch – but any ped-port will do in a sexual storm. I'd used it before, with extremely satisfying results. I pushed Melinda down onto the couch and knelt in front of her, in front of her feet, brushing her ped-tips off before taking up where I'd left off with her left foot.

I bit into the damp fabric of her stocking and savagely tore it open, exposing her creamy white toes as I'd done with her other foot. I teased them with my tongue, getting them all wet and wriggly, then sniffed them.

Melinda shrugged off her jacket and fumbled her blouse open, revealing her lush, pink-tipped breasts. She grasped and pushed them together, squeezed, primping her hardened nipples and moaning softly as I sucked and sucked on her toes.

I pulled her tootsie out of my mouth and slithered my tongue in between her toes, one at a time, down the wiggling row and then back up again from the other side. Did the same with her other foot. Then I pushed her peds together, side by side, and swiped my tongue back and forth between the delicious pair, licking and sucking toes as she shoved up a breast and licked and sucked her own nipple.

'Let – let me kiss your feet,' she finally whispered.

'Shure,' I slurred, mouth full of foot.

But as I climbed to my feet, the blood suddenly rushed from my head into my pussy, and I saw stars. I gazed down at the ped-heavenly lady, my head spinning and my pussy dripping with lust. I needed to come, and come now. 'Take off your clothes,' I hissed.

Melinda scrambled to her feet and hastily pulled away her blouse, unzipped and dropped her skirt and peeled off her panties. I had her beat by a heartbeat, and we stood there in our stockinged feet – hers considerably more tattered than mine – nude except for our sheer, sexy leg garments.

She reached out and fingered my blonde hair, closing her eyes and puckering her lips. But I was having none of it. Foreplay was over. I wanted, needed, to fuck. I pushed the naked hottie onto the couch and climbed aboard myself, positioning our limbs so that we were scissored pussy to pussy, fur on fur – one of the best ways for women to fuck while keeping their peds in play.

I undulated my hips, sliding my soaking blonde pussy back and forth over Melinda's dark, springy wetness. She groaned. I groaned back when she clasped one of my red-stockinged legs and brought my foot into her mouth.

'Yes, yes,' I urged, her sucking mouth feeling so very good on my outstretched toes.

She grabbed at the lacy top of my stocking and pulled it down and off my leg, swallowing my bare toes and tugging on them. I closed my eyes, my body flooding with heat, shimmering with excitement. I did what she was doing to me, sucking on her right foot, the two of us pulling on one another's toes as we rubbed our smouldering pussies together.

We moved faster, more urgently, the wet friction priming us for explosion, our ripe, rubbing clits tingling to the point of bursting with juicy orgasm. Melinda raked her fingernails up and down my leg, her tongue writhing in between my red-tipped toes. I sucked on her big toe, slotting my fingers in between her other toes and clenching them, digit to digit, in an intimate embrace.

'Jesus, I'm coming,' the foot-blessed babe yelped, her hot breath steaming over my slick toes.

Her body tensed, then jerked, her breasts shuddering and feet jumping as she was jolted by ecstasy. I desperately ground my pussy into her pussy and sucked on her big toe, until my own clit tingled out of control and orgasm detonated inside me. I hugged Melinda's trembling leg and quivered with raw, white-hot joy, my head spinning and body melting.

Eventually, we managed to unglue ourselves. And as I held and caressed Melinda's feet, she explained why she looked so familiar to me: we both had the same pedicurist. And it was that loose-lipped foot beautician who had tattled to Melinda about my ped peccadilloes.

It seems my reputation for loving ladies' feet is spreading, foot by foot. I can only hope there are more women like Melinda who want to take my passion for a test walk.

– *H.T., Manitoba, Canada*

Cheating

I know this is going to sound weird to a lot of guys, but I get off on being cheated. That probably makes no sense to you at all, but look at it this way. Where you might like big boobs, or leather, or whatever it might be, I like to watch another guy fuck my wife. Maybe you think I should have my head examined, but I prefer to face the truth. I'm a dirty little wanker and I deserve what I get.

I'm not worthy of my wife for a start. I can't keep her satisfied, and who needs a weedy little pencil-dick like me anyway, when the world's full of real men? She only keeps me around for the money, and because she thinks it's a laugh for me to know what she's doing with other men. Sometimes she even lets me watch.

I was always like that. I always knew I was unworthy. Women are just so far above me, and other men too, although men should always worship women. Even when I was young I knew it, and with the other boys I would look at porn mags with every bit as much lust, but in horror too, for my own dirty thoughts and for the mind-numbing outrage of me daring to look at a naked woman. I knew it was wrong, I could feel their disgust emanating from the pages, but I still looked, and alone in bed at night I still wanked my dirty little cock.

I really am truly pathetic. I've never been able to control myself or do what I know is right. No man should be privileged to look at a naked woman without her specific permission, and no woman should ever, ever be obliged to expose herself for the entertainment of men. Yet again and again I find myself masturbating over dirty magazines, lost in grovelling worship of the beautiful, divine beings displayed so cheaply in those flimsy pages even as I tug my cock over them. I can't help it.

All through my teenage years and my twenties I was completely useless with women. I knew none of them could possibly be interested in me, but still I dared to dream, of being an obedient, servile husband to some wonderful woman, or any woman, but what right do I have to pick and choose? None whatsoever.

I ought to be whipped for just daring to think I might be allowed a preference, let alone expressing one, or just plain spanked, naked over the knee of some magnificent woman, any woman, spanked like the dirty snivelling little brat I am. And when I've been soundly spanked and I'm snivelling on the floor, she should tie my hands behind my back to stop me playing with myself and make me watch while she makes love to some powerful masculine man, a real man, with a cock big enough to satisfy her.

I'm very lucky indeed to be married. Certainly I don't deserve my Mistress, but She deigned to have me and to make me Her husband. To me She is the Goddess, the perfect being, and so far above me I'm not even worthy to use the name She does with her friends. To them, other women and real men, She is Katrina. To me, if I am privileged, she is Mistress Kat or, usually, just Mistress. I hate it when other men don't address Her respectfully, and yet who am I to criticise?

At first, I think, She just regarded me as somebody who could be helpful to her. She is from Poland, and wanted to live in the UK, so answered one of my many pitiful attempts to attract a wife. Although uncertain at first, She very soon learnt what I was, and since shortly after our marriage has treated me with the contempt I deserve. I serve Her in every way I am able to, I support Her and count it a privilege, and while I do not claim to have any right to witness Her pleasuring herself with other men, that is what I desire more than anything else in the world, and which I am occasionally permitted.

More usually, I am simply left at home while She goes out to meet men. If She finds somebody she likes She will either go home with him or bring him back to the house, in which case I pretend I am just a lodger. In the first case I will do my chores until about midnight, then go upstairs to masturbate as I think of Her with Her man, imagining his cock sliding in and out of Her body, even in Her mouth, a privilege I have never been and will never be permitted, or even in Her anus, into which I would never even dare to think of intruding my penis, but in which She sometimes enjoys other men's, and which I am occasionally permitted to kiss. In the second case I will wait until they have gone up to Her room and creep into the box room next door, in which I sleep, from which I will listen to them making love, until I can bear it no more and am forced to take my cock in my hand.

Then there are those very rare occasions when She finds somebody who doesn't mind if I watch, occasions that for me represent the pinnacle of Heaven. Most men wouldn't put up with having a little wanker like me tossing off in the corner while they fuck my wife, but a few don't mind, and fewer still actively take pleasure in it.

Seven times in all it has happened, five times with men who are prepared to tolerate me, twice with men who enjoyed my presence. Mistress prefers black men, who she says give her more pleasure, and of the seven, six have been black. The very first was a young man with the body of an athlete She met in a bar one night and brought home. She had told him She was married and that Her husband wouldn't interfere but would like to watch. He had agreed, far too strong and confident to care if a little shit like me was there or not, or whether I lived or died.

Oh how I hated it, every second. Watching him kiss Her. Watching him take off Her clothes. Watching him touch Her divine body and comment rudely on the size of Her breasts. Watching him take out his big black cock and demand that She suck it. She did. She took that huge dark penis in Her hand and then into Her mouth and She sucked it, enjoying every moment, while I know for a fact that the thought of my penis makes Her feel physically sick.

They didn't care that I was watching at all. After a bit I think they'd forgotten I was even there. They did all sorts of things, the sorts of things that make me so excited and so jealous, but which I know could never be permitted to me. She even allowed him to enter Her from behind, on Her knees, a position no woman should ever have to adopt for any man. How that hurt, to see my Mistress despoiled, to see Her most intimate secrets exposed to his lust-filled eyes and to see that long black cock slide into her body, to hear Her moans of pleasure for what he was doing to Her, and how it excited me. By then I had spunked in my hand.

There have been similar scenes with four other men. Some were utterly indifferent to my presence, some were irritated by me, and who can blame them?

121

Three of the five told me to stop wanking and I had to be content with finishing myself off over the memories of what I'd seen and the thought that he was still in bed with Her, enjoying Her body while I lay alone in my room masturbating like the perverted little wretch I am.

Then there were the two, the two who took pleasure in me being made to watch as they despoiled my beautiful Mistress. The first was one of the biggest men I've ever seen, maybe six foot six, and so full of confidence and power it made me cringe on the floor just to look at him. Mistress thought he was wonderful, a real man among real men, as She told me while kissing him and stroking his ebony skin.

He enjoyed being cruel to me, and laughed as She showed me his penis and told me to pull out my own. Mine looked like a maggot next to his, and She told me to make myself erect while She did the same for him, leaving me wanking naked on the bedroom floor while She caressed his magnificent cock and balls, stroking and licking until She had coaxed him to a full, towering erection. He was twice as long as me, and more than twice as thick, a real man's cock.

How they tormented me, for hours. I was made to kneel in one corner with my hands tied behind my back to stop me wanking at my dirty little cock while they made love. He talked to me as they did it, showing me my own wife's body, Her breasts and bottom and sex, which he touched intimately, as if he possessed Her, and She didn't mind. He told me that he was going to put his cock in Her mouth, and as She sucked him he told me how good it felt to be in my wife's mouth.

Never had I felt so wretched, or so excited. My cock had stayed rigidly hard, sticking up like a pathetic little finger to betray my feelings. Yet I could not touch, could not bring myself to that much-needed climax, even as I watched my Mistress lie back to accept him inside Her. He took Her legs. He rolled her up into a thoroughly vulgar and inappropriate position, with Her sex spread to his monstrous cock and the cheeks of Her divine bottom split apart to show the tight orifice I have occasionally been permitted to kiss in worship. He put his cock to Her sex and rubbed it around, telling me how wet She was and how excited She was for him, not for me, Her grovelling little dirt bag of a husband, but for him. He put his cock inside Her, and as he did I nearly came despite having no power to touch.

As he fucked Her he called me a shit and a worm. He told he how good it felt, using dirty words like 'slut' and 'cunt' to describe my divine Mistress and Her perfect body. Oh how I writhed, how I begged for release, but they only laughed at me and grew more passionate still. What he then did I shall remember to my dying day. He had fucked Her well, leaving Her in such bliss that Her dignity was forgotten as She lay with Her thighs wide in acceptance and Her hands on her breasts. He asked Her to roll over, and my heart jumped at the outrage of such a suggestion, that my Mistress, my own perfect Mistress, should be asked to adopt such an undignified position.

Yet She did it, perhaps because She knew how much it would hurt me to see her so abused, and with Her bottom lifted She allowed him to penetrate Her from behind. That, I thought, would be the climax of their encounter, but no. He gave only a few firm pushes and then withdrew once more, his long black cock now glistening with my Mistress's juices, and he pressed his face between Her open buttocks.

I thought, naturally, that he was worshipping Her, giving obeisance to Her as a man should to a woman, if She permits it. But no, he was licking Her not to show how low a creature he was beside Her, but to prepare Her for the ultimate degradation, sodomy.

How I stared. It was hard to take in, to believe that he really intended to do such a thing, and worse by far for the soft moans and sighs issuing from my Mistress's mouth. I could have cried, and when he stopped and held apart Her cheeks to show Her now moist and open anus I screamed in pain. He laughed and jerked his thumb at me, calling me white boy and making a joke of how I didn't want to see Her sodomised. She laughed too, and told him to do it so I could see.

He did. He held Her cheeks open as he put the head of his cock to Her anus, so that I could see Her hole spread to take him, pushing in and then opening around the thickness of his meat. I watched as it went in, the full monstrous length. I heard Her moans and pleas to go slowly, and Her breathless ecstasy as She was sodomised. He came inside Her, up Her bottom, and in the dirtiest manner imaginable, with half his cock inside as he masturbated inside Her. Worse still, he had reached around Her belly and made Her climax while he was still in up Her bottom, and as She came, She called out his name.

Never had I felt more wretched, but as they left me there, tied in the corner, Her last action was to spit on me before they went to the bathroom, laughing. I could do nothing, my head hung low and with Her spittle trickling slowly down my face and my cock so hard it hurt. They showered together. She made him coffee, which they drank together, now utterly indifferent to me, but at last She took pity on me and released me.

How I masturbated that night, pulling at my cock until I had come more times than I can remember, until I was sore and could no longer get erect, yet still I wanted to come again, and always over that same awful image, of his cock penetrating Her anus. And all the while as I lay there in my frenzy of masturbation they were next door, making love the night through. I never imagined an experience could be stronger, or more appropriate for me. I was wrong.

The Turk was worse. He was a big man, very masculine, so much so that so far as he was concerned I was not a man at all, which he made abundantly clear. He was laughing at me from the start, and the way he treated my wife, my Mistress, was an outrage to Her and to the Goddess herself. He made Her strip for him, dancing to music as She peeled off Her clothes until She was nude, as She showed off Her breasts and wiggled Her bottom in a manner so lewd I could scarcely believe that it was Her doing it, and yet She seemed to enjoy every moment.

With Her naked he sat down in a chair and demanded that She bring him a beer, which She did. He sat there, drinking the beer and smoking a cigarette while She fellated him, on Her knees with his great brown cock in her mouth, my Mistress, sucking cock in the nude as I watched grovelling in the corner, already wanking at my own pathetic penis.

After a while he pushed down his trousers and underpants and told Her to do something that still makes me shudder to think of it. He told Her to lick his balls and anus. He told my Mistress, my beautiful, divine Mistress, to take his scrotum in Her mouth and put Her tongue to his anal orifice. And She did it. She did it while She played with Her breasts and stroked Her sex, exciting herself even as She was made to commit that filthy act. I saw. I saw Her tongue touch his hairy, horrible anus, licking him.

He saw me looking, and how he laughed. He laughed to see my pain at how he was treating my Mistress and he laughed to see how pathetically small my penis was next to his, which was now hard, towering up over his great hairy belly as She pulled at him and lapped at his anus and balls. He asked me if I wanted to watch him fuck my wife and I was forced to admit I did.

With that he did it. He stood up and made Her kneel in the chair with Her bottom pushed out so that he, and I, could see every secret detail. He felt Her up, rubbing his cock between the cheeks of Her bottom as he groped Her breasts, then putting it to Her sex, so that I could see as he slid it deep.

How hard he fucked Her, and how he abused Her, sometimes holding Her by Her hips or Her breasts, sometimes slapping Her buttocks as he called Her a bitch and a whore. I had to speak out, to tell him that such foul words were not acceptable, but She told me to shut up, and with that his attention turned to me. He asked if I was a bitch and a whore too, and all I could answer was that if he felt it proper, then I must be. He asked if I was a man at all, to let him fuck my wife while I masturbated in the corner. I told him I was no man. At that, he said I was certainly no man, and that he would make me a bitch and a whore, his bitch and his whore. He said he was going to make me suck his cock.

I could only stare, appalled, but She was laughing, my own wife, my wonderful Mistress, laughing at the suggestion that I be made to suck another man's penis, and when it was still wet with Her juices. I could not resist. He came to me, laughing as he held it out. He told me to open my mouth. He told my wife to watch. He put his cock in my mouth and told me to suck him.

Oh, the bitter shame of having to take another man's erection in my mouth, but my Mistress had spoken. How She laughed at me as I sucked on his penis, and worse, She began to play with Her sex as She watched, and She told him to finish off in my mouth. I thought he'd say no. I thought he would want to have Her. I was wrong. He was far too virile to think his orgasm wasted. He made me suck him all the way, and spunked in my mouth, and made me swallow it, and as I gulped down his spunk my wife came, providing me with my whole life's perfect moment.

– Anonymous, Watford, UK

Gagging the Press

Note: the editorial staff at ...... magazine might be a bunch of dim sloanes but the legal department are very sharp and diligent indeed. I have, therefore, changed the names of everyone involved to protect myself from being sacked and sued for libel and, of course, that of the magazine!

'Strip!'

It wasn't a request, it was an order and the woman who gave it did not look as if she was used to being disobeyed. She was tall with long black curly hair pulled into a ponytail. Beautiful, certainly, but with a hint of cruelty in her dark, almost almond-shaped eyes, and full lips made more striking by a dark crimson shade of lipstick.

'I said, *strip!*' she repeated, this time almost hissing the last word and picking up the riding crop that I had been trying to ignore from where it lay on the coffee table. She wore black leather gloves that reached above her elbows, a black leather top and short skirt too. Her flesh by contrast was almost icily pale.

My first response to her order to strip was quite involuntary; I felt my face go bright red. The tip of the crop quivered under my nose as if in suppressed fury. Swallowing hard and deciding that the situation called for abject cowardice, I began to unbutton my blouse.

'Quickly, you little bitch!' the woman ordered as my anxious fingers fumbled the buttons. At last I got them undone and with my cheeks flaming even hotter I took my top off. The skirt had a side zip and did not take a moment to undo. It hit the floor, forming a puddle around my feet.

'Bra and panties too!' she said, full lips curling in distaste. 'Take them off, at once!'

She punctuated her order by slapping the end of the crop into the palm of her hand with a noise that made my belly tighten. The crop was at least four feet long, very slender and sheathed in black leather. At its end was another six inches or so of stiff-looking, knotted crimson cord.

I had thought that my face was as red as it could get but as I unhooked my bra and felt my breasts swing free I could feel even more blood rushing to my cheeks. The panties were the last thing and the hardest. I hooked my thumbs into the waistband but then I looked up and found myself impaled on her ferocious gaze. I doubt I would have been able to peel them down at all if she had not curled the wicked-looking black crop between her hands before swishing it through the air, the tip inches from my face.

'Now!'

Almost paralysed with humiliation, I somehow managed to peel my panties down until they joined my skirt around my ankles. The tip of the crop tapped against my quim.

'Brazilian, that's something I suppose,' she said in a slightly less harsh tone. 'Though I prefer slaves to be totally shaved! Now, get on your knees, like the bitch you are!'

I said a silent prayer of thanks that I had decided to go through with the bikini wax, painful though it had been, and got down on my knees.

I found myself looking at her legs. Long and shapely and sheathed in sheer black nylon, they seemed to go on forever. My eyes were drawn up to her thighs where I could just see the dark welts of her stocking tops beneath her short leather skirt.

'Are you looking at my cunt, you little slut?' she demanded in an outraged tone.

'No, ah, I . . . I mean . . .' I babbled until a slap across the face shut me up. It wasn't really hard but the shock of it took my breath away.

'Get on all fours while I get the things ready,' she ordered. 'From now on you will speak only when you are spoken to, and when you answer me you will address me as *mistress*. Understand?'

'Yes, um . . . mistress,' I managed somehow, watching furtively as she took what looked like a set of manacles from a drawer. Stainless steel and gleaming and connected by heavy chains. There was something bigger, also made of steel, which I realised with a shock was a sort of collar. I quickly looked down at the carpet.

Why didn't I keep my big mouth shut? I thought.

'Well . . . ? Anyone?' Miranda had drummed her elegantly manicured nails on the teak conference table. Dave, the deputy editor, and Trish, the features editor, looked around accusingly. The rest of us just looked at the table or our pitiful notes as if this might somehow produce an idea.

'Something, *now*,' Miranda went on in her sloany accent. 'Something *sexy*.'

'What about SM?' put in Victoria, the beauty editor, with a distant smile.

Dave and Trish both groaned.

'Didn't we do that last month?' Dave had asked.

'No, we haven't done it for three issues, actually,' said Trish gloomily, 'but it is still all a bit 90s.'

'Yes, but, but . . .' Victoria said with more animation than I had ever seen before, in my short time at the mag. 'What about *lesbian* SM? That is really happening just now; in Chelsea anyway! Some girls are even paying for it. And others are getting into it for the lifestyle . . . Um, so I heard in the Ivy the other night.'

Christ, I remember thinking; she is wetting her pants about this. I think she wants to do the article herself. That would be a first!

'Oh really?' Miranda said, perking up. 'Are there men you can pay to spank . . .?'

'I think Victoria means dominatrixes,' Dave put in gently. Then, seeing the puzzled look on Miranda's face, 'Women. It wouldn't really be *lesbian* SM if they were doing it with men.'

There was a brief pause whilst we all tried not to snigger too obviously. I didn't manage very well.

'Deborah,' Miranda had said in a distinctly acid tone. 'Why don't you do it? Find one of these dominatrixes for women and write the article.'

I had felt, briefly, elated. Since joining the magazine I had been running other people's errands and the only writing I had got into print had been making up short bits of ridiculous nonsense for a column called *Weird Wide World* when Google failed to provide.

'Sure, I can do that,' I had said, trying to sound casual. 'Do you want me to interview a few or just do one in depth?'

'Oh no.' Miranda had smiled icily. 'I wasn't thinking *interview* exactly. I was thinking more *investigative*. What was it that you said at your interview?

You would do *anything* to write for *Chichi*? Well, darling, here is your chance! Why don't you go and try the service and then write about it?'

I must remember not to snigger at the editor, I told myself grimly on the way home.

Miranda, or more accurately Doug the legal guy, had decided that paying might be dodgy, but Victoria clearly had a very healthy interest in the subject because she had come up with a woman who was apparently a 'lifestyle domme', which seemed to me to mean that she dominated women for the fun of it. What's more she was quite happy to demonstrate her techniques to, not to mention on, me as long as we used a pseudonym for the piece. I have to say this seemed a bit strange to me as I doubted if Mistress Zenobia was her real name anyway.

Mind you, as she walked slowly around to my now completely naked rear, the chains and things in one hand and the crop in her other, I was more concerned about what her 'techniques' might involve than what she chose to call herself. Of course, the plan was simply for me to try enough to get the gist of her services; a bit of being bossed about and some mild bondage. That was the idea. I am a big girl and I can manage that, I told myself firmly.

'Ah . . .' I gasped as the startlingly cold metal of the steel collar closed around my neck, equally cold chains dangling down and brushing my back. There was a click as she secured the collar with a solid-feeling padlock. Then she took the chain and the brutal collar pressed against my throat as she hauled me back onto my feet.

'Put your hands behind you!'

As I did so she grabbed my left hand and pulled it up a little before a steel manacle was clamped around my wrist. The procedure was repeated with my right arm and now I really was helpless. The chains securing my wrists to the collar were heavy but short enough that I was forced to keep my hands up just above the small of my back.

'Oh!' I gasped as her leather-gloved hand grasped my bottom.

'Silence! You have a fine bottom, slave. Plump and juicy and just ready for the whip!'

I know it sounds a bit corny in the cold light of day, but believe me at the time, with that evil-looking crop in her hand and maniacal gleam in her eye, it sounded little short of terrifying.

'Turn around!' she ordered, releasing my bottom cheek.

Slowly, I turned to face her. Above the little black leather skirt she had a sort of strapless leather basque on which pushed up her full breasts so that there was a dramatic cleavage. She was taller than me anyway and her steeple heels gave her another five inches or so – which meant I found myself only just above the canyon of her bosom. Not that I was the only one whose attention was drawn to tits.

'You appear to be excited, little slave.'

A leather-gloved hand went to my left breast and pinched the nipple which, it was true, did seem to be already stiffly erect. I winced as she pinched and twisted hard enough to hurt, gasping with relief when she let go of it.

My relief did not last long. A leather-clad arm traced a path down the under curve of my breast, then down my ribs and belly until . . .

'Ooh, please . . .' I gasped.

'Silence, you little slut!' she hissed.

If my blushes had subsided, they came back with a vengeance. The finger slipped in easily. I was dripping wet and had been since she first ordered me to strip.

Despite her warning to keep quiet, and my fear of the riding crop, it was impossible to suppress a fair few squeaks and moans as her leather-encased finger probed and penetrated. My loudest sigh, though, I have to confess, was when she languidly withdrew the digit.

If it was possible to die of pure embarrassment, I would have expired right then. She held her finger up, inches from my face.

'Look at that, you horny little tart!' she said, and for once her stern face melted as she chuckled evilly. 'Look what you have done to my glove!'

It was an order, so I had to. The black leather around the finger glistened with the fluids of my arousal.

'You dirty little whore,' she said, her voice now husky with excitement. 'Suck it off!'

I am not sure exactly what happened to me then. When the heavy steel collar closed with a click about my neck something seemed to melt inside me. I am not saying that I would have dared to refuse her, with my hands secured behind my back, my body naked and the crop still in her other hand, but it wasn't simply fear that made me bend my head forwards and take the finger in my mouth, sucking hungrily, almost desperately. Nor was it entirely fear that made my thighs tremble and my belly flutter. It was as if I *had* to obey her, almost as if some unsuspected part of me *needed* to be humiliated like this.

'Are you going to put this in your article?' she asked with a sneer.

'What . . .?' I said, stunned into a recollection of what I was doing there.

The slap was harder than before and almost knocked me over.

'*Silence!* It was a rhetorical question!' she said contemptuously. ' "I was naked and chained and licking my own juices from Mistress Zenobia's finger", ' she continued facetiously. ' "Only I am such a dirty, perverted little whore that this turned me on so much that the cunt juice started trickling down my thighs . . ." '

As journalism went it wasn't exactly *Chichi* house style, but to my abject embarrassment there was truth in what she so mockingly said. I could feel it. I was not so much wet as dripping. Oh God, I thought, oh no, it is true. I really am loving this at least on some level. That was the most humiliating part of all.

Lady Zenobia gave me no time to dwell on this discovery.

'I think I will give you a spanking now, just to warm you up for the whip . . .' she said in a more thoughtful tone.

'The – the whip?' I blurted, as she had not said anything about whipping me during the pre-scene interview. Then I was squealing as she grabbed and twisted my left nipple, very hard.

'Are you going to hold your tongue, or shall I have to gag you, bitch?' she demanded furiously.

'Aow, ooh, yes, mistress . . .'

'Very well!'

I had meant, 'yes, mistress, I am going to hold my tongue,' but it seemed that she interpreted my answer to mean, 'yes, mistress, you will have to gag me.' In any event she took a thing from the same drawer my collar and chains had come from. It was a sort of black leather strap with a rubber ball in the centre. I took one look at the object and closed my mouth in a quite involuntary response.

'Open!'

Her eyes were inches from mine; cold, grey-green, determined and utterly pitiless. Reluctantly I opened my mouth and the rubber ball was thrust between my teeth. She was buckling the strap behind my head when I remembered something.

The address that Victoria had given me turned out, to my surprise, to be in the East End. I had not imagined that she knew anyone beyond Kensington and Chelsea and perhaps Westminster. But this was in the run-down bit of London that the Docklands Light Railway flies over in between the City and Canary Wharf. I was even more surprised when I got down to street level from the elevated Docklands Light Railway platform. It seemed to be all 1930s council blocks of flats, and most of the people in the street were Bengali.

I was less surprised when I got to the block itself. Set back from the main road, it was clearly not a council place at all but an older building redeveloped with Docklands-type yuppies in mind. For a start it was completely surrounded by a security fence and I had to buzz Zenobia to get her to let me in. The grounds were not extensive but, inside, the fence was hidden by a border of expensive and exotic-looking shrubs. Lady Zenobia's flat turned out to be up a lot of stairs. If the outside of the building was utilitarian, inside it was plush and felt expensive.

She greeted me in a long silk dressing gown, and looked me up and down in cool appraisal.

'Come and follow me. We need to get a few things sorted out first,' she said crisply.

The lounge she had let me into was comfortable and expensively furnished with a deep pile carpet, with nothing unusual about it. I followed her to an unobtrusive door which she opened and beckoned me inside. This was more like it, I thought. The room had a parquet floor, one wall was covered by an enormous mirror, and there were a slightly disturbing number of whips and other sinister things hanging from the walls.

'I have a few questions first,' I countered, standing my ground. I might be a virgin journalist at *Chichi* but I was reporting for the local rag before I came to London and no one ever accused me of not being assertive – quite the opposite in fact.

She came over to me and looked into my eyes and spoke very quietly but very, very firmly. 'Let me be quite clear. If you want this to happen, you will sit down, shut up, and listen. Otherwise get out.'

There did not seem to be a lot of choice if I was going to get my article. Biting my lip and surprised to find myself blushing from the telling off, I sat on the indicated stool as she took the only comfortable chair.

'To do an SM scene with a novice we need to get a few ground rules sorted out . . .' she had begun. 'Do you know what a safe word is?'

Safe word! We had decided to use *Chichi* if things became too much. How the hell was I going to yell out *Chichi* now? I wondered, frantically, especially if she really does intend to use the whip.

Madame Zenobia did not give me long to worry about it. Pinching the same now distinctly sore nipple, she led me over to the solitary chair. This she sat on, retaining her grip, and then used the nipple to pull me round and right over her knee. If something had melted when the collar went round my neck then all my self control seemed to slip away as my bare belly met the cold leather of her skirt. One of her hands grabbed me firmly by the waist and held me in position. Upended, with my hands secured by chains, my bare bottom completely vulnerable to her whims, I felt more helpless than I had since I was a small child. It was not entirely an unpleasant sensation. Her short leather skirt did not completely cover her thighs and my belly and the tops of my legs pressed down on sheer nylon as well as leather and one of her suspender tabs pressed into my skin with slight but rather exciting discomfort.

In fact, I could have stayed like that quite happily, babbling into the gag and letting myself drift away and luxuriate in the helplessness of my situation. Madame Zenobia had other ideas, however.

The first slaps from her gloved hand were quite gentle. Little more than pats really; rapid little smacks that rained down on my bare bottom and the backs of my thighs. It might have been quite pleasant if she had not kept making the most humiliating comments.

'Now this is a fine smacking arse! Firm and full and bouncy as a beach ball . . .' If this had been part of her act it would have been bad enough, but she sounded genuinely delighted and that was worse.

'It is a peach!' she said as the smacks got a little harder. 'Lovely colour too, coming up a nice blush pink now. This bottom was made for beating, and you are a lucky little tart because someone is going to do just that for you!'

Muffled babbling was becoming muffled moaning now. Little by little her hand spanks had got harder until my whole behind now felt as if it were glowing. My pelvis was writhing involuntarily not in direct response to the smacks but because I needed to rub my clitoris against her thigh as hard as I could.

But she had not stopped. The slaps got harder and then got harder still. Now the sound of her leather-gloved hand impacting on my naked bottom echoed round the playroom. The smarting became stinging and the stinging, burning pain. My muffled moans became stifled squealing. The frantic writhing about on her lap was now as much a futile attempt to escape the stinging rain of slaps as anything. Not that lust had fled, it had just melded into a red-hot cocktail with the pain. At that moment I could not have said if what I was feeling was pain or pleasure, nor if my cries were pleas for her to stop or to continue. As I writhed and squirmed ever more desperately on her leather-clad lap, however, my clit pressed down on the long bone of her thigh once too often.

And then the sounds the gag suppressed were definitely screaming, but they were screams of un-diluted pleasure as I came.

So I had my article and then some, and it was time to go. Well, not right away because I had to do a bit of moaning first and shuddering as my orgasm subsided in what seemed like aftershocks from some erotic earthquake. I think I was lost in a sort of post-orgasmic delirium for a while, but after a few minutes I began to come back down to earth and awareness of my now perspiring, naked body. At some point I must have fallen to the floor, where I lay, my hands still chained behind me.

So I looked up at Mistress Zenobia, who was sneering down at me, and politely asked her to unlock my shackles. The trouble was that I was still gagged so what actually came out of my mouth was a sort of muffled moan.

One thing that I noticed as I looked up, my eyes beseeching in a way that I hoped she would under-stand meant 'you can let me go now', was that she had picked up the crop again and was flexing it between her hands in a way that caused my belly to go fluttery. This also made me very aware of my bottom which was still glowing as if it had been badly sunburned.

Rather than unchain me, Mistress Zenobia bent and grabbed me by the hair, hauling me up onto my knees, then she took a step back and sliced the crop through the air, producing a seriously scary low whistle.

'You really are a desperate, perverted little slut, aren't you?' she said with supercilious delight, made all the worse since her amusement was so clearly genuine. 'Coming like a train after a few slaps! What will you do when I give you a proper flogging?'

If the parquet floor of her playroom had opened up and swallowed me at that moment, I would not have been sorry. She might have been exaggerating; it had hardly been a few slaps, more like a royal spanking, but there was some truth in her words. More immediately worrying, however, was the talk of flogging.

'Do you want to thank your mistress for your lovely orgasm, then, slave?' she asked.

I wanted to go home and write my article but the way she kept swishing that evil-looking black crop around made me decide to nod my head.

'Good girl! Now kiss my feet!'

Easy for her to say! I thought. With my arms still shackled behind me I could not lean forwards and down without collapsing. First I had to lower my upper body until my breasts nearly brushed my knees, and then crawl forwards until I could obey her order. Her shoes were brilliantly polished, impossibly high-heeled pumps. But that was not the only difficulty; I was still gagged. While I was wondering what to do I felt her hands unbuckle the gag.

I gasped with relief as the rubber ball came out and thought about asking her to unchain me then. However there was a whoosh and a vicious stinging feeling in my bottom.

'Aaow!'

'Silence, bitch, and kiss your mistress's feet!' she ordered.

I decided not to risk another crop stroke as something told me she had only stung me with the little cord bit at the end. I got down and saw myself, hair mussed and eyes looking dazed, reflected back in the brilliant polished surface of her shoes.

Something, as I mentioned earlier, had seemed to melt inside my brain, and perhaps my groin, when she put the collar on me. Something else seemed to dissolve when I pressed my lips to the cold leather of her shoes, my eyes on the sheer black nylon sheathing her foot and ankle.

'Lick!' she said, and there was something excited in her tone now. 'Lick, you little slave bitch!'

I did as I was ordered; licking her shoes, first one and then the other. Then experimentally I tongued her stockinged foot.

'That's right, you little tart! Now get up and lick me higher!'

I was in no doubt what she meant by this. I could hear the blood pound in my ears as I raised my body, my eyes slowly travelling up her shapely legs. Above the inky stocking tops her thighs were almost white. I swallowed hard. Mistress Zenobia had pulled up her short leather skirt and she was not wearing panties.

'Go on then!' she said warmly. 'What are you waiting for, a touch of this?'

She flicked the crop down so that the cord tip hissed into my naked thigh, making me yelp with pain. I did not wait for her to give me another.

Her pubic hair was neatly trimmed, though it was not a Brazilian wax. The hair around her labia had been carefully removed, but above her clitoral hood there was a black triangle of fur. Her vulva was quite obviously swollen and something was glistening on her pussy lips. I blinked hard and then quickly kissed her pussy lips.

'Don't peck, you silly bitch!' Mistress Zenobia said in a slightly hoarse voice. 'Put your tongue right in there!'

I did as I was told and tasted her juices, the scent of her arousal almost overwhelming. Mistress Zenobia let out a groan and I felt my hair grabbed, pulling my face harder against her crotch, pressing my nose into her mons so hard that I made a few alarmed but muffled squeaks. I pushed my tongue in as far as I could, hungry now to lick her vaginal juices, but I was not given long to explore her tunnel.

'Higher,' she grunted in a very strained voice. 'Higher, you little bitch, or I will whip the hide right off you!'

Her grip was released enough to let me obey, so my tongue licked upwards until it met her swollen clit, the glans of which was already protruding from its hood. I started to circle the little nub of flesh when my face was rammed against her crotch once more and Zenobia started shouting.

'Shit! Fuck! Yes! Yes, oooh, shit that's it, you bitch!' she yelled before her cries turned into more incoherent shrieking. Grinding her cunt brutally against my face, she came explosively.

My face felt squashed and smeared with Zenobia's juices. My bottom was still throbbing. I was still naked and in chains. It was definitely time to go now. The trouble was that I still seemed to be aroused after my orgasm, and being made to go down on Zenobia and lick her shoes only seemed to have turned me on more. I was completely unable to think straight about what was happening to me.

'I do believe that you are gagging for it again!' Mistress Zenobia said once she had recovered her composure. 'Your nipples are stiff as sentries and you are panting like a bitch on heat. I expect you would like me to fuck you with a strap-on, wouldn't you, tart?'

I did blush at that and bit my bottom lip in chagrin. She seemed to have the knack of saying things that humiliated and aroused me equally.

'Yes, mistress . . .' I managed to mumble somehow, a desperate hope rising in me that she would fuck me and relieve my awful need.

'Of course you would. Slave bitches like you always want it up you!' she said with a laugh. 'But you have not deserved it, have you?'

There was a pause before I realised that this was not a rhetorical question.

'No, mistress.'

'What have you deserved, do you think? Come on, answer me, slave!'

I had no idea what to answer, until she lashed the crop through the air once more, to give me a clue.

'Oh, please . . .' I began.

'Silence, get down flat on the floor, and spread your legs wide.'

I no longer seemed to have the power to disobey her, scared though I truly was of what she might intend to do. I got down flat, my naked body on the cold, hard parquet, my face towards her feet and, with desperate reluctance, spread my legs apart.

'Wider than that! Wider! Stop whimpering, slave, you know that you need it.'

I knew no such thing, but I did know that I was in a bad position to argue about it. I held my breath and bit my bottom lip hard and waited for the inevitable.

There was that horrible whistle once again and a nasty snicking sound. But of course I was most aware of the pain. The tip of the crop had caught me right between my spread legs. It stung like fury and I let out a desperate squeal.

'What are you doing? I did not tell you to close your legs, you little bitch! *Open them this instant!*' She was yelling.

I simply could not make my legs obey her. The fear of the long crop and its wicked tip had seeped into my soul and I was too scared to comply. In dread I listened to her heels clack on the parquet as she came around to my side. Then there was that dreadful whistle and a meaty crack of impact. This time she used the leather-sheathed shaft of the crop and lashed square across my bottom.

I opened up my mouth to let out an agonised squeal but that was cut short by a second, even harder stroke which took my breath away. The third followed with pitiless precision. I believe I screamed.

'Now open your legs!' Mistress Zenobia ordered.

As if by magic I found that I could obey her again. The pain in my bottom was intense enough to have eclipsed the fear of exposing my pussy. Once again I heard the awful clacking of her high heels as she walked leisurely around to my head.

Blinking away the tears of pain and raising my head a little, I saw that she now stood with a foot either side of my head. Then she bent forwards, leaning over my body, and I closed my eyes again.

Again she lashed, judging the stroke so that only the cord tip struck me. This did not feel like she was being merciful as the knotted whipcord stung my pussy. It felt like I was being stung by hornets in my most sensitive parts. Every time the cord cracked I ground myself hard into the parquet as if somehow I could escape the pain by burrowing through the floor.

And I did, in a manner of speaking. She whipped me rhythmically, these light, stinging strokes tormenting my exposed pussy, and I suppose I must have rubbed my clit against the floor, though I was more aware of the lashes at the time. Then, suddenly my body was convulsed and I was shrieking as great waves of pleasure flooded through me. I don't know how long I was screaming in ecstasy, but when my orgasm finally subsided, I found that I had screamed myself quite hoarse.

'I can read an *A to Z*, you know,' Zack said with a grin.

'I know, but I have to go out that way anyway,' I lied. 'I had to promise her copy approval.'

'There is this new thing called e-mail . . .' he replied facetiously.

'Ha ha, but it really is quite hard to find . . . and . . .'

'I know, I know,' he said wearily, packing the last of his camera equipment. 'It's *your* article!'

The usual thing with *Chichi* was to take the photographer with you in the first place, but for obvious reasons I had preferred to see Mistress Zenobia alone for the . . . interview. Zack was a freelance who we used a lot as he was both reliable and good, so there was really no need for me to hold his hand for the shoot. Still, I wasn't overwhelmed with work that afternoon and I might be able to suggest some shots, I thought.

This time, when she answered the door she looked absolutely breathtaking. Clearly, I thought, a little piqued, she had gone to a lot more trouble for the photographer than she had for me. Mistress Zenobia was wearing a long black satin corset. It had balconette-style cups with a wisp of fine lace that failed to veil rouged nipples. The thing was so tightly laced that I am quite sure that she must have had some help to get into it.

Her already impressive figure now looked astonishing. Broad black suspender straps held up the sheerest fully fashioned stockings and the heels of her patent pumps must have been eight inches high, a two-inch platform sole making it possible for her to walk on the things. A black ribbon with a cameo set in the front graced her long white throat and black lace opera gloves and small black satin panties were all the rest of her clothing.

Zenobia had piled her luxuriant mane up above her head which, with the platforms and heels, made her seem even taller. Zack was a biggish guy but she seemed to tower over him. Confronted with such an amazing vision most guys would have been dumbstruck.

'Hi there, Jenny tells me you have a playroom, shall we take a look?' Zack said, completely unfazed. I have to say I was impressed with his professionalism.

'Yes,' Zenobia purred. 'Why don't you show him where it is, girl?'

I felt myself turn into a beetroot once again, and prayed that Zack was too concerned with his cameras to notice. A vision of the guys back at the mag drinking at Soho House and sniggering as they discussed my lezzie SM encounter forced its way into my head, and did not help me to regain my composure. Funnily enough, though, Zack and Zenobia did. Both became very focused and professional and I was left to hang around the fringes of the shoot; now and then, when she raised a crop dramatically or turned to fix me in her stare, getting a jolt of confusing, guilty pleasure.

'That should do,' Zack said at last and began to pack up his kit. 'You going to give me a hand back with this lot, then?'

'No, Zack!' I said as crisply as I could. 'I wasn't your assistant last time I looked and anyway, I told you I need to go through the copy with Zenobia.'

He shrugged amiably enough and shouldered another bag, picked up his tripod and with a waved goodbye left us together.

'Right . . .' I said when the door had closed, turning to get the printed copy from my bag.

She took the A4 sheets from me and started to read as she walked, gesturing me to follow. I swallowed dryly as I followed her back into the playroom. Nervous, I suppose, that she would dislike the article. I had to stand awkwardly as she read the whole thing through, trying to suppress the urge to say something stupid.

She finished and simply tore the pages up and let them drop without a comment. I was about to ask her if there was something she objected to but the slap was quicker, almost knocking me over, her action so vigorous that the bones of her corset creaked audibly.

'You don't call me *Zenobia*, you little bitch. Not ever!' she hissed furiously. 'To slaves like you I am *always* mistress!'

My face burning from the slap, I was about to protest, but she spoke first.

'Now *strip*, you little object. I am going to give you a sound thrashing for insolence. And then, if you are very lucky, I *may* get the strap-on out.'

147

What answer could I make except to start to take off my clothes?

– *Debbie Palmer, London, UK*

Family Girlfriend

When Mom told me and my sister that her friend, Jayne, in California had invited us all to stay at her place for a couple of weeks, I was happier than a prick in a balloon factory. I'd just completed my first year of college, and was looking forward to a much-needed break before sweating out another year's tuition at the local lumber yard. And there's no better place to take a break than sunny Southern California – sand, surf, and snatch!

Cady and I flew out ahead of Mom – she had some work to finish up, but promised to join us in a couple of days – and Jayne was there to greet us at the airport. And what a greeting it was! The freed Iranian hostages weren't as happy as I was when I googled the foxy, forty-something lady. I hadn't seen her in ten years, since her husband's funeral, and the intervening years had been very, very good to her – and to my hormonally supercharged libido.

She was barely clothed in a red tank top and short white skirt, and the plenty of skin showing was tanned a golden-brown. Her sun-bleached blonde hair was tied back in a ponytail, and she had just the right amount of make-up on to really highlight her sky-blue eyes, her high cheekbones, and her full cushiony lips. Her legs were long and slender, smooth-looking, and her plump round butt cheeks jostled provocatively under her tiny skirt. But what really held my eyes, and breath, were her huge top-bursting tits! They were truly mountainous, peaked by jutting nipples that just about punched holes in the thin fabric of her top.

'H-hi, Mrs Kudlow,' I stammered, ogling her tremendous tanned chest like every other unbent male at the baggage carousel. The ultra-sexy MILF was exhibiting enough cleavage to be ticketed for indecent exposure, and her massive mams filled my orbs like my hardening dick filled my jockeys.

'Hi, Kyle!' she responded enthusiastically, throwing her arms around me. 'You sure have grown since I saw you last, and please, call me Jayne – Mrs Kudlow makes me sound so old.'

'S-sure,' I mumbled, squeezing the mature hottie tight against my body, her over-fluffed pillows pressing heavily into my chest.

'Don't squeeze all the air out of her,' Cady cracked.

I reluctantly gave up the erotic chest-clench, and Jayne hugged my sister, and then we snagged our bags and walked out to Jayne's minivan. I followed close behind the red-hot mama's bouncing bottom, and then pushed Cady aside and jumped into the front seat of the van, securing for myself a splendid view of Jayne's straining whoppers during the long, hard ride back to her place.

Later that night, Cady strolled into my room and plopped down on the end of my bed, clad in only a pair of panties and a sleeveless undershirt, her sleeping attire. She's the spitting image of our mother, with the same long brown hair, warm brown eyes, and lean supple body, and as I glanced at the eighteen-year-old's pert titties, I did a mental size comparison with Jayne's. It was no contest. My little sister, however, had in mind another type of contest.

'Sooo,' she said, 'when's the K-Man gonna put the moves on our well-endowed hostess?'

I looked at her over the *Sports Illustrated* I'd been using to cover up my Jayne-inspired hard-on and shrugged. 'Hey, if the sweet lady happens to fall victim to my innate charm, there's nothing I can do about it – other than cushion her fall, of course.' My plan was to put the full-court press on the busty babe the next day, take it to the twin hoops, so to speak.

Cady wrinkled her nose and grinned. 'Yeah, well, just remember that two can play at that game.'

'Hey!' I cried foul, but the come-of-age cutie had already scampered off my bed and out the door, her tight, twitching buttocks telling me it was Game On!

After a restless night, I woke up, blew off some steam in the bathroom, took a shower, and then shuffled out into the living room in search of some breakfast. I was hungry like the wolf, but what was served up to me did absolutely nothing to satisfy my hunger – only increased it tenfold!

Jayne and Cady were bobbing up and down in the swimming pool, in each other's arms. 'Damn!' I grunted. The early bird was getting what my worm so desperately wanted.

The two females were in the deep end of the kidney-shaped pool, and Cady, the three-summer lifeguard, was making out like she couldn't swim, clinging to my Mom's breast-blessed friend like she was terrified of drowning. The girls were dressed for pleasure, Cady in a hot-pink string bikini, Jayne in a more subdued blue one. I quickly slipped behind the curtains on the glass sliding doors that overlooked the pool, and then slipped my shorts down to let my swelling dick catch some air, and hand.

'Don't let go of me!' Cady squealed, gunning for an Oscar, her arms coiled around the neck of deep-chested Jayne.

'I've got you,' Jayne soothed.

'You sure have,' Cady cooed, looking up into the luscious lady's bright-blue eyes. Then, sure enough, the sassy lass kissed the mother I'd love to fuck square on her pouty lips.

Cady held the womanly lip-lock, her hands gripping Jayne's wet blonde head, the two babes' bodies pressing together in the sparkling clear water, Jayne's twin buoys smothering Cady's teensy tits. Then Cady pulled her head back with a smack, and Jayne gazed at the sultry young seductress like she'd been struck by sexual lightning.

'I-I'm not sure ...' Jayne stammered. 'Your mother and I –'

'Fuck my mother!' Cady interrupted, mashing her lips back into Jayne's.

That did it! The overwrought MILF hugged Cady's slim body against her own big-bumpered body and the two girls sucked face in all sincerity, their inhibitions down the drain. This was California dreamin' at its finest, and I gave the horny honeys a one-handed standing ovation, fisting my dick with gusto.

The sun-drenched babes kissed hard and long, hungrily devouring each other's mouths, until Cady darted her kitten-pink tongue in between Jayne's parted lips and the naughty little minx and the woman old enough to be her mother started frenching each other, their thick slippery tongues swirling together in a heated, jumbled rush.

'Yes, Mrs Kudlow!' Cady moaned, Jayne's tongue filling the teen's mouth, painting her glossy lips.

The two hotties feverishly frenched for what seemed like forever, the blistering sun beating down on them, their hands diving into the shimmering water to urgently feel up each other's bods, me waxing my dong like it was a surfboard and a huge breaker was heading for shore. Cady eventually ended the sensual tongue-swiping, then towed the sexed-up Jayne to the shallow end of the pool, swimming the short distance with an assured stroke. They stood in the waist-deep sun-dappled water, facing each other, and Cady slid the twin strained-to-the-max straps holding up the mature gal's bikini top off her shoulders and exposed Jayne's magnificent mammaries.

'Beautiful!' Cady and I breathed in unison, eyeing the older woman's humungous hooters.

Her tits were the size of over-ripe melons, their all-natural goodness certified by the slight saggage they exhibited, and they were capped by rigid chocolate-hued nipples of at least an inch in length. Cady reached out and cupped Jayne's bountiful bronze breasts.

'Yes!' the chest-heavy ma'am moaned, her giant jugs heaving, obviously super-sensitive to the touch.

I polished my pole and watched wide-eyed and open-mouthed as Cady squeezed and kneaded Jayne's thunderous tits, the teenager's tiny hands not quite up to the gargantuan task. She bent her head down and lashed at one of Jayne's obscenely dis-tended nipples with her mischievous tongue, and Jayne moaned with the erotic impact.

'Suck my tits, Cady!' she urged, grabbing my sister's head and pulling it into her knockers.

Cady grasped the groaning gal's well-seasoned casabas as best she could and applied a serious tongue-pasting to them. She earnestly licked at first one fully flowered nipple and then the other, teasing them to what had to be painful erection. Then the teen queen latched her puffy lips onto Jayne's rock-hard right nipple and sucked on it like she was trying to suck the air, or liquid, right out of that lady's fantastic flopper.

'God, yes!' Jayne gasped, her eyes half-closed, her silver-lacquered fingernails digging sharply into Cady's bare shoulders, her sun-burnished body rippling like the water around her.

Cady mouthed as much of Jayne's round mound as she could, which wasn't much, her cheeks billowing in and out as she greedily sucked on the woman's throat-plugging nipple and tugged on her huge hanger. Then she disgorged the one over-swollen nipple in a shower of saliva and went to work on the other, vacuuming it into her mouth and sucking hard on it, feeding on Jayne's boobs, her innocent brown eyes staring up into the ecstatic face of her big-breasted, more-than-twice-as-old lover.

'Enough of that, young lady!' Jayne finally commanded, regaining some of her sexual equilibrium. She pulled Cady up off her chest and kissed the panting teen, then untied the girl's bikini top and exposed Cady's schoolgirl titties to the sunshine, and her hands. She excitedly mauled and mouthed Cady's girlish boobs for a while, before grabbing the hard-breathing hottie's hand and leading her out of the pool and onto the diving board.

She pushed Cady down flat on her back on the quivering springboard, then reverse-mounted her, so that her knees were straddling Cady's head, and Cady was looking up into the mature lady's bikini bottom. Jayne quickly unfastened Cady's skimpy cunny-covering and dived tongue-first into the teenager's shaved snatch.

'Fuck, yeah!' Cady howled, fumbling aside Jayne's bikini bottom so she could attack the woman's quim in kind.

I gazed deliriously at the dripping, drop-dead gorgeous babes' bodies as they desperately sixty-nined each other, my sweaty palms providing just the lubrication I needed to buff my wood. Jayne hastily spread Cady's pink pussy lips with her slender fingers and licked at the writhing girl's slit, over and over, thumb-rubbing clit while she urgently tongued twat. Cady buried her pretty face in between Jayne's trembling legs and lapped anxiously at the furry clam that was served up to her.

And just as I threw back my head and grunted with joy as I blasted an opening salvo of white-hot jism against the heated windowpane, Cady cried out with her own personal ecstasy and gushed girly-juice into Jayne's gaping mouth. The two of us spewed cum like twin geysers, me splashing the window, Cady splashing Jayne's face, again and again and again.

Cady's hot little bod quivered with girl-inspired orgasm, but she still somehow managed to jam two of her fingers into Jayne's gash and piston them in and out, which proved to be the trigger for Jayne's all-out release. The MILF's heavenly hooters undulated with euphoria as she was blown away by Cady's muff-pumping digits and clit-lashing tongue.

It was the most thrilling threeway I'd ever experienced – without being an actual participant.

I vowed to follow up my sister's trailblazing seduction with some mother-fucking of my own, and I didn't have to wait long to get my chance. After a hearty breakfast interrupted repeatedly by Jayne and Cady glancing at each other and giggling, we three sun-worshippers enjoyed a leisurely lounge around the swimming pool. And after toasting ourselves for an hour or two, Jayne suggested we have a picnic lunch at a local park that afternoon.

'I'll pass,' Cady said, eyeing me over her shades and smiling. 'I'm not very hungry for some reason; I think I'll go shopping instead.'

So, come noontime, Jayne dropped Cady off at a mall, and then she and I drove out to a small secluded park which commanded a spectacular view of the ocean. We shared small talk and chicken salad sandwiches, before I casually mentioned that I'd seen some rather arousing aquatic activity only earlier that morning.

'What!?' Jayne shrieked, spraying me with cola.

I nodded sagely, gave her my Valentino stare, and then stood up and strolled over to her side of the picnic table. I placed my hands on her smooth sun-freckled shoulders and started some sensual massage, my dick pitching a tent in my shorts. She mumbled something about her responsibility to my mother, but I was too busy feeling up the buxom beauty's buff shoulders to listen.

She was wearing a purple tube-top literally bursting at the seams and a pair of hanky-sized pink shorts, and her silky blonde hair was loose around her shoulders, just like my hands. I let them roam down her arms, then her sides, before not-so-subtly reaching around and grabbing onto her big, bold breasts and squeezing.

'Oh, God, Kyle!' Jayne breathed, her head lolling back as I buried my face in her soft scented hair, kissed and tongued the hot brown flesh of her neck, worked her tits.

I licked in behind her delicately shaped ears, inside her ears, clutching and kneading her massive mams all the while, and the shapely babe on the shady side of forty responded exactly as I hoped. She pulled her legs out from under the picnic table, shook off my hands, and climbed on top of the rustic eating platform. She sat up on the table, looked me in the eye, and then rolled her tube-top down, displaying her eye-popping jugs for me and the seagulls to see.

'Come to mama!' she said saucily, shaking her tanned ta-ta's at me.

I took a quick glance around, saw only green trees and blue ocean, and then dove into the fired-up female's cleavage like a Spanish explorer diving into the fountain of youth. I jammed my face in between Jayne's awesome bumpers and lapped happily at her warm, moist tit-canyon, and she shoved her boobs together and urged me on.

I kissed and licked her humid, depthless cleft, her blue-veined titties feeling great against my shaven cheeks. Then I pulled back and anxiously grabbed up her boisterous boobies again, juggled them around some, my wrists almost snapping with the weighty exertion. I pushed her fleshy fruits together and played my tongue across both her pointed nipples at once, coating her rigid inchers with my hot spit.

'Enough of that, young man!' Jayne suddenly intoned, after I'd tongued her rubbery tit-caps for a glorious couple of minutes. 'Show me your cock!'

I gave the MILF's monster mounds one final lick and squeeze and then yanked down my shorts, my steel-hard cunt/tit-splitter springing out into the salty sea air. Jayne surveyed my seven-inch fuck-stick approvingly, then gestured at me to climb aboard the wooden table where more than food was being served. I scrambled to comply, and was soon teetering on the sagging seat planks, my throbbing rod only inches away from Jayne's plush, puckered lips.

She laid a firm experienced hand on my dong, then started sliding her hand back and forth, her fingers swirling up and down on my manhood, around and over the top of my bloated purple hood, while my body jerked like a puppet with its strings cut. I seemed to blissfully hang in mid-air, with only Jayne's gripping, groping hand on my pulsating cock preventing me from floating away, or falling over backwards.

Then she grasped my dick at the furry base and stuck out her silver-tinted tongue and flicked the tip of it across my yawning slit. She twirled her warm wet tongue all around my mushroomed cocktop and teased the super-sensitive underside of my shaft, before sucking my knob into her mouth and tugging on it.

'Fuck, yeah, suck my cock, Mrs Kudlow!' I howled, sending seagulls sailing into the air.

The breasty blonde didn't need any encouragement, or instruction. She quickly and expertly inhaled three-quarters of my stiffy without batting a blackened eyelash, and then bobbed her head up and down on my prick, her bee-stung, red-painted lips gliding easily and erotically back and forth on my meat. And as she expertly blew me, juggled my balls around and pinched my nipples, she occasionally hoovered my entire dong into her mouth and throat and held it there, her nose nuzzling my pubes, before disgorging a third of my rod and taking up with her hummer again.

It quickly became way too much for a freshman like me to handle. I clutched at the sexy mama's sun-bleached hair and was just about to blow hot seed down her throat when she sensed my distress and spat out my jacked-up cock. 'Tit-fuck me!' she yelled.

I grabbed my slickened schlong and slammed it in between Jayne's proffered jugs, started churning my hips with everything I had, frantically polishing the wicked lady's tit-tunnel with my prick. She spat into the superheated chasm between her knockers to give me extra lube, and the incendiary heat and slimy friction felt fucking marvellous! I plunged my cock into the babe's amazing cleavage faster and faster as she shoved her pillows together and urged me on with some dirty talk.

'Fuck almighty!' I bellowed before long, tearing a hole in the surf-softened air. My balls boiled out of control and my cock jetted white-hot jism, a devastating orgasm detonating inside me.

'Cum all over my tits!' Jayne shouted, sperm splashing against her neck, onto her face. She opened her mouth and stuck out her tongue, and I wildly rocketed semen directly down her throat, coming in a frenzy, like a MILF-virgin with years and years of pent-up, pressurised frustration behind him.

It was only when Cady and I witnessed Jayne and Mom greet each other at the airport that we stopped congratulating ourselves on our powers of seduction – the two super-hot women excitedly embraced and hungrily kissed one other, demonstrating for all to see that they were a lot more than just old friends.

'Your kids and I have really bonded, Marion – just like you said we would!' Jayne gushed, as Mom winked at me and my sister over the buxom blonde's shoulder.

– *K.W., Minnesota, USA*

Moving On

Afterwards I blamed Gary. He was totally responsible for what happened because he started on me –
again!

'Look, Bridie, we know you've tried hard,' he said.
'But you still can't pay your share.' I recall dreading
the next stage. 'Since you gave up being a Goth you
look fantastic so why not trade on your assets?'

'What do think I've been trying to do?'

He rolled his eyes, suggesting a hopeless case. 'I'm
not talking about auditions for jobs you don't get, or
a single advert on telly.'

'The only way is up!' I know that sounded flippant
but on my CV there's more. 'Don't forget my stint as
a bunny at that sales promotion. If you had your way
I'd be working the strip clubs.'

'I'm just saying that here's a firm offer – a gig that
pays the rent, and gives you some breathing space to
look around.'

Stubbornly I held out.

'And here's the other plus,' Gary insisted. 'You'll
be doing it with me. It's not as if you're being tossed
into a pack of strangers.'

Clive leant forwards intently. 'I'm sorry, Bridie, but
supporting you for three months is enough. If you
can't pay your rent you'll have to move out.'

I brushed crumbs of biscuit, the remains of lunch, off my scraggy jeans. No rent, tatty clothes, and no proper food. All I have, for a short while, is a bed and a shared bathroom. 'I'm not experienced in that stuff,' I grumbled. 'What makes you think I can do it?'

'Follow my lead,' Gary answered promptly.

Where do blokes get their massive confidence? I played for more time. 'Who is it for?'

'Mr Buchan. He's way past doing it but enjoys looking. Why not think of it as a drama school production? He's the talent scout in the audience. You're straight in, centre stage, do the business, and off you go with cash in hand.'

'I think you need to work on your chat-up line.'

'Bridie . . .'

I couldn't mistake Clive's warning. They'd closed down every option until, weary of arguing, I caved in. I stood and flounced to the door – as in *Lady Windermere's Fan* – and threw back a defiant shot. 'Just be sure you have a bath. And a shave!'

'Any chance of rehearsal?'

I slammed the door. On stage the scenery would have rocked.

The following evening I remember trailing some distance behind, cold and miserable. Those huge houses, divided from the pavement by iron railings, were intimidating. Gary moved along the row inspecting the polished brass numbers on each door. He came to a halt and asked, 'Still OK?'

'Not really.' My college ambitions were supposed to work out better than this. I had no idea how to cope with the crippling embarrassment – doing it with one and watched by another, an old wheezy geezer. My tutor, Mr Elliot, used to say: 'There's nothing

161

worse than a rainy matinee in Bolton.' He'd obviously never had a booking like this one.

As Gary rang the bell I clutched my threadbare coat, huddled like a pathetic waif to the only familiar person in this alien place. When the door opened it cast over us a bright yellow beam. A maid with narrow exotic features and cascading black hair stood in the entrance. She surveyed us with eyes of liquid jet. Her black uniform ended in a short skirt which showed plenty of thigh in black stockings. 'You . . . expect.' I reckoned she came from somewhere in the Middle East. She turned to lead us inside and Gary showed his appreciation by raising his eyebrows and leering at me. In exchange I rudely poked out my tongue.

The interior – wow! It glowed with warmth, glittering glass and ceramics on polished tables, shiny paintings, ornate lamps with tasselled shades, and a carpet that compressed like a cushion. Immediately I felt right at home. If I could somehow persuade the wheezy geezer to marry me all this could be mine. In a small room the maid said, 'Ere . . . dis-robe.' She pointed to herself, 'Renata,' rolling the R, then to a group of bottles at the side, 'Refresh.' Spreading five fingers she added, 'Minute. Then Señora Buchan . . . er, ready.'

I rounded furiously on Gary, who flinched. 'You said it was a man! What kind of woman would pay to watch this?'

'One who wants an eyeful of me,' he said. 'Or, if your nasty mind is thinking she's a dyke, remember the rent.' He poured a glass of white wine and held it out as a token of peace.

I drained the glass too quickly, poured a second, and bolted that too. The wine was the best I'd ever tasted. Maybe, I thought woozily, I didn't care too much if the rent's paid. Ashamed of my coat I peeled it off and made my protest clear to Gary. He winced at the word WHORE printed across my T-shirt. I turned away to lift it over my head, slid my tattered jeans to the floor, stripped off my cotton bra and dropped my panties. Bare-arsed, I paused for one deep breath then swivelled to face him.

He looked satisfactorily dazed. 'Bridie! I had no idea. You look superb.'

Pleased but tense, I watched his dangling penis which, to a novice, seemed weighty and fat. I wondered how much it would change when fully erect and shuddered with a tremor of fear. Gazing at me must have affected him too because unconsciously he started playing, stroking the length in light well-practised motions. I didn't realise how sexy it was to see a man rubbing his own dick, and slightly threatening too, preparing himself to take me. But when it grew into a rigid pole it would fill me and make me sore.

'We should warm up.' Folded in his arms, my breasts flattened onto Gary's chest and the touch of his skin, plus the push of his cock, affected me. Our impressively deep kiss finally parted at a cough from behind. I turned to the maid, embarrassed at my nakedness in front of her, the first of two women who would look at me.

'Come.'

As Renata led us along a corridor I tried once again to think myself into the role but with the same result. I had absolutely no idea how to shape my performance. We entered a large sitting room with too much light for comfort where a large tufted rug in the centre of the floor defined our space – a kind of display ring for the public event. At the far end a motionless form sat in a large chair and I briefly noticed a gaunt face, a shawl covering her lap, and bony linked fingers lying on top. She might be perverse and far wealthier than we would ever be, but the shrivelled figure appeared pathetic in contrast to us. We had firm bodies, raw energy and the lust of youth; possessions her money could never buy. Let her look, eaten alive by envy!

'Every nerve is a tingling wire,' Mr Elliot used to say. 'Get out in the spotlight, hit your mark and then – project!' Following his advice I took the initiative by placing Gary's hand to my breast and drew him into another kiss. Leading through every stage I nurtured his tool with my hand, then in my mouth's seductive warmth. I had no need to think at all – every stage flowed naturally from sheer instinct. I gave my succulence to his tongue, his roving fingers and later to his erection which speared me to the maximum. In my creamy sleek heat I slowed his first frantic pace, then roused him again, soaking up his relentless power. Judging the moment carefully I began to shriek, writhing and bucking my pelvis while Gary plunged on, gasping and wild-eyed, brutally fierce in the last throes. Heaving out of my cunt he spewed long streaks over my belly, forming a dense pool with heated vapour curling upwards. I heard a dry quivering sob from the chair.

As he slumped beside me we sank into the after-glow and our strained breathing relaxed. The room remained silent and still. I hadn't expected spunk on my belly and wondered how to deal with the problem. Mostly I felt smug at passing the test. Opening night is always the worst and that may have been my best performance. Some time later Renata leant over Gary and touched his shoulder, helped him to stand, and led him away. In her place came a smiling figure, not withered or stooped but with handsome features.

Though her skin was seamed with the lines of age she had abundant wavy hair of silver-blonde and crystal eyes, wise and wicked, of vibrant blue.

Mrs Buchan reached for my hand, lifted me up, and led me to a chair at the side where we sat facing each other. The pool started to creep down my belly.

'In a state of nakedness you're quite magnetic,' she said. 'With a little acquired sophistication I can make you beautiful.'

The sperm began seeping between my thighs. 'If you don't let me mop this I'll be staining your cushion.'

'Call me Allison. And don't worry about that.' Leaning forwards she scooped up a thick wad of viscous fluid which drooped in strands between her fingers. She sniffed, tentatively licked a sample and then the whole, and swallowed enthusiastically.

Stunned, I wondered how she could. Where was the satisfaction in doing that?

'Uhm . . .! I enjoyed watching the way you encouraged your young man to produce the goods. I believe you have real talent – and he's certainly given delicious value for money. You, however, are a nasty cheat to fake your orgasm.'

Thinking I'd blown the rent I muttered nervously, 'That's what actresses do, they play a role. Just like you, Miss Haversham!'

The old girl actually giggled. 'I thought I did rather well.'

'Anyway, he's not "my young man".'

'Excellent. You could do better. Would I offend you by saying how much I admire your bush – it's glorious, completely untamed. I keep Renata shaved.' Stunned again, I jerked back. 'May I –?'

Allison reached into my soaking hair and fondled the strands. Though her touches were respectful I only just managed to control my reaction.

'And your nipples. I love the way they form the whole front of your breasts. Immensely attractive. I simply must –'

She cupped and stroked my left, smearing the teat in cold fluid while I clung desperately to the need for her money. 'I ought to dress now,' I choked.

'Do you really want to?'

'Gary's probably waiting.'

'He has already left.'

I shot up from the chair, my heart pounding. 'What do you want?'

'To make a proposal.'

'Forget it, I'm not a lesbian.'

'Sit down, please. You remind me of myself when a girl. Unfortunately with advancing age I have abandoned many sexual hopes, though regret for lost opportunities remains. Through you I could, in an empathetic sense, experience what I missed.'

She had me way out of my depth. 'I don't understand.'

'Having once had sex for payment, would you object to doing it more? I can offer a regular salary, the best food, and foreign travel. I'll buy you some clothes and you have a choice of the vacant rooms upstairs.'

'All in exchange for what?'

'Of course, your inexperience is obvious and you would need to be trained.'

I screeched, 'For what?'

'Helping me to realise my fantasies.'

In the right circumstances it doesn't take long for a person to change. For me it was like returning to drama school and learning a special part, different from anything I'd tried before. I took to the training so naturally it was a part I might have been born to play. I've always enjoyed being directed – having parameters set for me – and loved the way Allison positioned me as she wanted. Her intimate touches combined the gentleness of a woman with a man's assurance.

I finished brushing my hair, dyed blonde, a colour that flattered me. I had thrown away my old WHORE shirt; a word I never use now, nor any of the similar words that describe my new career. I'm Young Allison, living the fantasies that excite her imagination. On many occasions I share the feeling.

Leaving my bathroom I started to walk along the landing. On the top floor we're often naked but I chose to wear a satin slip that barely covered my sex. Split on both sides up to the hips, the front panel flapped loosely and my buttocks bunched and lengthened at each step, disturbing the rear flap. My breasts swayed and my smooth inner thighs lightly caressed each other. I'd become aware of every part of my body and had learnt the ways to use it effectively for provocation.

With no need to knock on the door I entered to find Allison spread-eagled on the bed and Renata kneeling for the personal daily chore. The maid's head bobbed up and down, exploring our employer's labia, and in leaning forwards her uniform's short skirt lifted high. Against her bare copper skin, red silk panties wedged in her crotch. This view is one of my own favourites and I'm not surprised that visitors request me to adopt the pose. I raised the skirt over Renata's back, exposing the expanse of her butt, and fondled up and around, to raise her temperature. Moving beneath I cupped the squashed flesh of her labia, a soft warm lump in my palm. Weakening, I took hold of its waistband to drag the tiny garment down her thighs. Her smooth dark genitals above the stretched fabric are another good sight. As the maid continued her duty I took it slowly, first rimming her steamy slit before separating the supple membranes. At last I gave in to what we both wanted and inserted fingers deep in her passage, spreading her groove to a gaping incision. In her soft velvet heat I could thrust easily while the hussy squirmed back against my pressure.

From Allison's wavering moans I could tell she was close. But when Renata stopped sucking and collapsed on her belly, gasping convulsively, Allison opened her eyes to plead, 'Let her finish me first.'

I contented myself with gently tickling the maid's clit, keeping her tension high but watching Allison. Renata resumed the task urgently until Allison's voluptuous shudders and tiny shrieks like a wounded bird tore apart her authority. For a short while she was washed by the hot pulsing waves and eventually she lay back, quietly fulfilled. The maid reached for a brush to comb Allison's thin pubic hair. The bristles flopped the labia apart and pushed the pliable tissues from side to side. Renata finished by using the handle as a dildo, deep in the humid funnel, bulging Allison's lips. I'm still not sure if it's a game when she leaves it sticking out or an act of revenge to make our employer look obscene. When my friend looked around at me, gleaming lubrication coated her mouth and chin. I plugged her vagina a few more times but decided she would not be allowed to come this time. Instead I pulled out, smeared her cream over my lips and drew her into my arms. The poor girl desperately wanted to go all the way, which made our kisses more passionate, sharing and mingling our different flavours. Gazing up from her pillow, Allison enjoyed us performing together and jiggled the brush handle to and fro. 'Don't take too long,' she murmured. 'It's nearly time to get ready.'

Allison's policy is to launch me into one of her fantasies and see where it leads. She dictates what I wear but never prepares, or warns me, so whatever happens – whether good or bad – I bear the consequences. Mostly I enjoy the game but a few weeks ago I had a different experience. On a quiet evening, almost dark, I walked around the central square of a Cretan village. Around the perimeter the tables outside tavernas were filled with men drinking, arguing, and playing cards but no other women – only me, walking steadily, loud heels striking the cobbles. I wore long black stockings which showed off my pale skin, held by a matching suspender belt. The waistband and long straps down the front of my thighs nicely framed my triangular thatch and my bare breasts bounced at each impact of my heels. As I passed their tables the men stopped talking and stared, unable to believe what they saw. I ignored them all, feeling immense power in strolling magnetically, embracing their attention as my natural right, like a real actress. On my approach I sensed the pressure of lust-filled eyes roaming my face, breasts and pubes, transferred to my swaying rump as I moved on. Sizzling electrically I patrolled one side of the square but then, as I crossed the open space to the opposite side, I began to quiver, not at the cooling air but the silent danger all around. I've never felt so alone or exposed but I kept going – what else could I do? – head high and striding evenly. I remembered, with wild animals, the absolute need to show them no fear. The eyes of more men ripped parts off my body, and flooded my mind with images of threatening cocks provoked beyond endurance. But I dared not turn or look as some men stood up, either for a better view, or preparing to pounce. Naked, I had no chance to defend myself and I'm sure that figures moved towards me, unclipping their belts. My heart hammered, I started to sweat, and cursed Allison while calling on St Christopher. Just in time, as darkness cloaked visibility, I reached the corner and left the square. Renata and Allison drew me into a doorway and hustled me up a flight of stairs where, from an unlit room, we watched the men searching suspiciously. Allison's huge pleasure did nothing for me and through her usual post-fantasy interrogation I stumbled to explain how it felt. I admitted the gut-wrenching exhilaration but all the while trembled as if in a bath of ice.

At home in her garden I sunbathe nude with Renata. When I caress her springy breasts the erect nubs rock like stiff springs between my fingers. There, exhibitionism is safe and a great freedom. So now I wondered what kind of fantasy required Allison to dress me in more clothes than I'd worn for weeks.

After a final check in the mirror I left my room. At the foot of the staircase I approached the much larger room where Gary and I had first performed. I heard the hum of conversation and inside discovered six men grouped around my employer, looking radiant swathed in grey silk. Her hair had been piled on top of her head and her eyes sparkled like diamonds. Renata offered a drink from a tray and the sweet mellow taste relaxed my tension. I started to weigh up the men, making intuitive judgements and waiting for the tingling that occurs in my nipples. It goes without saying that I'm looking for confidence, but also latent animal energy lurking beneath the elegant and courteous exterior. I see the way a man holds himself and the unconscious fluent power when he moves. I often imagine that if he has big expressive hands he will also possess a sizable cock although experience tells me that's not so. Usually, if I find the right qualities, I decide to fuck him and set about letting him know that I'm interested. I enjoy the game, especially when, caught in a sexual aura that excludes everyone else around, there's only us, alone and aroused. Tingles confirmed a couple of likely candidates.

Allison broke off her conversation and came across. 'You're up from the country and off to Harrods,' she murmured. I'd stopped even trying to guess what she meant by remarks like that. Taking my hand she led me to a couch at one end of the room where we settled down. 'Sit with your knees together. Hands on lap, head up, prim and proper.' As I followed the instructions the buzz of conversation dwindled and the men focused on us, particularly on me, over-dressed and out of place. 'Here is my niece,' Allison announced. 'I have enticed this shy girl from the solitude of the country where she has been unbearably lonely. She is desperate for company and will agree to almost any polite proposal. Her name is Victoria and like her namesake, the fruity plum, she is brimming with juice. So I want you to rack your brains. What kinds of suggestion would you like to make to my dear Vicky?'

A silence descended. I could see the visitors pondering what line they should take, until one at the back called out, 'I'm willing to buy the hat.'

'An auction! A splendid idea,' Allison cried. 'Start the bidding.'

A process began but so half-heartedly it suggested that no one had any particular interest. Eventually, when the price satisfied the auctioneer, she told me to take it to the highest bidder. I stood and walked slowly, poised on high heels. In the bunch I threaded sinuously through bodies that seemed to be packed together. Reaching the new owner I graciously offered him the chance to remove the hat and while he did so remained passive. The return journey was more difficult with the bodies pressing closer, permitting only a little room. Hard chests and arms brushed against my breasts, my buttocks and thighs until, breathless and flushed, I emerged from the pack and sat again at Allison's side. Holding my hand affectionately she asked, 'Is anyone interested in having her skirt?'

When Allison mentioned Harrods she gave me no clue that my clothes would be the objects for sale and I realised immediately where the process would lead. So did the men, and the bidding picked up rapidly. In a few moments my skirt had been sold and again I swivelled and turned through the bunch to reach the bidder. He insisted on a little space and knelt for a slow unzipping while his free hand explored my belly and thighs. The loose garment slid down my legs and as it settled around my ankles I stepped out, displaying stocking tops, suspenders and flashing flesh. Returning to the couch proved to be a squirming struggle with so many fingers from all directions touching my bared skin, and so many kisses on my cheeks and neck. How densely could six bodies stand together? As I cleared the edge and crossed the open space to the couch I knew that every eye would be staring at the taut gusset of tiny panties drawn tightly into my crotch, leaving the rounded slopes of my buttocks completely exposed. And when I sat I was aware of the fixed gazes along my thighs into the shadowed area.

'You have made my niece very keen to disclose more. What should be next?' She kept us all in suspense before adding, 'I expect you would like to give Victoria the chance to show off her lingerie?' A couple of the men nodded eagerly. 'How delicious! Who wants her jacket?'

For my last outer garment the process speeded up vigorously with bids overlapping. At last, flaunting myself, I wriggled through the crowd to reach the buyer. Again the men separated for a clear view as the top came off and the purchaser took his opportunity to caress my shoulders and the length of my arms. With so many men standing so close how could I hope to stay calm? I breathed uncertainly, acutely conscious of the amount of flesh on display. In addition to tiny panties and stockings my only other covering was an underwired bra that jacked up my breasts and barely covered my areolae.

'Time's up!'

The men obeyed Allison's call by providing narrow gaps to sidle through with twelve hands caressing my bared skin. By the time I reached sanctuary I was trembling but Allison would not let me sit. Instead she allowed the assembly to study the hard tug of lace over my pouch and the prominent rounded tops of my breasts above the bra. In addition she looped her arm around my buttocks, conveying to the men our intimacy.

'We're all getting nicely warm, aren't we? As you can see, I won't let her shave.'

Stricken, I glanced down at strands of pubic hair poking out of my panties.

'Are you pleased you came up from the country, my dear?'

'Oh yes, aunt,' I choked.

'It's much more exciting than riding your pony. Gentlemen, you have uncovered one of Victoria's secrets. She simply loves exhibitionism. Do you favour her in stockings and suspenders, or want them off?' A majority voted for them to stay. 'What would you like her to liberate next?' An impatient consensus chose the bra. 'I approve your choice. I happen to know that her rosy nipples are a glorious sight so I expect high bids.'

The amounts offered rated me topless at such a value that I began to consider setting up on my own. As tension mounted I walked again into the crowd. The bodies pressed closer than ever until I stood before a silver-haired man. 'Look only at me,' he said. 'I've paid for the first sample.' His arms circled my back, drawing me onto his chest, my arms splayed helplessly out to the sides. His fingers found the clasp, snapped it open, and my breasts slumped as the bra released. He stood back and gradually pulled it away from my chest. I tried breathing calmly to smooth their rise and fall, and watched his gleaming eyes. I began to enjoy myself through his pleasure before he turned me round to the waiting group. He gave them a few seconds to relish the sight and then, from behind, decided he'd bought more than a view. He cupped both my boobs in his palms and moved the supple bowls in heavy rotations. My distorted teats stuck out from between his fingers and my senses reeled. As I groaned, my back arched against his chest.

Allison permitted him a lengthy taster before calling, 'Time!'

When the man let me go I had to get back to the couch but the packed figures fondled every part of me, front and back, as I attempted to wiggle through. The stimulation of their jackets' coarse cloth on my sensitive peaks meant that by the time I reached safety they were jutting out invitingly, advertising my aroused state.

Again Allison kept me standing. 'There, you see? You are having a riotous effect on my niece's body and I expect by now she is leaking down here. Shall I find out?'

Staring at my remaining garment, the men agreed. From the rear Allison's hand snuggled between my thighs and slid to and fro along my labia through the cloth. I clutched her shoulder, straining at the manipulation with strangers watching. 'Oh, yes, she's nicely wet.' Provoked by her stimulation it may have been true, and my face showed it, but without being asked the bidding started urgently. Were these real or pretend amounts of money? At the end I tottered back into the lion's den and I must have been nudged in the right direction. When I reached the buyer he also knelt at my feet and took hold of the waistband. Teasing himself, or getting his money's worth, he dragged down the flimsy garment very slowly. When it dropped to the floor his palms enclosed my haunches and their pressure forced me onto his face. He breathed my scent and worked his lips in my pubic hair as if he wanted to adore my cunt. I'd never had anyone do that before and it made me feel proud; arrogant too. He began –

'Time!'

The man stood, leaving me swaying giddily. I don't recall the return journey except for complete susceptibility to every brush of fabric, wandering hand or pinching fingers, and the fleeting kisses to neck and shoulders. They regarded my body as belonging to them more than to me and everyone wanted a piece. I struggled onwards, almost tearing myself out of the grips that could easily have swallowed me up.

As I staggered to Allison's side she reported to the group, 'Victoria really enjoyed your attention – I have never seen her so terribly roused. My dear, do have a rest. Lean on my knees.' Facing her, I inclined forwards, head low, acutely aware of presenting my rear view to many eyes. Silently, Allison allowed them a good look. Then: 'Who would like to open her?'

I heard a quiet tussle then bodies against me. From either side hands spread my legs and sets of fingers groped in the folds of my labia, now definitely wet with lubrication, and pulled them apart. A cold wave swept over me. Everyone would see beyond the spread tissues into my dark channel. I couldn't imagine any exposure more humiliating. Firmly gripped on both sides, I moaned aloud and writhed wretchedly.

'She loves it,' Allison whispered to the men holding me. Vengefully I dug my nails in her thighs, causing her to yelp in alarm. Before I could repeat the action a fleshy club invaded my entrance and pressed hard. With one smooth glide to the hilt a hairy groin impacted my rump. The raider's force rocked me to and fro while I clung desperately to Allison's legs. At each inward thrust his pendulous balls banged my clit and I gasped painfully at each strike on the sensitive bud. The sliding shaft seemed to be of unusual girth, stretching my vagina's walls, but as it continued I started to climb towards a glorious peak of ecstatic release. In a few more strokes the inexorable surge would carry –

He stopped and held himself rigidly, his cock in spasms, pouring its seed deep inside me.

Dimly, I heard Allison cry: 'Vicky welcomes you all.'

Dragged away from her lap I was bundled onto the white rug and laid down. Fingers thrust into my belly, dragged out a package of sperm and wiped it over my breasts, like a sort of 'blooding' at the end of a hunt. The crush of bodies, some clothed and others naked, pressed so close I could see nothing at all of any surroundings. They captured me, imprisoned me, in a wall of moving flesh and more reddened rampant cocks than I'd seen before at one time. And they all wanted to penetrate me without fussing about a particular aperture. One reoccupied my sex while another man straddled my chest and moved up until his thighs pressed the sides of my head. Shadowed under his belly his livid member stuffed my mouth and my nostrils filled with a strong masculine scent. Hands clawed at my breasts and multitudes of competing sensations unravelled my senses. Unable to control anything I could not predict the next touch, or lunge, or revolution onto my front for another shaft to enter my rear. Following my body's instinctive urge I could only breathe in harsh gasps and revealed my own carnality, occasionally snarling in response to the hammer blows. Braided into the maelstrom I occasionally glimpsed Allison watching it all with burning eyes and a rapt expression. Scorched in shame I heard her say, 'I had no idea that Vicky's a nymphomaniac. She's insatiable.'

The constant changes and varying positions bewildered me. All my confused impressions were of raw lust and the opening, and the hasty thrusts, or a stifling gag of rigid flesh and the flood of semen I had to swallow. As my panting eager body strained beneath them the mounting heat of sexual arousal combined with my churning emotions. One of them masturbated, dragging his flesh in his bunched fist with frightening barbarity and spouting his hot viscous load over my face. The bodies were so big and hard, built like teak blocks, and pinned in the centre there was only me convulsing and, though younger than them, more frail at every penetration sapping my fading energy.

Unexpectedly the violent energies faded away and a hush descended. Sprawled out on the floor I resembled an accident victim, legs wide, throbbing and sore, and reeking of mixtures of spunk. But as my senses returned and gradually assembled to consciousness I swelled with a new kind of emotion. I felt proud of my power, and proud of my ardour, full out at fever-pitch. And proud too of the tattered remnants of spirit when I crawled around, searching for any penis with a spark of life that could still be roused in the heat of my mouth.

Hours later I found Allison in her bathroom with mirrored walls. She lay in a deep tub of soapy foam with globs and smears over her breasts. While she chatted on her mobile phone, one leg hooked over the rim, I gazed around at multiple reflections of her head and arm. Then I realised she was recounting to one of her friends the events of the afternoon, describing the ways the men had used me and my own enthusiasm for more. I snuggled my hand under her raised leg, sliding around the smooth wet surfaces until my fingertips encountered her slit. As she continued to talk, panting and gulping in the middle of sentences, I probed her passage in a gentle finger-fuck.

When the phone snapped shut she gasped explosively as if she'd been holding herself under tight control. 'How cruel you are,' she protested.

'Stand up and lean forwards. I want to see you in the same way as you let the men look at me.'

'Do you hope for an apology? I cannot. It was truly wonderful to observe a persistent fantasy. I suppose for you, however, on the receiving end it did present quite a demanding challenge.'

'That comes nowhere close.'

Allison smiled bravely. 'Oh well, it's only fair to give you some fun in exchange. Assist me.'

I tugged a languid arm and hauled her upright. Foam streamed down her lean form, creamy patches dripped from her crests, and her flat belly glittered in crystal light. As she turned and assumed the pose I gazed at the wads of white foam clogging her anal hole and drooping from the dark tissues of her glistening lips like obscene drooping fangs. I'd never seen anything so compulsively sexual and after a moment, strangely affected, I embedded two fingers up to the knuckles in soft wet heat. Through a silent interval the only sound was the quiet slick, slick, of juice as I pushed in and out.

'You enjoy fingering me,' Allison panted. 'Shall I put you on the roster for daily sucking?'

'I have a better plan. One of those men you left me with wants me again in a couple of days.'

'You know I don't allow you to freelance.'

'I said I would consider it, on one condition.'

'And what is that?'

'That he fucks you first. I told him this tight hole would grip his cock like a leech, and that age makes you like seasoned wine.'

Allison writhed and gasped, 'I hope he didn't agree.'

'He did, immediately.'

'That is not one of my fantasies.'

'But it's one of mine. And I intend to watch, as you do to me. After that I'll find you another.' I concentrated all my attention on the stiff bud of her clitoris, rotating it unmercifully. 'I should thank you for teaching me one thing this afternoon.'

'Yes?' Allison gasped faintly, unable to concentrate.

'There's a huge difference between acting sexual and being sexual. So I'm moving on.'

'Oh, Bridie! Ah! Oh! Ooooh . . .'
'Now I'm in it for real.'

— *Bridie Mohan, Knightsbridge, London, UK*

My Wife is a Lesbian

'What the frig is this?' I exclaimed.

Carol came running. I guess she thought I'd found another spider. The hairy little buggers are not a big favourite of mine and she knows I need help when dealing with them. She burst into the room, momentarily dishevelled, and saw I was holding a silver disc. Usually Carol holds herself with the deportment of a catwalk model. She's 5′11″, taller in her customary heels, and, although she's twenty years older than me, she's the one who always turns heads and inspires the wolf-whistles whenever we are out together. I don't know if it's the lemon-blonde hair, the slender waist or her ample boobs. I only know that I would love to look half as good as her when I reach forty. We've been best friends since Philip and I moved into the house next door two years ago.

'What the frig is what?' Carol asked. She was already regaining her composure, clearly realising this was not a spider emergency. Manicured nails brushed stray locks from her otherwise immaculate fringe.

'This?' I demanded, waving the disc at her.

She blinked. 'It looks like a CD or a DVD,' she said coolly. 'They're a marvellous invention of modern technology that can either play –'

I pursed my lips. 'I can see it's a DVD,' I snapped.

'I can also see it has the word PORN written on it. I want to know why it's in my house?'

Carol raised an eyebrow. 'I'm not trying to pretend that I'm Sherlock Holmes,' she began dryly. 'But if you've not been watching it, then it sounds like Philip's been enjoying a bluey.' Her pristine smile broke to reveal sparkling white teeth. 'It's elementary, my dear Watson.' She frowned and asked, 'You don't mind him watching blue movies, do you?'

I paused, not sure how to answer that one. As naïve as it sounds, I'd never had the chance to watch porn of any description. It wasn't something I ever saw before meeting Philip and, since marrying, the opportunity had never arisen. However, the idea that Philip was doing something sexual that didn't involve me seemed like an act of betrayal. I could feel tears on the lower lids of my eyes and I covered my face to hide my distress.

'You're upset,' Carol exclaimed. Her tone was rich with genuine sympathy. She folded me in a maternal embrace. 'That is so sweet,' she gushed. 'No wonder I find you so adorable.'

I pulled out of the hug. 'It's not sweet. And it's not adorable. It's frigging horrible. Why would Philip need to look at a pornographic movie?'

Carol shrugged. 'Masturbatory fodder?'

'Why would he want to keep it hidden from me?'

She didn't answer.

I tossed the DVD onto a chair and then collapsed on the settee. 'Filthy piece of frigging filth,' I spat. 'He's a bastard. How can he do that to me?'

'It's only a bluey,' Carol said, sitting beside me. Her tone was soothing and she made me feel as though I was blowing the discovery out of proportion. She reached for the DVD, picked it up and asked, 'Fancy glancing at Philip's masturbatory fodder? It might help put things in perspective.'

I blushed, horrified she had made the suggestion. 'You wouldn't really want to watch a pornographic movie, would you?'

Carol laughed with mock disdain. 'I've watched them before,' she grinned. Kneeling on the floor, as she pushed the DVD into the slot on the front of the machine and pressed play, she said, 'Hell! I've even sta–' She stopped abruptly and turned back to grin at me. 'I've got no problems watching it,' she said calmly. 'I enjoy the occasional porn flick.'

And then we were sitting next to each other as the film came onto the TV screen. I wondered what she had been about to say, dismissing the idea that she was about to confess she had starred in a pornographic film and deciding it was more likely she would have said she had *started* watching them with her husband, or *stayed* in some glamorous location where a pornographic film had been made. There was little time for me to dwell on what Carol might have said because, as soon as the film began, I couldn't tear my eyes from the screen.

The title said: MY WIFE IS A LESBIAN. A busty brunette sat on a settee between two blondes. She was not spectacularly beautiful. But, because she wore a short dress with no panties and had her legs wide open, there was something that made her appearance sexually exciting.

I squirmed against the settee.

Carol chuckled. 'Home-made porn,' she grinned knowledgably. 'Your husband is a true connoisseur.'

I didn't know if Carol was being sarcastic or if it was a genuine compliment. The word that had stuck in my mind was *home-made*. 'Are you saying Philip made this himself?' I screeched hotly. The background did look uncomfortably familiar. The accents sounded disturbingly local and, although I didn't recognise any of the women on screen, I had the vague idea that I might have seen some of them before.

Carol laughed again and told me not to be so excitable. She explained the movie was low-budget (the constant buzz on the soundtrack had told me as much) and nothing more than the output of some opportunist with a camcorder, some decent editing software on his PC, and an obliging woman or two at his disposal. I said, aside from having access to obliging women, she could have been describing Philip.

Carol shushed me and insisted we watch the film.

The movie started with stilted dialogue between the blondes and the brunette. The premise of the story seemed to be that the brunette was married but had always wanted to have sex with a woman. The blondes were there to help her achieve that ambition. I sniffed with disdain, horrified by the open way the characters discussed their sexual requirements, and appalled to see one blonde stroking the brunette's thigh while the other gave her a gratuitous French kiss. Bare boobs were soon exposed. All the breasts were silicone-enhanced and looked like oversized beach balls decorated with horribly large nipples. Before the DVD had gone four full minutes into the movie all three women were naked. They showed off their surgically reconstructed bodies and a disturbing absence of pubic hair. They kissed. They licked. They touched, fingered, stroked and moaned. I watched bright pink vaginas being lapped by dark purple tongues. The flesh looked wet and perversely inviting. It had never crossed my mind to think about having sex with a woman before but, as I watched Philip's movie, I found myself yearning to know what the experience was like. The blondes devoured the helpless brunette, feasting on her breasts, lapping at her pussy, and pushing their fingers eagerly between her labia.

I watched, sweating with embarrassment and unexpected excitement.

After fifteen minutes, the camera, thankfully, broke away from the action. The three central characters had screamed themselves to climaxes that sounded pathetically overacted and enviously enjoyable. When the film resumed the blondes wore plastic penises. The sight was so unexpected and horrifying I almost burst into hysterical laughter. I choked on my giggles when I realised what they were going to do to the sweat-plastered brunette they had already devoured.

'This is obscene,' I whispered.

Carol glanced at me and tut-tutted. 'You're not watching it properly,' she complained. She grabbed my right hand, placed it on the settee between my legs, and pushed it back until the ball of my thumb touched the crotch of my jeans. It wasn't until she told me to sit forwards, and I felt my pussy being squashed against my arm, that I was struck by a flourish of sensation. It was so strong and unexpected I squealed as I pulled my hand away.

'Carol!' I gasped.

She tut-tutted again, put my wrist back in place and told me to sit that way through the remainder of the movie. 'That's how a lady should watch a porn flick,' she explained. She made the declaration as though this was a common lesson of deportment taught in finishing school.

And, because I'd always depended on her advice, I sat that way for the remainder of the film. Each time I rocked forwards I could feel the mouth of my vagina being squashed by my wrist. Admittedly, the hard seam of my jeans was in the way, as well as the thin veneer of my panties. But there was no mistaking the sensation of being coarsely caressed. And, although the stimulation wasn't quite what I needed, it was enough to heighten my arousal.

Only once, while the film was on, did I dare to glance at Carol. She sat in the same position she had made me assume and rocked gently back and forth. Her attention was divided somewhere between the movie and her own personal pleasure. The satisfied grin on her lips was simultaneously beautiful and terrifying. I was shocked to realise that my best *female* friend and I were sitting on our settee, quietly rubbing at our private parts as we watched my husband's porn. But that horror didn't stop me from following Carol's example and rocking my hips more assertively.

By the time *My Wife is a Lesbian* had finished I was sweating and flustered. My anger at the discovery of Philip's porn was muted by a heady arousal that needed satisfying by more than just the weight of my wrist. The inside of my pants was obscenely moist. I could feel the shape of my vulva and knew the flesh would be sticky and warm to the touch. The thought made me want to shiver. Trying not to show how I had been affected, I snapped irritably at Carol, 'That was disgusting.'

She nodded agreement. 'The focus was off in a couple of shots. And that audio track could have given me a migraine with its constant buzzing.'

'No,' I said indignantly. 'It was a disgusting piece of filth.'

'It turned you on, didn't it?'

I flushed angrily and then lowered my gaze. I was on the verge of arguing that it had done no such thing but I knew the words would have been lies. I hadn't enjoyed the movie but I couldn't argue against the liquid heat that now sat between my legs. I trembled with all the sensations that usually indicated I was aroused. My breasts felt swollen and full and they ached from the tension in my nipples. My sex lips bristled as though they carried a small electrical current. It hadn't escaped my notice that Carol's colour was unusually high and her smile had inched a little wider than was usual. Again, I was unsettled to think we were two women, alone in the house, and both buzzing with a fever of arousal. After the lurid events that had occurred in the film I felt as though I was stepping into a world I didn't know or understand.

'Didn't it?' Carol coaxed. 'It turned you on, didn't it?'

It was easier not to answer Carol's question. 'I don't know which hurts worse,' I began. 'The fact that Philip watches this sort of filth. Or the fact that he kept it secret from me.'

'Are you going to confront him?'

I pictured the embarrassment of that conversation and cringed from the concept. 'I couldn't!'

'Are you just going to pretend you never saw it?'

'That's the cowardly option,' I whispered. I thought it sounded preferable to any other. Aloud I said, 'I can't do that, can I?'

She studied me coolly. 'Then, what are you going to do?'

'What can I do?'

'I know how you could get back at him.' Carol stood up with sudden eagerness. 'Imagine the scene: you've gone to bed; Philip is alone down here, erection in one hand, tissue paper in the other, and the DVD onscreen.'

I shuddered at the image. It felt tawdry enough that Carol and I had both become so excited by the hateful film. It was disgusting to think of Philip sitting on the same settee with all the accoutrements he needed for masturbation.

'He starts to stroke himself . . .'

She gestured with her wrist gliding back and forth.

'Carol!' I cried.

'. . . he glances at the screen . . .'

'I don't like the sound of this idea.'

'. . . and, instead of seeing those silicon blondes and that dippy brunette, he finds he's watching us!'

I stared at her in amazement. If I said anything I can't remember what it was. The idea was so shocking it was like a slap across the face and it left me without words.

'You said yourself that Philip's got all the necessary recording equipment,' Carol said quickly. 'And, if he didn't have, we could use the stuff from my home. I know you're pretty handy with DVD software. We could act out our own lesbian movie for him and . . .'

'No.' I intended the word to come out and put an end to her suggestion. Instead it sounded like I was considering the idea. My head was filled with images of Carol and me naked, embracing, touching, stroking, kissing and licking. The room was incredibly warm and I had caught the scent of my own excited musk. Now I wondered if that earthy perfume might also be coming from Carol. A twisted part of my curiosity wondered how it might taste. I wanted to sob with revulsion at my own lurid train of thought.

'What would Philip think if he saw your face buried in my pussy?'

I gasped and placed a hand over my mouth. It was almost as though she had read my thoughts. Indignantly, I shook my head.

'What would Philip do if he saw me ride you with a strap-on? Do you think he'd stroke harder? Do you think he'd finish himself off before asking you what the frig you were doing as the star of a porn flick?'

My stomach churned. I wasn't thinking of Philip's responses. I was only thinking that I wanted to try all those things she had suggested.

'Wouldn't it be the perfect payback?' Carol murmured. Her words had taken on a hypnotic quality. 'Remember the sense of hurt and betrayal you felt when you found that DVD? Don't you think Philip would feel something similar, and maybe understand what he put you through?'

'I couldn't,' I whispered.

But in the back of my mind I had already made a different decision.

She continued as though I hadn't spoken. 'Philip would be forced to confront you. He'd want to know what you were doing in a porn movie. You'd be able to take the argument away from him and ask him why he was watching porn without including you.'

'And you think we could really make one?' I asked, still not admitting that I'd come to a decision.

Carol's grin was triumphant. 'Set up the camera. I'll pop back home and grab a couple of props.'

In less than an hour we were ready to start making the film. Carol and I were both dressed in bra, panties and hold-up stockings. I wore black and she wore red. We'd applied make-up, set up the camera so the view it captured was visible on the TV screen, and we were ready to start.

We sat facing each other on the settee – uncomfortably close with our lingerie-clad bodies touching. Carol operated the camcorder with a remote control and, when she pressed the button to record, I asked her if we had a script. She laughed, placed a hand on the back of my neck, and whispered, 'I don't think we need to spoil this movie with words.'

And then she lowered her face over mine.

The kiss was exhilarating.

Her tongue plunged into my mouth, teasing and tasting me, and suggesting a greater intimacy that we both knew would soon be ours. Feeling stilted and awkward, constantly aware of the camera's eye, I tried to caress her body as we kissed. The movements felt halting and ungainly at first. Yet, as I found myself stroking her breasts, her hips and then her thighs, I began to feel more comfortable.

'Just relax and enjoy it,' Carol whispered.

It sounded like good advice.

Carol moved her kiss from my mouth down to my breast. She was positioned so that the camera could see exactly what we were doing. On the TV screen her leg rubbed against mine. The image didn't relay the fantastic sensation of having stockings rub together, but I could see it captured my response. My mouth gaped open. My eyes were wide with shock. When she eased the bra strap from my shoulder, exposed my right breast to the camera and then cooed appreciatively at the sight of the rounded orb, I watched the incident onscreen and was slapped by a thrill of excitement. When she lowered her lips to the nipple, sucking, nibbling and provoking so many incendiary responses, I stopped watching the TV and concentrated on what was happening between us.

The sensations were fantastic.

She had set out markers before we began. Neither of us was meant to stray from between the goalposts of two strategically placed scatter cushions, otherwise the camera wouldn't catch all the action. Occasionally Carol muttered for us to stop, adjusted the camera's angle, its height or the zoom. But, for the majority of the afternoon, the camera was a forgotten voyeur as we became acquainted with the important task of making our own porn movie.

And, all the time, I was thinking: *I'm having sex with a woman*.

The thought melted the walls of my pussy.

Carol sucked against my nipples until I begged her to do more. My fingers had pushed against the crotch of her scarlet panties, exploring the shape of her vulva and fingering the labia through the thin denier of the gusset. Her pussy was warm and damp and she rubbed it against my hand like the most shameless of the blondes from Philip's DVD. She finally broke her mouth away from my breasts. I gasped, partly with relief and partly with frustration. I squealed when she moved her mouth down to my pussy.

For the first hour of our filmmaking Carol worshipped me with her lips, fingers and tongue. I struggled not to climax as she licked and touched me but, eventually, that seemed like a fruitless waste of energies. Whatever part of me still insisted I was wrong for having sex with a woman had finally accepted that I wasn't going to heed its advice.

The orgasms came in a screaming rush. I shrieked, shook, quivered and groaned. Afterwards, Carol said they would look sensational on camera.

But then it was my turn to work on her. And, although I was hesitant at first, I quickly got into the action of kissing her, stroking her and then suckling against her breasts. I had never thought tonguing a nipple could be as rewarding for the person doing the tonguing, but there was a genuine thrill of pleasure when I took her breast in my mouth. That arousal only became stronger when I found my nose buried against her pussy lips while my tongue stroked at the salty flesh of her sex. She tasted so exciting – a flavour that defied description – and the thrill I achieved from lapping her to climax was almost enough to inspire another burst of pleasure in my own body. Eventually, when she was sweating and weary from the sex and I was gasping for more, Carol pushed me away and told me we ought to start filming the second scene.

I don't know how much longer we would have spent making the film. I suppose there was a danger our movie-making could have continued until after Philip had returned from work and spoilt the surprise we were planning. Fortunately, the end of the filming was decided for us as we were completing the second scene.

I was on my hands and knees staring at the carpet. Carol was behind me, riding in and out of my pussy with her strap-on dildo. She handled the length more skilfully than Philip handled his penis and, even though this was the second time she had ridden me, I found myself responding to her as though it had been the first.

Carol explained that we had to do the scene twice: once with the camera behind us, and once with the camera in front. She added, unnecessarily, that this would allow us to edit the two scenes shot with one camera to look like one scene shot with two. I digested the information without thinking about it, more anxious to get on with having her pound those ten inches into my pussy. My clitoris was sore from having too much tonguing and the insides of my pussy ached to be penetrated. I didn't know why Carol possessed a strap-on: I only wanted her to fill me and ride me hard.

I admit that I was trying to make my responses a little theatrical for the benefit of the movie. My cries were exaggerated and I rolled my eyes in excessive gestures of ecstasy. But, being honest, Carol rode me so well, I would have been groaning and moaning even if we were trying to keep our liaison quiet.

My pussy was stretched by her dildo. Carol's hands rested firmly on my hips. She muttered some glib dialogue about me being a horny little bitch who was desperate for her cock. I concurred and told her that was exactly what I was. Carol pushed hard into me and screamed as though she was in the throes of her own climax. The sound of that cry, and the force of her penetration, were enough to give me an orgasm. It was a release that should have had me quivering on the floor for an hour afterwards.

But, as I came, I saw the spider. It crept across the floor, less than twelve inches away from my hand.

By the time I'd finished screaming and Carol had disposed of the hairy intruder, we both realised it was time to stop filming and transform the camcorder footage into our own pornographic movie. The editing turned out to be almost as much fun as the filming. Once it was complete, Carol and I sat clothed on the settee, watching the finished result with our wrists jammed firmly between our legs. I don't know if our remake was better than the original, but I do know that I reached orgasm once while we were watching and I'm fairly sure that Carol climaxed twice.

She kissed me farewell before leaving, and said she had to know what Philip thought of our foray into sexploitation. I promised that, as soon as he had seen it, she would be the first and only other person to know about his reaction.

But, after three days, and with Philip making no mention of the movie, I felt forced to bring up the subject myself. He'd clearly found a new hiding place for the DVD but I had no idea whether or not he'd viewed it, or where it was now concealed. I innocently asked if he'd seen the disc that had been stuffed down the side of the settee. I explained that I'd noticed it earlier in the week, meant to tidy it away, but never got round to it. He laughed, and seemed a little embarrassed when he said it was a porn film.

'Carol's husband lends them to me,' he explained. 'And I don't have the heart to tell him that we don't watch that sort of thing.'

I flushed and tried not to sound too panicked. 'So where is it now?'

He shrugged. 'I gave it back to him yesterday,' he explained. 'So it's either back in his private collection or he's lent it out to some other sad wanker who needs that sort of stimulation.' Cocking an eyebrow, he added, 'Why do you ask? You don't think we should watch one of those films together, do you?'

And I thought, for the sake of our marriage: that was probably something we should never do.

– Jan, Redditch, UK

The Officer and His Bitch

'You are an idiot!!' I shouted, my ears still ringing from the impact.

Just as the red-haired drunk began to lunge at me, a cruiser pulled up and, before I knew it, his unstable body slammed against the hood of the car. I was shaken, but my temper was savage enough to have taken him on. I had seen his car barrelling down the road towards my car and there was nothing I could do to stop it – at least not without hitting someone else. Once the initial shock of the impact subsided, I was on the jerk like a dirty shirt! It was only seconds before I realised that he was intoxicated.

I watched in sheer delight at the sweet justice as an especially large officer manhandled the drunk and couldn't help but laugh out loud at his sarcasm, which made him glance over at me amidst the struggle and flash an arrogant grin. He was scrumptious; well over six feet tall with auburn hair and the bluest eyes I had ever seen.

There was something about his mischievous little-boy grin that made me forget about the accident for a moment. As I stared in sexy awe of this giant who saved me from the bad man, my cell phone rang – the display showing that it was my boyfriend who I had temporarily forgotten about! By the time I finished recounting the details of the accident to him, my handsome saviour was gone, leaving me with a heavy-set balding cop to take my statement.

That evening I found myself feeling especially restless, which I chalked up to anxiety from the accident, but I knew the truth; I couldn't get that policeman off my mind. My boyfriend, being the sweet guy that he was, wanted to do all he could to get my mind off the incident with a massage, but his well-meaning gesture soon turned to the ideal plateau for my erotic fantasy about the cop. Each caress of his hand took me deeper and deeper into my fantasy until I was so wet that I had to climb on top of him. As I slid up and down on his hard cock, I closed my eyes, shutting out the puzzled look on his face, and imagined the beautiful officer until I came. My boyfriend slept soundly after the romp, but I remained restless – unable to shake the sexy stranger from my thoughts.

A couple of days passed and I had surrendered to the fact that I would never see him again, when my cell rang.

'Hi, this is Constable Dover, am I speaking to Anna?' asked the familiar voice.

My insides fluttered wildly as I responded, 'Yes you are. What can I do for you, officer?' I asked, putting on my most seductive voice.

'Just thought I would update you on that jerk that hit your car – if you have time,' he said, cockier than ever.

'Sure, go ahead,' I said.

'I was thinking over a coffee would be better.'

'Oh . . . um . . . sure . . .' I stammered, distracted by the warmth building between my thighs.

'How's tomorrow morning? Let's say about ten? I should be out of court by then and can meet you at the coffee shop next door – I know it's not far from your place,' he said.

'Wow – guess that's one of the perks of being a cop – access to personal info?' I joked, trying not to show my excitement.

'Well, I normally don't go there, but, to be honest, I've been thinking of you ever since that day,' he replied.

'Now how could I not meet you after that? Ten it is,' I giggled.

From the moment I hung up with him until I got out of bed the next morning, I was plagued by guilt for what I was doing and more so for what I wanted to do. My intentions were clearly displayed in the outfit that I chose – pouring myself into a pair of very tight jeans and a flimsy little top that, though not tight, was so low-cut that my cleavage and the lace trim of my bra cups were brilliantly showcased. I watched myself in the mirrored closet door as I bent to slip on my stilettos and was impressed by my ample display as it hung beautifully beneath the fabric of my top.

On the drive over my mind raced with different scenarios of how the day could go, and by the time I reached the coffee shop I was in such a state of arousal that I could barely ignore the moist heat emanating from between my thighs, and it only got worse as I glanced up to find him standing there waiting for me. He was even sexier than I had remembered. I couldn't have imagined anything hotter than his huge body clad in his police uniform until I saw him dressed for court. He was in a black suit that seemed perfectly tailored to his large frame and broad shoulders. When his lips curled up in a sexy grin above his goatee I was certain that I felt myself truly swoon for the first time in my life.

'Wow – you look great!' he said, his eyes quickly homing in on my cleavage.

I just smiled and let him take my hand as he led me into the coffee shop. We made small talk until our coffee arrived and while I was in mid-sentence, he leant over, dropped his card in front of me and cut me off. 'Put that in your purse. I know you're gonna need it.'

I paused for a second, a little put off by his arrogance, and then went back to what I was saying only to be interrupted again. 'OK, here's the deal – I don't know if you have a boyfriend, though a pretty girl like you probably does. I don't even really care if you do. I think you and I could be great together in and out of bed, so if you are seeing anyone – ditch the loser and give me a shot.'

I was stunned. 'Being a little presumptuous, aren't you? We haven't even finished coffee – shit – you haven't even let me finish a sentence and you're already talking about bed?'

I could feel the rage beginning to overpower the arousal and considered getting up and leaving.

'I'm just being honest. Come on, you wouldn't have worn that or even come here for that matter if you weren't attracted to me too, so let's just cut through the crap,' he said seriously.

I glared at him in disbelief; he was certainly not the chivalrous officer that I had been imagining in my fantasies, but I couldn't deny my longing for him, especially since it was already so apparent to him. He matched my stare, only instead of contempt, his look had an almost amused undertone to it. His blue eyes sparkled wickedly as he stood up and walked towards the door. 'Let's go,' he practically commanded.

'You're a jerk,' I said angrily, following behind.

We walked past my car and around to the side of the coffee shop and I didn't question why. My heart raced with an equal infusion of anger and lust. We stopped in the alleyway between the café and a pile of wooden skids and he again flashed a wicked grin and took me by the shoulders, standing me against the cold brick wall.

'I'm a jerk? Maybe so – but you love it,' he sneered before leaning in for a kiss.

At first I resisted, pursing my lips and trying to push him away, but he persisted.

His big hands engulfed my face and his body pushed into me, sandwiching me between him and the rough brick wall. His goatee scratched at the skin around my chin as his tongue continued to fight its way into my mouth. He had to crouch down to meet my height even in spite of my spike heels. I hated him for his arrogance and for not being the romantic gentleman in my fantasy, but when his tongue managed to break through my stiff lips and I felt its warmth in my mouth, it quickly spread down to my cunt. He clued in to my surrender right away and his hands released the tight grip they had on my face and began to explore my body hungrily. His mouth went straight for my breasts as his hand moved in between my thighs and played with me through my jeans – rubbing hard and pushing the thick seam against my swollen clit and causing my pussy to drip right into it. There was nothing romantic or tender in the way that he touched me. It was nothing like my boyfriend's touch, but maybe that's why I didn't stop him. His hand continued to rub my cunt through the denim while he quickly found my nipple with his lips.

'You like the way my hand feels, don't you? You're a slut. A gorgeous slut.' His breath was as harsh as his words.

As if he knew I would get upset and try to pull away, he pushed his body against me, slamming me back against the brick wall and laughing. 'Don't deny it. Your cunt is dripping even through your fuckin' jeans. There's nothing wrong with liking this . . .' His voice once again became muffled by tit.

He was right – I loved it with every inch of my being and could feel my knees buckling from the pleasure. I felt his hand fiddling with his belt and glanced down to see him taking out his fat cock. He grabbed my hand and placed it there and I welcomed it into my little grip and began stroking it fervently. It wasn't very long, but definitely thick with a slight curve and harder than any cock I had felt before – my own little personal victory.

'Make me cum,' he commanded.

I'm not sure why I felt I needed to oblige, but I stroked him faster as I pushed my tit further into his mouth, determined to do what he asked. His breathing soon turned to a series of quiet moans and his hand rubbed my aching cunt faster, making the heat between my thighs unbearable. I wanted him to kiss me, to press his lips to mine and show me some resemblance of the man I had dreamt him up to be, but when I tried to wriggle my way towards his lips, he manoeuvred around me and instead bit my nipple, causing me to flinch. I should have slapped him for his lack of respect but instead stroked even faster, making sure to slide my thumb over his swollen head for extra kick. He somehow managed without even saying a word to make me feel as if he could be won over if I gave him the pleasuring of his life. I felt myself aching not only to be touched but also to gain his affection, even though deep down I knew he didn't deserve it.

I peeked about to make certain that no one would see and squatted in front of his cock. I thought that he would be excited, but instead he said flatly, 'I'm glad you know your place,' and then pushed his cock deep into my throat.

I attempted to move my mouth over his flesh sensuously to show him how sexy I could be, but he began fucking my face so savagely that I could barely breathe. With each thrust, his curved cock would hit the roof of my mouth and bring tears to my eyes, but I continued to take it. I wrapped my lips as tight around his pumping wand as I could and used my hand to free his balls from his briefs. With each push of his dick into my mouth I squeezed the fleshy sac, tugging on it lightly. My attempt to breathe around his fat cock caused a sound that stood someplace between a moan and a whimper and this seemed to stir something in him as he began to moan as well. The rigid flesh that was consuming my mouth turned to rock as I sucked away. His thrusts became less co-ordinated and finally turned to uncontrolled jerks, each topped with a squirt of hot cum. Though hornier than ever, the sensation that overwhelmed me was one of smug victory over my feat. I savoured his tart milk, swirling it about with my tongue, and looked up at him as I licked what dribbled from the head after the quivering had stopped. His face was beet-red and he had trouble containing his satisfaction – finally offering me the look of approval that I had needed.

He took my hand and helped me up and smiled down at me, causing me to blush, and asked, 'Now what are we going to do about you?' looking at the wet spot between my legs.

As wet as he had left me, I felt a satisfaction that I had never known. I knew that I could cum on my own or even get that from my sweet boyfriend later that evening, but for now my strange gratification came from having pleased him.

I stood up on my toes and brought myself as close to his ear as I could and whispered, 'All I want is to be your bitch.'

He nodded and walked back towards the car, and I again followed behind and then went on about my day.

Though I continue to be plagued by guilt over cheating on my boyfriend, I am strangely intoxicated by the combination of guilt, shame and rage each time I service Constable Dover.

– *A.D.R., Ontario, Canada*

Pounce

One minute we were just three friends who'd gone to university together, catching up over dinner and drinks; the next we were feverishly calling for the bill. Marguerite, who always imagined herself, when tipsy, as something of a leader, tottered off in her high heels to hail a cab while Nathan and I stayed behind to pay.

'She barely touched her salmon,' grumbled Nathan. 'Maybe she's thin because she's anorexic, not because she's broke.'

'Maybe.' I did a double take over the size of our liquor bill. 'It suits her.'

'Great cheekbones. I'd forgotten about them.' He grinned at me; I think he saw me as a co-conspirator although the truth was, the whole thing had been my idea.

Nathan was lanky, with long straight brown hair that fell over his pale-green eyes. His impressive forehead took up half his face. He had a fine nose and sensual lips. His mouth wasn't lush so much as long. Wide soft lips and a big mouth. Nathan was a great kisser, one of the best.

Marguerite waved frantically (she did a lot of things 'frantically'), to get our attention through the front window of the café. She'd flagged down a taxi.

'Do you think she's going to be all right?' Nathan asked. My co-conspirator again. 'If she freaks, I'm out of there.'

'She's going to be brilliant,' I said. I wiggled my expressive eyebrows at him. My eyes are grey. I have bedroom eyes. They come in handy at times, like then. 'Trust me, Nathan, there's a raunchy side to her randiness.'

He listened. He had to grant me superior knowledge – I was the one who'd actually had sex with her. I mentioned we met in college. Marguerite and I had gone through the same-sex curiosity phase together.

'She's in the groove, Nathan. The question is, can you handle us both?'

'Hah! Just so long as you have plenty of booze.'

'I just stocked up.'

'I think I'm going to need it,' he said.

I laughed. I laugh a lot when I'm tipsy, if I'm not moaning about the state of the world, which I decidedly was not, that night. 'Not too much I hope,' I said. I wiggled my index finger at him, then let it slowly droop.

'Not wiggling a *pinkie* at me?' He gave me his classic one eyebrow up, one eyebrow down look. We both knew why, even in jest, I wouldn't wiggle a pinkie at him.

At college he'd been so sensitive I think the size of his equipment embarrassed him. We'd been lovers for a while, shortly after we met, which seemed a long time ago to me, although only a couple of years had passed since we'd graduated and we'd met only a couple of years before that. Since then, he'd scored a lucrative gig with Public Broadcasting, writing an animated series.

I remembered that when he came from a blowjob he laughed out loud. I was about to ask him if he still did when the waiter arrived with our change. Nathan grabbed a bill from the tray with one hand and my hand with the other. We sprinted towards the exit.

'I told the driver we had no time to waste,' called Marguerite.

'Hear that? No time to waste!' I whispered to Nathan.

Nathan motioned to Marguerite to get into the cab and entered next, so he'd be seated between the two of us. Fair enough. I got in and gave the driver my address.

It was almost Christmas and really cold. I remember the festive lights through the breath-fogged windows of the cab and asking the cabbie to crank up the heat. The whole thing is cast in the soft glow of Christmas, or better yet, in blurry holiday colours.

We'd met to celebrate the season. We'd ordered a few rounds of drinks and there'd been a nice meal. We'd touched on a lot of topics but, as usual, *passion* had been our favourite theme. All three of us were passionate about passion. Perhaps I shouldn't have been surprised when my impromptu, half-kidding proposition ('Let's continue this at my place! I've stocked up my bedside fridge with wine') had been eagerly accepted. But I was.

Had we actually established the sex part, I wondered. Yes, Nathan and Marguerite were already kissing. It had been Nathan who'd said, 'We can have sex!' and Marguerite who'd agreed with enthusiasm. 'Yes, let's!'

She and I had met in an improvisation class. 'Yes, let's' was an improv game. I leant in to the two of them, so close my lips caressed their faces when I spoke. 'Tonight, let's make a Nathan sandwich,' I said, and when she mumbled, 'Yes, let's,' I followed with, 'Let's try anal sex!' and before she thought about it she said, 'Yes, let's,' and then we all three gasped.

I placed her hand on Nathan's incredibly long hard-on. It ran most of the way down his thigh. She screamed! Nathan and I giggled as we hushed her up. Man, this was going to be so much fun.

It's long been a puzzle to me why so many multi-orgasmic easy-cum women are neurotic. Or, alternately, why neurotic women are often multi-orgasmic cum-queens. Marguerite would likely have several killer climaxes long before I even got close. Because I, a low-maintenance woman, can only hope for one big one per encounter. I'm not complaining. It just doesn't really add up, but then, what about human nature does?

Our cabbie was casting disapproving glances in his rear-view mirror. My fault, I was the one who'd put Marguerite's hand on Nathan. I took it off again. We sat up nice and held hands until we got to my house.

'I'll need to have a bath first,' said Marguerite.

'No problem,' I said. 'You'll love the tub.'

'I'll need to borrow a nightie.'

'I have the perfect thing. It's long and pink with soft lace at the neck and a slit up the back. There's a coat to match.'

'Coat,' snorted Nathan.

'Peignoir, silly,' said Marguerite.

Of course I'd done it on purpose so they could correct me and feel superior. I know it seems like I was cold-blooded about it but that's not the case at all. I really wanted to do this thing, and I wanted to do it right. I loved both of them more than either loved me and much more than they loved each other. I'd had sex with each of them, too. I knew best. I really wanted to see if there were such a thing as free sex, if we could have sex that could be all fun, no consequences. There was enough affection and enough attraction, but was there enough sense – adventurous tonight, common tomorrow – to prevent complications? I believed there was.

'Sorry,' I said. 'I forgot. I have a lovely pink *peignoir* set.'

'What'll you wear?' Nathan asked me.

'Same as you,' I replied.

'Boxers?' asked Marguerite. She laughed, just a touch hysterically. I made a mental note to dilute her wine.

'Nothing,' I said.

When we got to my house we didn't try to keep our arrival a secret. It was almost a mansion. Five bedrooms, all original. Mine was on the top floor. It had a desk and a dresser and futon and some posters and that's about it. We were all just starting out.

My housemates were gay guys, one couple and one single. It was Saturday night. The couple was out but the single guy, Drew, was home. He gaped when I escorted my friends past the living room and up the staircase.

We burst into my room in a flurry of wet wool coats. I kissed each of them in turn as I took their outer garments and hung them in a closet to dry. When I came back I had the pink peignoir set over my arm. Nathan had one hand on Marguerite's tiny left breast and the other wrapped tightly around her narrow waist, pressing her to his body. They kissed passionately. It was gorgeous.

She had long straight black hair and a willowy body. She was fond of a sort of East Indian look, little mirrors and embroidery and scarves and silk. It looked great on her. She was five-ten to his six-two. I'm five-four and voluptuous, but well proportioned. I don't look top-heavy or anything. My hair is dirty blonde and curly and I have a good kissing mouth too, like Nathan, and those grey bedroom eyes I mentioned.

Nathan twirled her like they were dancing. I caught her and she and I kissed while Nathan watched. We hadn't kissed in years but everyone knows kissing, even same-sex kissing, is like riding a bicycle. The kiss became passionate immediately. I moaned and she moaned. No giggling, not from us and not even from Nathan. Just us moaning and him breathing deeply.

'I need a drink,' he said.

I broke the kiss to perform my duties. Marguerite took the peignoir set from me. 'I'll take my bath now,' she said.

'I'll bring you a glass of wine,' I promised.

'Thank you.' Without another word, she left. I was proud of her for not insisting I escort her to the bathroom. She has a rules-of-etiquette list a mile long, amazing these days, and I wanted to be sure I measured up to it as much as possible. I wanted her to feel at home.

I chose a bottle of Chardonnay. Nathan and I drank in unison, each taking a fairly long, thirst-quenching draught of tangy white wine. The air seemed suffused with warmth when I set my glass down.

Nathan and I wrapped our arms around each other. I tilted my face up to his. He murmured sweet stuff about how beautiful I was but I cut him off with a greedy kiss. He made me slow down, stroking my cheek as he nibbled my lips before slipping me the tip of his tongue. What a kisser! I opened my mouth. He slid his tongue inside, where mine waited to dance with it. We sucked and teased; the ending of each kiss was the beginning of the next, and we did that until I had to lean against him for support because my knees were weak.

Nathan started unbuttoning my blouse. I stopped him. 'I promised her a drink,' I mumbled. I was breathless from kissing and anticipation.

The bathroom door had no lock. She'd drawn the shower curtain for modesty. 'It's me,' I said when I entered.

Her hand snaked around the shower curtain for her glass. 'Hurry up,' I said, 'I can't wait.'

'Take this,' she said. Her hand appeared again, holding the glass. 'And hand me a towel.'

I did. She opened the shower curtain and our eyes met. Her slender body was barely covered by the towel. Her eyes shone with anticipation. 'Don't watch me,' she said, so I turned my back while she dressed. I didn't laugh.

She said, 'I love you.'

I said, 'I love you too.'

When we got back to my room Nathan was under the covers.

'Wow,' he said when he caught sight of Marguerite. 'You should wear the slinky look more often.'

Marguerite posed. She did look stunning. I locked the door behind her. She stretched out beside Nathan. They both looked at me expectantly. I gulped my wine.

I stripped awkwardly, not sure what to do next. It's not that I was having a change of heart. I just wanted to make sure I did everything right. I was orchestrating this thing and I didn't know who to put in the middle first. If I lay down beside Nathan he would be in the middle. That made sense, as there were two of us and only one of him. But perhaps I should lie beside Marguerite, since she was our flightiest member.

They shifted, making a nest between them that was just my size. 'Well, come on,' said Marguerite. She patted the covers between them.

Nathan did the same. 'Here, pussy,' he cooed.

I pounced.

I don't know how long we were at it. I know at one point the room was so dark I lit candles and Marguerite told me later that when she'd blown them out they were more than half-melted. That suggests a fair bit of time passed, maybe four hours?

It was glorious! When Marguerite saw Nathan's erection in all its naked splendour she gasped. I swear she *blanched*. Her eyes became saucers. She stage-whispered, 'It's a club!'

Nathan blushed.

'See, what did I tell you?' I said.

Marguerite and I fell on it like famished sirens. We licked our way up that impressive shaft to the head and then we licked it until it was purple. I knelt over Nathan's mouth so he could eat me while I licked him. Marguerite and I alternated between licking and sucking him and kissing each other. Big, sloppy, open-mouthed, panting kisses. Nathan worked me until I was sopping wet. I turned around and lowered myself onto his stiff cock. I rode it for half a dozen deep, satisfying strokes before Marguerite interrupted us.

'Let me!' she cried. I hopped off. She lay on her side so Nathan could take her a little more gently than he had me. He parted her thighs to lick her pussy first. I kissed her mouth to keep her calm. He slid inside her. I watched her eyes dilate with pleasure as he sunk inch after fat inch into her. Her moan was delighted.

Later, we attempted to initiate Marguerite into the joys of anal sex. Though both Nathan and I took turns lapping at her sphincter before he coated it with lube while I scooped more onto his erection, she screamed like a banshee when he tried to enter her. It sounded like someone was being murdered and anyway, her sphincter had tightened, not loosened, at the touch of his cock. Nathan said there was no way he could get in there without *ruining* both of them so we abandoned the idea.

Instead, Marguerite gawked as he mounted me from behind and fucked my ass. Anal slut that I am, I opened like a flower to the rubbery head of his big dick. He thrust it so deep, so fast, I was sure I would tear but even so, I didn't scream. Of course, inside of six strokes I'd been reshaped to accommodate him. Then he fucked me so that his balls slapped my ass and I was driven across the bed on my hands and knees until my head touched the wall and I dropped to my elbows and lodged my head in them so I could keep taking it. I tried to slither my hand down to my clit, because I need direct stimulation to come, but it was impossible. Then I felt Marguerite's feminine touch. She planted her fingers between my splayed pussy lips, and with each thrust from Nathan I was rubbed in the same place, the same way, hard and slick against my pubic bone. I couldn't change a thing because Nathan was fucking me and Marguerite was fingering me, so I wasn't in control of anything but protecting my head from hitting the wall.

Marguerite had numerous orgasms along the way. She was one of those women who actually came from intercourse. All she had to do was lie with her legs together with Nathan on top, fucking her fast, and she came for the first time. I made her come by giving her head with Nathan telling me what to do. That was hot. He'd show me and then I'd try and it was while I was eating her that she went off again, like firecrackers. Pop! Pop! Pop! She shrieked then, too, but we didn't worry about it.

Though Nathan had three more glasses of wine through the night he was still rock-hard and horny. We'd sucked him and he'd fucked us and we'd finger-fucked each other but he never came even close to climax. I, on the other hand, had been close for so long it was bothering me.

But now, with Nathan and Marguerite working me over in tandem, I crashed helplessly into a full-tilt orgasm that shook me from top to bottom. I could hardly stand the double onslaught of his cock and her delicate fingers. I wanted to beg them to stop or go faster or harder or something, I didn't know what, so I didn't bother articulating real words beyond 'Yes!' and 'Oh!' and 'Uh-huh'. It's possible that the memory of that event is so exciting it's colouring my recollection, but I don't think so. It honestly seemed, at the time, that my orgasm was twice as intense and twice as long because there were two people fucking me. At first I groaned into my arms but when I kept coming and coming I threw back my head and roared with triumph.

Nathan held my ass cheeks and stayed still, his cock buried fully inside me. Marguerite kept rubbing me with her two stiff wet fingers until I finally stopped shuddering. I dropped my head to the mattress. My groans faded to moans and she slid her sticky fingers from between my thighs.

I couldn't bear it any more. Nathan slowly withdrew and sat back on his heels. I was a boneless puddle of pleasure. Marguerite started blowing out the candles.

Nathan groaned. 'What about me?'

'If it doesn't happen, it doesn't happen,' she replied. 'We can't be greedy.'

I laughed. 'Easy for you to say.'

'Maybe I've had too much to drink,' said Nathan. I could tell he was disappointed. I was too, sort of, although I was also exhausted. He elbowed me. 'Come on!'

I rolled over. 'What can we do?' I asked. Marguerite knelt beside me.

'Let me come on your hair,' he blurted.

Marguerite and I looked at each other. We shrugged. 'Sure,' she said, for both of us.

We lay on the futon, kissing, and Nathan stood above us. He used both hands, lubed, to pump himself while she and I languidly kissed. We kept our heads close so our hair mixed together, my damp blonde curls with her long chestnut mane, until he grunted and came. It was a delicate sensation, a man's jet hitting my hair; I could only just feel it. His aim was true but still, a little jism trickled down my cheek. I kept my eyes closed so I didn't see him right when it happened but a moment later, when he fell onto the bed, whispering, 'Thank you,' I saw the satiation in his eyes.

Someone pulled the covers up and we slept.

I didn't get up until it was my turn to shower. Marguerite had gone first; she was already dressed and making breakfast by the time Nathan finished his. I had a fast shower and threw on the first jeans and T-shirt I could find. I wanted to get to the kitchen to make sure the morning went smoothly.

Marguerite set an omelette down before me. Nathan had finished his; he was drinking coffee and reading the paper.

It was a clear, cold morning. The sky was very blue. There were no blurry lights; all the lines were clean. We bundled up in our coats and scarves and gloves. I walked them to the bus stop. We didn't talk. Nathan stamped his feet. I watched my breath puff white and disappear. The bus came. I pushed my scarf down and kissed Marguerite, then stood on tiptoe to kiss Nathan, goodbye.

The bus rumbled off. I walked home. There would be a little teasing from my room mates, and of course the next time I saw Nathan we blushed and the next time I saw Marguerite we giggled, but other than that, life simply went on. We'd had sex without consequences. It didn't drive us apart, or draw us closer together.

Now, five years later, Marguerite is a journalist, not a poet. The last time I talked to her she was behind on a deadline and trying to lose five pounds. Nathan's in America, directing motion-capture animation. He's going bald, so I guess that big forehead was evidence of hair-loss, not brains. I hear he got married. I didn't move anywhere. I stopped writing murder mysteries and started writing about the greatest mystery of all, people. I'm a biographer. I haven't seen either of them for ages. We're all still friends, though. I'm sure of it.

I've had 'group' sex since but I've never again achieved sex without consequences. Things don't always turn out the way it looks like they will. Still, when something good comes along that looks like it just might turn out right, I believe it's best to pounce.

– *Connie Summers, Toronto, Canada*

Annie's Bum Deal

I suppose I ask for it. I mean, giving in to Jamie's
kinky obsession has been a painful experience for me,
more times than I care to remember. I knew it from
almost the very beginning. Of course, I never should
have agreed in the first place, but that's an easy thing
to say *now*. Besides, shouldn't a girl keep her man
happy, or risk losing him altogether? And Jamie's
never been the sort of guy to settle for cosy,
lovey-dovey missionary sex in bed with the lights out.
No, girls! My man needs something more to bring out
his true sexuality, and in his case it seems to be my
bum that does it. I don't mean that he just likes my
naked buttocks in their pure and natural unblemished
state. Nothing so mundane for him! He likes it when
they've been nicely striped with crimson welts.

To begin with it was just a few humble spanks, and
then later with his little French martinet whip. The
silly sod bought the wretched thing on holiday a few
years back, and stupidly I let him! That's not to say
I didn't object at the time – strenuously so, in fact.

'Don't think for a moment that you're going to use
that fucking thing on *me*, Jamie!'

He grinned wolfishly. Of course, that always has a
strangely irresistible effect on me. He's got that look
– sort of a cross between a naughty schoolboy and a

215

sadistic slave-master. His eyes light up with guilty mischief and, whenever that happens, I know that I'm shortly in for an uncomfortable time. It's that boyishly persuasive air about him that could charm the knickers off a virgin nun. His eyes narrow and crease up with crow's feet at the corners and he looks at me all doleful and hurt if I don't agree to his lustful demands. And then there's all the emotional blackmail stuff – like, 'if you don't want to let me do it, it means you don't love me', and all that sort of manipulative crap.

We were staying at one of those upmarket campsites in the South of France and Jamie couldn't wait to get back to our chalet, his suntanned cheeks glowing with illicit excitement. I, on the other hand, would have much preferred to do some more shopping in town, but he was already in a state of ecstatic anticipation at the thought of trying out his new toy. I could see that he had a hard-on even as he drove back, his mind already planning the illicit event.

He'd put the martinet on my lap, and I studied the wretched thing with grim fascination, giggling nervously. Out of the corner of his eye he was watching my face, enjoying the moment. Like a fish in a pond I was going to take the bait, and he bloody knew it! But I wasn't about to give in quite so easily. A girl has her dignity to consider, after all. He kept begging me all the while, and of course I told him repeatedly to forget the whole idea, but as always my resistance was gradually worn down, his pleas growing ever more persuasive. With one hand on the steering wheel, he kissed me and fondled my boobs, rubbing his fingers suggestively over my thighs.

Finally, shaking my head in mock despair, I laughed and he grinned back like an impish little boy who's got the candy prize – against all the odds. And that was that. He knew then that he'd won.

'Hmmm. Well, I guess as you've taken me on holiday I'll have to be *very* generous to my man, even though he's a rotten sod . . . and a right kinky one at that!' I told him, sighing deeply then as if I'd just committed myself to something I'd later regret. 'But you'd better be gentle though, Jamie boy. And it's *only* for this once, OK?' I warned, glaring intently at him as if I really meant it.

He nodded, looking annoyingly smug and pleased with himself. Then we both giggled again, like we always do when sex is on the cards.

I was going to be a lamb to the slaughter, but he'd be a very happy bull. And I quite like it when he's a happy bull. Sure, Jamie always gets his wicked way with me in the end. That's my trouble. I'm a right softie – or, if you like, a right mug and a glutton for punishment.

It's because he's so utterly irresistible when he's in his spanking mode. All the more so when he knows that I'll be submissively compliant. His whole demeanour is like a smouldering fire, quietly burning away but ready to flare up with excitement at any moment. And that cunning look he gives me! Yes, it's the wolf about to devour Little Miss Red Riding Hood. And I'm completely helpless, putty in his hands.

I don't really understand why, but yes, I *do* get a kick out of the knowledge that he enjoys spanking me. The fact that he gets so turned on also turns me on just as much. He gives me all the standard chat of how he adores me, and that my naked body drives him crazy. And I suppose I like being worshipped, even if being worshipped has its painful drawbacks. Of course, he's very slick with his persuasive approach. He knows all my weak points, and plays on them ruthlessly. He even manages to excuse his 'funny ways', as he calls it, by telling me it's all quite normal. *Normal!* But maybe I'm not normal either – putting up with all the indignity! He refers to it as 'light domestic spanking' as if it were as natural a function as doing light domestic housework!

I say 'spanking' because up until the time of that French holiday that was all it ever was – a few playful slaps from his long sinewy hands on my naked cheeks, accompanied by a few girlish yelps from me. When he thought that my bum was sufficiently reddened and glowing, then he'd make frenzied love to me, and I can't say that I didn't enjoy every moment. Despite the discomfort, I'd climax every time and he'd shout the bloody place down! But there are limits to the pain a girl can take, whereas Jamie experiences none of that – although he always says that his poor hands smart as much as my poor bum! A likely story! And, yes, of course I know it's not fair on me. But it gets even worse. His obsession for beholding my punished rump has led him to ever greater ambitions.

I can't say that the very first time he suggested spanking me didn't come as a mind-boggling shock to my innocence. At that time we'd only been an item for a few months. From the very first night, sex was always good, but even so I sensed that there was something more about him that desperately wanted to rise above the surface of his own sexuality – as if some long-suppressed desire simmered dangerously beneath his lean muscled torso. I giggled at first, not taking him very seriously, but he was very persistent, looking at me with those smoky eyes of his that always made me melt.

'Your bare arse is so juicily tempting, Annie. I could eat it . . . but I'd prefer to spank it, actually. It wouldn't be painful, I promise. I'd be very gentle. But it would be such a fantastic turn-on. I'd be like on cloud nine! My bursting passion would erupt like a rocket to the moon!'

Rocket to the moon, indeed! I giggled with nervous delight. How could I refuse such a poetic request? I was simply overcome, my mind suddenly incapable of rational function. So I agreed – with reluctant trepidation. It would certainly be a new experience for me. Little did I know then that it would be such a fateful prelude to so many more such experiences.

And that was how it all began – with just an innocent hand-on-bare-bum affair. I became a compliant but not necessarily willing participant in his games. But then he graduated first to this bloody martinet whip thing, and then over the last couple of years to an assortment of canes, and then riding whips. Each new punishment implement is always more painful than the last, and consequently my poor bum is seldom free of the trace evidence.

The first time he was very gentle, just as promised. The next time was less gentle, and thereafter it gradually went from tolerable pain to excruciating agony. Ever since that first spanking he never made any real promises, because he knew that he couldn't keep them. We had a sort of tacit understanding, however. The moment I started to shout insults at him, that was the signal for him to stop. I could moan and gasp and scream out loud, or stamp my feet. That was all OK and within the accepted boundaries of the game. But the moment I called him a cruel fucker or a slimy little shit, he knew that it was game over!

Anyway, let's return to the French holiday. We'd just got back to our chalet, which was wedged between two others. Our neighbours were an elderly German couple on one side, and two gay French guys on the other. We were hardly through the door when Jamie virtually ripped my thin cotton dress off me. I quickly found myself bent over the table, my rump proffered in the way I know he likes – that's to say naked and taut, my legs apart so that he can see all the way into my crease, particularly at my back-facing vaginal pouch. I could hear his heavy breathing behind me. He doesn't like me turning my head round to see what's going on, because he says it spoils his fantasy. I must be like a remorseful schoolgirl getting her comeuppance in the headmaster's study, or I'd be the housemaid deserving her master's chastisement, and so on.

When Jamie advanced on me with this martinet thing in his hand, I got a fit of the giggles, but that didn't last long. After the first few swipes I was gasping and groaning with pain. If you've ever seen a martinet, you'll know that at first glance it appears to be a fairly tame object, comprising a solid handle and a dozen slender and lightweight thongs of suede, each about a foot long. But first appearances can be deceptive. Lightweight suede or not, I can assure you that those thongs are anything but tame. More like bloody lethal! My poor bum can vouch for it. I had streaks like thin tails of red across both buttocks, and after the sixth stroke I yelled out so loud that Jamie told me to shush it. The neighbours would hear! Oh yes, Jamie, I should bloody care less! He's bloody flaying my nether regions with his new toy, and I must button my mouth for fear of disturbing the neighbours in the next chalet!

By the time he'd finished I was sweating profusely, not so much from the summer heat, but from the pasting he'd given me. I was even shaking, but that seemed only to drive him all the more into a frenzy of lust. We had sex there and then, with me still bent over the table and him coming into me from behind. And if you've ever experienced a guy's rangy thighs pumping against your welt-ravaged backside, you'll know how I felt! Nevertheless, despite the pain, I *did* climax – virtually at the same moment as he did. Our combined warblings of ecstasy must have shattered the peace of the French countryside that evening. So much for Jamie's consideration for our neighbours!

That next morning we got dirty looks from the German couple and barely concealed sniggers from the evidently delighted gay guys. And it wasn't long before the whole campsite became aware of Jamie's liking for domestic discipline, so we had to pack up and move on. The supreme irony is that most of those contemptuous stares were directed towards *me* – particularly those from my fellow women holidaymakers! Although I was the victim, apparently I was also the object of scorn, presumably because I'd allowed myself to be a compliant female who gives in to the perverted whims of a dominant male! As Jamie roared off in his MG past the other chalets, with me holding onto my sun hat for dear life, I did at least manage to poke my tongue out defiantly at all those watching, scornful faces! He and I laugh about it even now. His 'funny ways' are not without their humorous moments.

But your question is, why am I such a mug to put up with his CP fetish? I suppose the answer must be that I love him to bits, and I know that he doesn't do it sadistically – not really. He says that it's his way of showing his passion and desire for me.

'When I see you naked, Annie, I just can't ever resist the urge to whip that sweet little butt of yours to shreds!' he'd tell me all dolefully afterwards. 'Can't help feeling that way. It's so cute and firm, but as ripe as two fresh peaches. I know I must be bent, but I *really* do adore you, Babes. I guess it must be a sort of way of expressing my love.'

Expressing his love? Well, OK, I know that sounds just a teensy-weensy bit feeble. But which of you girls wouldn't instantly fall for that vulnerable little-boy act? If you could see his face you'd know that it fills with genuine remorse, his eyes brimming with emotion, as much as mine are brimming with tears of pain and sometimes anger. Even when he goes too far – which these days is quite often – somehow he always manages to appease me. He goes from being the wicked headmaster to the caring lover in an instant. His expression is all worried-looking as he views the damage he's just inflicted. He sort of stands there gazing at my steaming butt in a daze of disbelief, his trembling hand running gingerly across the freshly delivered welts.

'Forgive me, Annie Babes, please. I didn't m-mean to. I get carried away. You know I do. Can't help m-myself,' he stammers pathetically. 'But you look so ravishing . . . and when I've made your poor bum like that, it's . . . it's irresistible.'

And then he'd fetch the Vaseline jar, and get himself off again whilst he massaged my sore cheeks, kissing them all the while and muttering sweet nothings. And I allow myself to remain bent over the table while he administers to me, his fingers sometimes straying into my crease, where certainly my unpunished flesh there hardly needs his soothing treatment. And even when he's overstepped the mark and my buttocks are stinging and throbbing madly from one of his numbing and bum-blistering onslaughts, I somehow can still never blame him. I often get angry, of course, but I can never bring myself to condemn him or even deny him his pleasures next time.

So, yes I'm a mug. On the other hand, which of you girls can say that *your* man climaxes you *every* time? Yeah, *every* time! Sure, I have to put up with having a permanently smarting backside, but it's worth it – I think. And for the next few days after a session he's really attentive and caring, and he never forgets to buy me flowers on his way back from work. It's those little things that count, I guess. Those small tokens of his appreciation – or perhaps guilt – show that he's really devoted to me. And until the next occasion when he gets the urge, we're meanwhile blissfully happy, going about our daily lives just like any other couple. He's always considerate; never loses his temper; listens to me; chats to me as a friend; is very respectful to my mum; goes shopping with me without moaning; helps with the housework and never forgets to kiss me as he leaves for work in the morning. In fact, I can truthfully say that he's my soul mate, our destinies inextricably entwined. There's nothing we can't discuss together, and in every respect but one, he's a gentle person and a caring and devoted husband. Yes, *husband*! I even *married* the man, knowing beforehand all about his 'funny ways'. So I take the view that whatever unsavoury baggage he brought into our marital partnership, I accepted it, and must therefore live with it and take the consequences.

Well, up to a point, anyway. And that point came one fine Sunday evening last spring.

We'd spent a wonderful afternoon at a riverside pub with a few of our crowd. They, of course, know nothing of Jamie's 'funny ways' or, for that matter, the perpetual condition of my backside. I mean, there I was in the bar sipping my vodka and coke, laughing

223

and joking. All the while, my friends are entirely oblivious of the fact that I'm perched on the edge of my seat, trying to take the weight off my striped backside! Typically my punishments are administered once a week, but he makes an exception whenever he's been overly harsh in his delivery. In that case he usually lets me off for a whole fortnight – not so much for the sake of leniency, but more because he likes my flesh to be relatively free of bruising at each new session – like an artist who needs a clean canvas to work on, I suppose! That's not to say he doesn't like a few pencil-thin, black trace-marks to remain there – sort of as testimony both to his artistry and to my own rampant stupidity. He calls them my 'battle scars', and I'm some brave heroine like Boadicea displaying her war wounds! And war wounds or not, I'm still expected to make love to him, whether the wounds are fresh or stale.

Anyway, we're walking back home, arm in arm, both of us pleasantly tanked up from the afternoon's boozing. And then the bombshell comes, out of the blue.

'I've been having a chat with Mathew,' he announces all casual-like.

'Oh yeah,' says I warily. Mathew is one of Jamie's less savoury buddies.

'He knows this bloke who makes spanking videos, and he's –'

'*Forget it*!' I reply sharply before he's even finished. I can tell instinctively what kind of perverted little scheme Jamie's about to unleash upon my unwilling lugholes. 'Definitely *not*, Jamie. No way.'

And then of course he starts trying to twist me round his little finger, just as he always does. He's not at all put out by my brusque refusal, his face all wrinkled up in a coy smile and a sort of droopy puppy-like expression that I instantly recognise for what it is.

'It would be fun, Babes. Really it would. And nobody ever need know. Not even Mathew. Only Richard – that's the video guy – would know.'

'Oh? Fun? Fun for whom, may I ask?'

Jamie giggles.

'It really would be a right turn-on, Babes! I mean . . . the thought of you being filmed while another girl is caning your sweet –'

'Another *girl*? Caning *me*?' My voice is as indignant as it is astonished. 'You actually mean to tell me that you want this – this Richard freak to arrange for some low-life tart to cane my private ass, while you and him are watching? Is that your bent little caper?'

He laughs nervously, but this time he becomes all sheepish, that vulnerable and damaged little-boy look creeping over his handsome features.

'It's just that – that I'd like to watch . . . just for once, rather than being the person doing it, Annie. I can't explain. You know I can't. But it would be a mind-blasting experience . . . just to be able to watch a girl doing it to you, for a change. And it would only be for this one time, I promise. I'd never ask again. Never. Honest I wouldn't.'

I look at him angrily now. This is something that goes beyond even the boundaries of his own lustful extremities. It's already bad enough that he gets his sexual kicks out of beating me, but now he wants to take his 'funny ways' a stage further.

'Jamie, are you seriously expecting me to allow myself to be caned by a *woman*, and what's more while I'm being bloody *filmed* . . . and by some porn-movie perv who I don't even know? And all so that you can get yourself off on it?'

The sheepish grin remains frozen on his lips.

'Just once. Please, Babes. Even the thought of it gives me a hard-on. And – and . . . well, I know it's not important, but Richard pays two hundred quid to his models . . . just for two hours' work!'

So now I'm going to be insulted into the bargain. I stop in my tracks and tear my hand furiously away from his.

'You want me, your own wife, to be like a – a bloody prostitute, is that it?'

Now he's all shifty and confused looking.

'No . . . no, Babes. It's got nothing to do with the money. Call it an added extra, if you like. I mean, getting paid would sort of add to the illicit intrigue of the whole thing! I could watch, knowing that my beautiful wife was being videoed . . . and being paid for it!'

Well, I'm seething. He's on a good salary, drives a sporty car that he bought outright, and we live in a nice home in a respectable area. My dad was a director of a well known company, and my poor mum is a church warden . . . but her dumb daughter is married to a bloke who wants her to appear in a porn movie whilst having her butt flayed to buggery! And I'll get two hundred pounds for the privilege!

My eyes are blazing. Passers-by in the street look away.

'*Forget it!*'

But clearly he won't. His puppy eyes are looking at me pleadingly. He grabs my hand again and squeezes it tight.

'It's only because I'm so – so absolutely infatuated with you, Annie Babes! Really I am. Seeing you like that would – would drive me wild with desire. Afterwards we'd have the best bonk ever!'

'*What?* On film, as well . . . is that it?' I'm incredulous.

'No . . . no, of course not, silly. I mean after . . . when we got home.'

I let out another snort of indignation, but he's looking at me all doleful and with that hurt expression that usually makes me melt. But not today. I'm in a right huff and I pull myself away and flounce on ahead of him. He's really worried now and when he catches me up he tries to hug me, but I'm having none of it.

'Annie, I'm really sorry. I didn't mean to offend you. Honest. It's just that you know my funny ways . . . and I can't help it. I wish I could control them, but I can't. I know I'm bent . . . and . . . and you've been really very understanding . . . all this time . . . and always given in to me. And I'm so, so very appreciative. I love you all the more for it.'

He looks as if he's about to cry. I'm beginning to weaken. Yes, I bloody am!

We walk in silence for a while. He's holding my hand again, and I don't pull away.

'Jamie, I know you can't help it. But your – your fetish is getting worse, and more demanding every time. The spanking bit was already a shock to my system, but it was OK, I guess. But then it's progressed to canings and then whippings . . . and they're always more severe each time. I'm not a bloody donkey, Jamie. My bum's not made of fucking leather, for Chrissakes. There's only so much a girl can take. Call me a spoilsport if you like!'

'But you're *not* a spoilsport, Babes. Far from it,' he protests. 'You've been great about it, and I love you madly for it. You're the best wife a bloke could have . . . especially for such a miserable shit like me.'

I can tell that there'll be more. The hangdog charm is on full-power again.

'But isn't our sex life really fantastic, Annie? I mean . . . I never look at other girls. My eyes are entirely for you. It's only you that turns me on. I just have to look at you naked and I get the immediate hots. It just so happens that I'm turned on all the more when – when that cute little juicy bum of yours is thrust back at me, ready to be flogged. It's like an addictive drug . . . one that I can't resist.'

I've calmed down now and I listen sympathetically. My heart goes out to him as I hear his pitiful excuses. What a daft softie I am! I can sense his desperation, but I'm not ready to give in yet awhile to this new and yet more shocking demand. Perhaps I like that brief moment of power over him that I have. It's the same every time he wants to cane or whip me. And these days, of course, it's never something as mild as a mere hand-spank. That's all in the past. Like any drug, the craving always increases every time, the addict always needing more of a fix.

It's a part of the ritual, I suppose. I make him go through his pleading routine on each occasion, and I always know when he's in the mood for one of his sessions. He gets that randy look about him, and becomes all ingratiating, rubbing up against me and fondling my bum. Then he starts sort of breathing his usual pre-spank patter in my ear, telling me how he can't wait another minute for me to get naked, and how he's already hard at the thought of me bent over the desk. When I eventually give in to his pleas – and, of course, he knows that I always will – then he leads me by the hand upstairs, kissing me all the while, with both of us giggling like silly school kids embarking on some really naughty mischief. He takes me to the spare room, which doubles as his study. This, of course, is where the desk is and where his assortment of canes and crops and his martinet are kept locked in his 'special' cupboard. And it's here in this small room, behind closed windows and curtains, where it all happens, and where I shout the place down and dance around holding my throbbing posterior – whilst he's getting himself off on the whole scene!

As we go up the stairs I can't say that my mouth isn't dry with terror at what I know awaits me, and I'm conscious of that chilling emptiness in my tummy. If anyone thinks that the prospect of pain whilst being flagellated is like an aphrodisiac, then it's a load of crap. For me it's just a means to an end, although I confess to a sort of strange thrill beforehand. That pure illicit feeling of being in that bent-over posture, naked and compliant, and knowing all the while that I'm making my man as hard as steel, is really mind-blowing stuff. As he stands behind me sizing up my proffered hindquarters, with his cane swung out for action, I secretly revel in knowing that he's got that odd sick look of lust on his face. He's completely wrapped up in his own kinky world. If the house collapsed around us I don't think he'd even notice! And, as I've already said, the sex afterwards is explosively orgasmic. He gets my G-button every time.

Anyway, we're almost back at the house and I'm mulling things over, my fury spent. My resolve is on the wane, too, and he can see it in my face. He makes me a strong cup of coffee, aware that his moment of triumph is not far off. He's not saying much now, relying on that sort of wistfully apologetic look on his little-boy face to finally win me over. I'm not saying much either, pretending disdainful indifference. I sip my coffee without looking at him, but I know from his furtive glances that he's willing me to capitulate. Yes, my Jamie is a scheming little creep, but I can't love him any less for it.

Eventually he comes up behind me and strokes the back of my neck. As usual he's got some sexually explicit witticism up his sleeve. My pursed lips break into a reluctant grin, and then he's kissing me. And I giggle, my previously angry resolve at once blown to the winds. A while later we're in bed, and the sex is all warm and lovey-dovey, if rather subdued. Afterwards we smoke a cigarette and, of course, I'm at my most vulnerable now. It's not long before I've tentatively agreed, his face immediately lighting up. So, I'm a mug, all over again, and he kisses me like I'm the most wonderful thing on God's earth.

'But Jamie, I mean it. It's a one-off. I'll do it for you this once, but you must promise me faithfully that it'll *never* happen again. Never.'

'Promise. Cross my heart!'

He was already hard again.

I didn't want to know any details in advance, or even when it was to take place, except that he'd tell me the night before. He'd arranged it with this Richard bloke, and the day came quicker than I'd expected, although I could tell by Jamie's happy-slappy mood that it had been all too imminent. I'd never seen him so excited before. For days he'd been all over me like a hot rash, eager to please me, indulging my every whim and fancy, praising me at any opportunity, and brimming over with soppy affection. I was lapping it up, but now it was pay-time.

To be honest, Richard turned out to be not such a bad sort, after all. He's like a big overweight bear, and he's jolly with it, putting me at ease as soon as we came through the door of his place. The atmosphere inside the room was all kind of cosy in a masculine way, although my spine took an icy jolt as soon as I saw the two spotlights and the camera equipment! For a few frantic moments I went all goggle-eyed and panicky. With stark reality confronting me now, I was beginning to regret my rash decision. But Jamie's always ready for my last-minute wobbles. He knows precisely how to soothe nerves, sort of smooching all over me and rubbing up against me so that I can feel his excitement. And all the while he's whispering affectionate nothings and all manner of sexy crap into my ear.

'Babes, I can't wait for you to put the schoolgirl kit on. And when you've got to lower your knickers, those scrumptiously tight little cheeks of yours are going to blow the lens right off that fucking video camera!'

And of course I couldn't disappoint him now. I'd given my word. Besides, Amanda had just arrived, and she turned out to be the biggest surprise of the afternoon. She wasn't the tarty little slapper I'd been expecting. Far from it. She works as a receptionist at my local dentist! I don't know which of us was most gobsmacked! Certainly we both blushed like school-girls. She seemed so ordinary, almost prim and proper. I couldn't really imagine her doing this porn stuff. But then I suppose she couldn't imagine *me* doing it either – and she's got the better end of the deal! Apparently she's Richard's regular star dominatrix, but she only ever appears fully clothed and never on the receiving end!

She's quite attractive in her way and she looks every bit the youthful headmistress that she's sup-posed to be for the part. She even wears those regulation schoolmarmish spectacles and black nylon tights. Jamie's equally taken with her, although he was obviously a bit concerned at my initial reaction when we all realised who she was. I hope she's discreet, although a visit to our dentist will never be quite the same again!

Well, Richard's schoolgirl skirt and blouse were a bit tight for me. I changed into the gear with trepidation, my heart thumping at the prospect of the filming as much as the impending agony. Amanda stifled her giggles as soon as she saw me dressed like that. She's a nice sort of girl, quiet but sociable, and actually we've since become friends – not that I intend to succumb to her headmistress's skills again!

The rest of that afternoon went by in a sort of mixture of light-hearted banter and a daze of pain. Of course, I'd insisted that my face mustn't be caught on film. Surely my buttocks were enough! I can recall everything vividly – and agonisingly. Despite her quietness and that sort of meek and mild appearance of hers, Amanda was the very strictest of headmistresses. She played the part like a veritable actress, her practised script sounding really authentic. And of course I played my submissive role accordingly.

'Your behaviour in class today was so bad, my girl, that you're going to get a *very* severe caning indeed.'

She said it as if she really meant it, and apparently she did, because that's what I got!

'You understand why such appalling behaviour can't go unpunished?'

'Yes, Miss,' I replied timidly, my hands clasped demurely in front of my pleated skirt.

'Very well. Slip your panties down to your knees and bend down over here.'

'Yes, Miss.'

'Bend right over. Lower! Knees straight and touch your toes. Brace yourself. It's going to hurt.'

I had no illusions about that. The camera whirred. I took a dozen stinging strokes, but they were spaced out at appropriate intervals to give me time to recover. I had to count each cut out aloud, just to add to the overall fantasy. When it was all over I was sweating and trembling, but Richard was delighted with the result, having filmed me at various different angles, close-ups and long shots, and leaving nothing to the imagination.

My Jamie was certainly on cloud nine. He'd sat there out of camera-shot gawping at the scene in silent astonishment, his jaw hanging stupidly and his trousers jacked like a tent. At least that was what Richard laughingly told me afterwards as he handed me my money.

For the next few weeks Jamie was all over me, madly passionate, lovingly tender, praising me all the time. And just as he'd promised, our sex life was fantastic – although slightly uncomfortable for a while. Furthermore, apart from my new friendship with Amanda, there was one other consolation prize for me.

Richard had given a copy of the videotape to Jamie, and of course he plays it regularly now – so much so that I've been spared quite a number of what otherwise would have been real-life sessions. It hasn't actually curbed his enthusiasm, but it's given me a welcome breather. At least for the moment he's satisfied with just watching me on video. We sometimes even watch the tape together, careful to keep the volume turned down for fear of old Mrs Pascoe next door hearing my yelps.

'You were absolutely fabulous, Annie Babes. I nearly came just watching you. It was a stunning performance. I don't suppose ... er ... you'd consider –?'

'*No*, I bloody would *not*.'

'Even with Amanda? I mean ... something a bit different ... like the tawse or the paddle? Richard's planning another video and –'

'No, Jamie. Absolutely *not*. Don't push your luck!'

Even so, I enjoyed spending my two hundred quid on a pair of Gucci shoes.

On second thoughts, I might eventually agree to doing another video – but only once my bum has had a well deserved rest, and only when Jamie has begged and pleaded with me more than ever. That's my main adrenaline rush. But yes, I *do* need a couple of winter dresses, as it so happens. And I'm a resilient girl, even if I'm a mug.

– Annie Foster, Harrow, Middlesex, UK

nexus

The leading publisher of fetish and adult fiction

TELL US WHAT YOU THINK!

Readers' ideas and opinions matter to us so please take a few minutes to fill in the questionnaire below.

1. Sex: Are you male ☐   female ☐   a couple ☐?

2. Age: Under 21 ☐   21–30 ☐   31–40 ☐   41–50 ☐   51–60 ☐   over 60 ☐

3. Where do you buy your Nexus books from?

☐ A chain book shop. If so, which one(s)?

_____

☐ An independent book shop. If so, which one(s)?

_____

☐ A used book shop/charity shop
☐ Online book store. If so, which one(s)?

_____

4. How did you find out about Nexus books?

☐ Browsing in a book shop
☐ A review in a magazine
☐ Online
☐ Recommendation
☐ Other _____

5. In terms of settings, which do you prefer? (Tick as many as you like.)

☐ Down to earth and as realistic as possible
☐ Historical settings. If so, which period do you prefer?

_____

☐ Fantasy settings – barbarian worlds
☐ Completely escapist/surreal fantasy
☐ Institutional or secret academy

- ☐ Futuristic/sci fi
- ☐ Escapist but still believable
- ☐ Any settings you dislike?

_____

- ☐ Where would you like to see an adult novel set?

_____

6. In terms of storylines, would you prefer:
- ☐ Simple stories that concentrate on adult interests?
- ☐ More plot and character-driven stories with less explicit adult activity?
- ☐ We value your ideas, so give us your opinion of this book:

_____

_____

_____

7. In terms of your adult interests, what do you like to read about? (Tick as many as you like.)
- ☐ Traditional corporal punishment (CP)
- ☐ Modern corporal punishment
- ☐ Spanking
- ☐ Restraint/bondage
- ☐ Rope bondage
- ☐ Latex/rubber
- ☐ Leather
- ☐ Female domination and male submission
- ☐ Female domination and female submission
- ☐ Male domination and female submission
- ☐ Willing captivity
- ☐ Uniforms
- ☐ Lingerie/underwear/hosiery/footwear (boots and high heels)
- ☐ Sex rituals
- ☐ Vanilla sex
- ☐ Swinging
- ☐ Cross-dressing/TV
- ☐ Enforced feminisation

☐ Others – tell us what you don't see enough of in adult fiction:

_____

_____

_____

8. Would you prefer books with a more specialised approach to your interests, i.e. a novel specifically about uniforms? If so, which subject(s) would you like to read a Nexus novel about?

_____

_____

_____

9. Would you like to read true stories in Nexus books? For instance, the true story of a submissive woman, or a male slave? Tell us which true revelations you would most like to read about:

_____

_____

_____

10. What do you like best about Nexus books?

_____

_____

11. What do you like least about Nexus books?

_____

_____

12. Which are your favourite titles?

_____

_____

13. Who are your favourite authors?

_____

_____

14. Which covers do you prefer? Those featuring:
(Tick as many as you like.)

- ☐ Fetish outfits
- ☐ More nudity
- ☐ Two models
- ☐ Unusual models or settings
- ☐ Classic erotic photography
- ☐ More contemporary images and poses
- ☐ A blank/non-erotic cover
- ☐ What would your ideal cover look like?

_____

15. Describe your ideal Nexus novel in the space provided:

_____

_____

_____

_____

16. Which celebrity would feature in one of your Nexus-style fantasies? We'll post the best suggestions on our website – anonymously!

_____

THANKS FOR YOUR TIME

Now simply write the title of this book in the space below and cut out the questionnaire pages. Post to: Nexus, Marketing Dept., Thames Wharf Studios, Rainville Rd, London W6 9HA

Book title: _____

NEXUS BOOKLIST

Information is correct at time of printing. To avoid disappointment, check availability before ordering. Go to www.nexus-books.com.

All books are priced at £6.99 unless another price is given.

NEXUS

☐ ABANDONED ALICE Adriana Arden ISBN 978 0 352 33969 0
☐ ALICE IN CHAINS Adriana Arden ISBN 978 0 352 33908 9
☐ AQUA DOMINATION William Doughty ISBN 978 0 352 34020 7
☐ THE ART OF CORRECTION Tara Black ISBN 978 0 352 33895 2
☐ THE ART OF SURRENDER Madeline Bastinado ISBN 978 0 352 34013 9
☐ BEASTLY BEHAVIOUR Aishling Morgan ISBN 978 0 352 34095 5
☐ BEHIND THE CURTAIN Primula Bond ISBN 978 0 352 34111 2
☐ BEING A GIRL Chloë Thurlow ISBN 978 0 352 34139 6
☐ BELINDA BARES UP Yolanda Celbridge ISBN 978 0 352 33926 3
☐ BIDDING TO SIN Rosita Varón ISBN 978 0 352 34063 4
☐ BLUSHING AT BOTH ENDS Philip Kemp ISBN 978 0 352 34107 5
☐ THE BOOK OF PUNISHMENT Cat Scarlett ISBN 978 0 352 33975 1
☐ BRUSH STROKES Penny Birch ISBN 978 0 352 34072 6
☐ BUTTER WOULDN'T MELT Penny Birch ISBN 978 0 352 34120 4
☐ CALLED TO THE WILD Angel Blake ISBN 978 0 352 34067 2
☐ CAPTIVES OF CHEYNER CLOSE Adriana Arden ISBN 978 0 352 34028 3
☐ CARNAL POSSESSION Yvonne Strickland ISBN 978 0 352 34062 7
☐ CITY MAID Amelia Evangeline ISBN 978 0 352 34096 2
☐ COLLEGE GIRLS Cat Scarlett ISBN 978 0 352 33942 3

☐ COMPANY OF SLAVES	Christina Shelly	ISBN 978 0 352 33887 7
☐ CONCEIT AND CONSEQUENCE	Aishling Morgan	ISBN 978 0 352 33965 2
☐ CORRECTIVE THERAPY	Jacqueline Masterson	ISBN 978 0 352 33917 1
☐ CORRUPTION	Virginia Crowley	ISBN 978 0 352 34073 3
☐ CRUEL SHADOW	Aishling Morgan	ISBN 978 0 352 33886 0
☐ DARK MISCHIEF	Lady Alice McCloud	ISBN 978 0 352 33998 0
☐ DEPTHS OF DEPRAVATION	Ray Gordon	ISBN 978 0 352 33995 9
☐ DICE WITH DOMINATION	P.S. Brett	ISBN 978 0 352 34023 8
☐ DOMINANT	Felix Baron	ISBN 978 0 352 34044 3
☐ DOMINATION DOLLS	Lindsay Gordon	ISBN 978 0 352 33891 4
☐ EXPOSÉ	Laura Bowen	ISBN 978 0 352 34035 1
☐ FORBIDDEN READING	Lisette Ashton	ISBN 978 0 352 34022 1
☐ FRESH FLESH	Wendy Swanscombe	ISBN 978 0 352 34041 2
☐ THE GIRLFLESH INSTITUTE	Adriana Arden	ISBN 978 0 352 34101 3
☐ HOT PURSUIT	Lisette Ashton	ISBN 978 0 352 33878 5
☐ THE INDECENCIES OF ISABELLE	Penny Birch (writing as Cruella)	ISBN 978 0 352 33989 8
☐ THE INDISCRETIONS OF ISABELLE	Penny Birch (writing as Cruella)	ISBN 978 0 352 33882 2
☐ IN DISGRACE	Penny Birch	ISBN 978 0 352 33922 5
☐ IN HER SERVICE	Lindsay Gordon	ISBN 978 0 352 33968 3
☐ INSTRUMENTS OF PLEASURE	Nicole Dere	ISBN 978 0 352 34098 6
☐ THE ISLAND OF DR SADE	Wendy Swanscombe	ISBN 978 0 352 34112 9
☐ JULIA C	Laura Bowen	ISBN 978 0 352 33852 5
☐ LACING LISBETH	Yolanda Celbridge	ISBN 978 0 352 33912 6
☐ LICKED CLEAN	Yolanda Celbridge	ISBN 978 0 352 33999 7
☐ LONGING FOR TOYS	Virginia Crowley	ISBN 978 0 352 34138 9
☐ LOVE JUICE	Donna Exeter	ISBN 978 0 352 33913 3
☐ LOVE SONG OF THE DOMINATRIX	Cat Scarlett	ISBN 978 0 352 34106 8

☐ LUST CALL	Ray Gordon	ISBN 978 0 352 34143 3
☐ MANSLAVE	J.D. Jensen	ISBN 978 0 352 34040 5
☐ MOST BUXOM	Aishling Morgan	ISBN 978 0 352 34121 1
☐ NIGHTS IN WHITE COTTON	Penny Birch	ISBN 978 0 352 34008 5
☐ NO PAIN, NO GAIN	James Baron	ISBN 978 0 352 33966 9
☐ THE OLD PERVERSITY SHOP	Aishling Morgan	ISBN 978 0 352 34007 8
☐ THE PALACE OF PLEASURES	Christobel Coleridge	ISBN 978 0 352 33801 3
☐ PETTING GIRLS	Penny Birch	ISBN 978 0 352 33957 7
☐ THE PRIESTESS	Jacqueline Bellevois	ISBN 978 0 352 33905 8
☐ PRIZE OF PAIN	Wendy Swanscombe	ISBN 978 0 352 33890 7
☐ PUNISHED IN PINK	Yolanda Celbridge	ISBN 978 0 352 34003 0
☐ THE PUNISHMENT CAMP	Jacqueline Masterson	ISBN 978 0 352 33940 9
☐ THE PUNISHMENT CLUB	Jacqueline Masterson	ISBN 978 0 352 33862 4
☐ THE ROAD TO DEPRAVITY	Ray Gordon	ISBN 978 0 352 34092 4
☐ SCARLET VICE	Aishling Morgan	ISBN 978 0 352 33988 1
☐ SCHOOLED FOR SERVICE	Lady Alice McCloud	ISBN 978 0 352 33918 8
☐ SCHOOL FOR STINGERS	Yolanda Celbridge	ISBN 978 0 352 33994 2
☐ SEXUAL HEELING	Wendy Swanscombe	ISBN 978 0 352 33921 8
☐ SILKEN EMBRACE	Christina Shelly	ISBN 978 0 352 34081 8
☐ SILKEN SERVITUDE	Christina Shelly	ISBN 978 0 352 34004 7
☐ SINDI IN SILK	Yolanda Celbridge	ISBN 978 0 352 34102 0
☐ SIN'S APPRENTICE	Aishling Morgan	ISBN 978 0 352 33909 6
☐ SLAVE OF THE SPARTANS	Yolanda Celbridge	ISBN 978 0 352 34078 8
☐ SLIPPERY WHEN WET	Penny Birch	ISBN 978 0 352 34091 7
☐ THE SMARTING OF SELINA	Yolanda Celbridge	ISBN 978 0 352 33872 3
☐ STRIP GIRL	Aishling Morgan	ISBN 978 0 352 34077 1
☐ STRIPING KAYLA	Yolanda Marshall	ISBN 978 0 352 33881 5
☐ STRIPPED BARE	Angel Blake	ISBN 978 0 352 33971 3

☐ SWEET AS SIN	Felix Baron	ISBN 978 0 352 34134 1
☐ A TALENT FOR SURRENDER	Madeline Bastinado	ISBN 978 0 352 34135 8
☐ TEMPTING THE GODDESS	Aishling Morgan	ISBN 978 0 352 33972 0
☐ THAI HONEY	Kit McCann	ISBN 978 0 352 34068 9
☐ TICKLE TORTURE	Penny Birch	ISBN 978 0 352 33904 1
☐ TOKYO BOUND	Sachi	ISBN 978 0 352 34019 1
☐ TORMENT, INCORPORATED	Murilee Martin	ISBN 978 0 352 33943 0
☐ UNEARTHLY DESIRES	Ray Gordon	ISBN 978 0 352 34036 8
☐ UNIFORM DOLL	Penny Birch	ISBN 978 0 352 33698 9
☐ WEB OF DESIRE	Ray Gordon	ISBN 978 0 352 34167 9
☐ WHALEBONE STRICT	Lady Alice McCloud	ISBN 978 0 352 34082 5
☐ WHAT HAPPENS TO BAD GIRLS	Penny Birch	ISBN 978 0 352 34031 3
☐ WHAT SUKI WANTS	Cat Scarlett	ISBN 978 0 352 34027 6
☐ WHEN SHE WAS BAD	Penny Birch	ISBN 978 0 352 33859 4
☐ WHIP HAND	G.C. Scott	ISBN 978 0 352 33694 1
☐ WHIPPING GIRL	Aishling Morgan	ISBN 978 0 352 33789 4
☐ WHIPPING TRIANGLE	G.C. Scott	ISBN 978 0 352 34086 3
☐ THE WICKED SEX	Lance Porter	ISBN 978 0 352 34161 7
☐ ZELLIE'S WEAKNESS	Jean Aveline	ISBN 978 0 352 34160 0

NEXUS CLASSIC

☐ AMAZON SLAVE	Lisette Ashton	ISBN 978 0 352 33916 4
☐ ANGEL	Lindsay Gordon	ISBN 978 0 352 34009 2
☐ THE BLACK GARTER	Lisette Ashton	ISBN 978 0 352 33919 5
☐ THE BLACK MASQUE	Lisette Ashton	ISBN 978 0 352 33977 5
☐ THE BLACK ROOM	Lisette Ashton	ISBN 978 0 352 33914 0
☐ THE BLACK WIDOW	Lisette Ashton	ISBN 978 0 352 33973 7
☐ THE BOND	Lindsay Gordon	ISBN 978 0 352 33996 6
☐ THE DOMINO ENIGMA	Cyrian Amberlake	ISBN 978 0 352 34064 1
☐ THE DOMINO QUEEN	Cyrian Amberlake	ISBN 978 0 352 34074 0
☐ THE DOMINO TATTOO	Cyrian Amberlake	ISBN 978 0 352 34037 5

☐ EMMA ENSLAVED	Hilary James	ISBN 978 0 352 33883 9
☐ EMMA'S HUMILIATION	Hilary James	ISBN 978 0 352 33910 2
☐ EMMA'S SUBMISSION	Hilary James	ISBN 978 0 352 33906 5
☐ FAIRGROUND ATTRACTION	Lisette Ashton	ISBN 978 0 352 33927 0
☐ THE INSTITUTE	Maria Del Rey	ISBN 978 0 352 33352 0
☐ PLAYTHING	Penny Birch	ISBN 978 0 352 33967 6
☐ PLEASING THEM	William Doughty	ISBN 978 0 352 34015 3
☐ RITES OF OBEDIENCE	Lindsay Gordon	ISBN 978 0 352 34005 4
☐ SERVING TIME	Sarah Veitch	ISBN 978 0 352 33509 8
☐ THE SUBMISSION GALLERY	Lindsay Gordon	ISBN 978 0 352 34026 9
☐ TIE AND TEASE	Penny Birch	ISBN 978 0 352 33987 4
☐ TIGHT WHITE COTTON	Penny Birch	ISBN 978 0 352 33970 6

NEXUS CONFESSIONS

| ☐ NEXUS CONFESSIONS: VOLUME ONE | Ed. Lindsay Gordon | ISBN 978 0 352 34093 1 |
| ☐ NEXUS CONFESSIONS: VOLUME TWO | Ed. Lindsay Gordon | ISBN 978 0 352 34103 7 |

NEXUS ENTHUSIAST

☐ BUSTY	Tom King	ISBN 978 0 352 34032 0
☐ CUCKOLD	Amber Leigh	ISBN 978 0 352 34140 2
☐ DERRIÈRE	Julius Culdrose	ISBN 978 0 352 34024 5
☐ ENTHRALLED	Lance Porter	ISBN 978 0 352 34108 2
☐ LEG LOVER	L.G. Denier	ISBN 978 0 352 34016 0
☐ OVER THE KNEE	Fiona Locke	ISBN 978 0 352 34079 5
☐ RUBBER GIRL	William Doughty	ISBN 978 0 352 34087 0
☐ THE SECRET SELF	Christina Shelly	ISBN 978 0 352 34069 6
☐ UNDER MY MASTER'S WINGS	Lauren Wissot	ISBN 978 0 352 34042 9
☐ UNIFORM DOLLS	Aishling Morgan	ISBN 978 0 352 34159 4
☐ THE UPSKIRT EXHIBITIONIST	Ray Gordon	ISBN 978 0 352 34122 8
☐ WIFE SWAP	Amber Leigh	ISBN 978 0 352 34097 9

NEXUS NON FICTION

☐ LESBIAN SEX   Jamie Goddard and   ISBN 978 0 352 33724 5
  SECRETS FOR MEN   Kurt Brungard

--------- ✂ -----------------------------------

Please send me the books I have ticked above.

Name   ....

Address   ....

                   ....

                   ....

                   .... Post code ....

Send to: **Virgin Books Cash Sales, Thames Wharf Studios, Rainville Road, London W6 9HA**

US customers: for prices and details of how to order books for delivery by mail, call 888-330-8477.

Please enclose a cheque or postal order, made payable to **Nexus Books Ltd**, to the value of the books you have ordered plus postage and packing costs as follows:
   UK and BFPO – £1.00 for the first book, 50p for each subsequent book.
   Overseas (including Republic of Ireland) – £2.00 for the first book, £1.00 for each subsequent book.

If you would prefer to pay by VISA, ACCESS/MASTERCARD, AMEX, DINERS CLUB or SWITCH, please write your card number and expiry date here:

....

Please allow up to 28 days for delivery.

Signature ....

Our privacy policy

We will not disclose information you supply us to any other parties. We will not disclose any information which identifies you personally to any person without your express consent.

From time to time we may send out information about Nexus books and special offers. Please tick here if you do *not* wish to receive Nexus information.   ☐

------- ✂ -----------------------------